THE CHINABERRY ALBUM

a novel by
Ruth Coe Chambers

Mercury House, Incorporated
San Francisco

Published in the United States by
Mercury House
San Francisco, California

Distributed to the trade by
Kampmann & Company, Inc.
New York, New York

Mercury House and colophon are registered trademarks of Mercury House, Incorporated

Manufactured in the United State of America

Library of Congress Cataloging-in-Publication Data

Chambers, Ruth Coe.
  The Chinaberry album : a novel / Ruth Coe Chambers.
    p.   cm.
  ISBN 0–916515–31–1 : $16.95
  I. Title.
PS3553.H263C5   1988
813'.54 — dc 19   87–28748
                                                            CIP

For my husband, Jack,
and our daughters,
Melissa and Wendy

Acknowledgments

With deepest gratitude to my literary agent, Elizabeth Pomada, for believing in and titling *The Chinaberry Album,* and to Jinx Walton of the University of Pittsburgh, Michael Christ of the University of Georgia, and Carol Costello of Mercury House for expert and invaluable assistance.

1

Bay Harbor was a city as sure as if its population had been five or even ten thousand. Actually, there weren't five thousand people in all of Bay Harbor, not even in the summer, when people came to the beach, or when World War II forced its soldiers and sailors among us. It had nothing to do with size. It was a feeling among the people. We felt like city people. Maybe it was because of the water. The Gulf of Mexico touched places and people we never saw, and that made us feel bigger than we were. Then again, maybe we were just privileged. We had water around us and history behind us.

Once Bay Harbor had been a city even in population — a teeming city, sin city. A saloon on every corner. It had been a thriving port, a bustling, busy place, until a mysterious fever struck it down. It was difficult to imagine Bay Harbor crowded, bursting with people, when we never even had to step off the sidewalk to let someone pass. We knew the names of all our neighbors, what their wash looked like, and what kind of table they set. The Bay Harbor we knew was so different from its former self that the past seemed almost unreal. Its history was a picture we could look at without its changing us at all.

Only the Baptists tried to make it otherwise. So that we would always remember what God did to the wicked, they did their best to keep the memory of the town's evil history alive. First, there had been the fever, brought in on one of the ships. They had tried to contain it, of course, but a fever-crazed sailor escaped from the ship and swam ashore. In a town so crowded, the fever spread like wildfire. But that hadn't satisfied God. Bay Harbor might still have become the state capital. But following the fever, He sent a great tidal wave, and that's what really finished sin city.

When the town was rebuilt, she lifted her skirts out of the mud and sidestepped slightly to the north. Nothing prospered as well in the new location, not even sin, but so that people didn't forget—and the Baptists felt it was a measure of Bay Harbor's wickedness that God didn't leave something beautiful like a rainbow—the water never left entirely. Part of Bay Harbor still lay buried beneath the bay. The fact that in some places there was land where water had once been never entered the Baptists' accounting of things.

Bay Harbor no longer aspired to be the state capital. We didn't have to. We could afford to be unhurried because of those who had hurried before us. We lived secure in the knowledge of what we were and what we had been. We were proud to be Southerners. Not anything or anybody could ever take that away or make it any less than it was, and we knew it. When we talked, no matter what we said, it sounded soft and was gentle to the ear. Tourists traveled hundreds of miles to see things we took for granted. We didn't have to leave home to see the sun grow huge behind the tall palms as it sank slowly into the bay or cart home bags of curly gray moss or boxes of seashells. Almost at our doorsteps, we had beaches with sand so glistening white it hurt your eyes to look at it too long. And the Gulf water was salty to support us and warm to the touch. If the salt also burned our eyes and the undertow threatened to suck us away, it only taught us respect. We could leave if we wanted to, but we never had to be tourists.

Still, we didn't wonder that they came. Bay Harbor was beautiful. As clean and sparkling as a freshly washed shell, it had to be the brightest spot on any map. Our houses were mostly wood, mostly painted white and set comfortably back from straight black roads that softened in the summer sun and hardened to the winter wind. One main street ran through town, with a second, lesser street behind it for filling stations and offices for two doctors, a dentist, a lawyer, and the mayor. The lesser street became the winding beach road, lined with palm trees, and it got most of the tourist traffic. Sun-washed and treeless, the main street was bordered with smooth sidewalks, perfect for skating. The most important buildings were the drugstore, the post office, the police station, our new picture show, and the boarding house.

Helen and Chester Armstrong owned more than the boarding house; they owned the star in Bay Harbor's crown. Covered with white clapboard siding, its high upstairs porch trimmed with elaborate gingerbread lace, the boarding house towered over Bay Harbor like a giant wedding cake glistening in the sun. The lettering had long since worn off the swinging sign that hung out front, but there wasn't a soul in town who didn't know the name of the big two-storied building. It was our landmark. As sure a beacon as the mirrored, winding lighthouse that flashed to the Gulf of Mexico, it beckoned to us all. Forming a balcony that seemed to float suspended over the sidewalk, the screened second-story porch supported a row of wooden rockers, every one of which was familiar to me because Helen was Mama's best friend. Her dining room was the only public eating place in town, and the words *Dining Room* had once been lettered in blue above the small door cut, like an afterthought, into the side of the building. The rain and wind had rubbed that lettering off, too, but it didn't hurt her business any. The long tables, pushed together and covered with white cloths, were crowded with people every day at noon. Only a thin wall separated the kitchen from the long, narrow dining room, and the heat that was a nuisance in the summer was a necessity in the winter. But in the summer, tall fans, like giant trees, blew across the ends of the tables so that it was never too uncomfortable.

The dishes, like the tablecloths, were perfectly white. All the color came from wedges of corn bread, large, plump biscuits, or golden sweet potato soufflé topped with pale brown marshmallows. There were always greens of some kind, too — collards, turnips, or deep green spinach flowered with slices of boiled egg. There might be slices of ham fanning the length of huge platters or roasts or heaping mounds of fried chicken or freshly caught, pan-fried fish. But when the smell of chitlins settled over Bay

Harbor like a choking fog, I gave wide berth to the boarding house. I couldn't imagine that Helen liked chitlins, but no doubt the boarders did.

In all the times I'd been to her dining room, I'd never seen Helen lift a hand to cook a thing. She'd just walk into the kitchen, smile at the Nigra cooks, calling them each by name, and nod her head as she looked at the bowls of food and large platters of meat that would stretch the length of the tables when the noon whistle blew.

Helen's detachment fascinated me. She was somehow removed from the rest of us and above the kinds of things that involved Mama and most of the other women I knew. I could never even recall seeing her eat because she was always standing, making sure everything was okay. Because she was Mama's best friend, I could eat there any time I wanted and not have to pay. I had only to walk in and sit down, and at some point during the meal Helen would come by and rest her soft white hands on my shoulders.

"Everything all right?" she'd ask. She'd say it to me, but all the men would answer, waving forks and talking with their mouths full of food. They liked Helen and were eager to please her. She was in the right business all right. Men were drawn to her like bees to honey. It was a good thing, too. Chester couldn't attract a gnat.

Age was as kind to Helen as it was gentle to Bay Harbor. Bay Harbor might mellow, its corners give way to gentle curves, but it never looked old or worn. There was something ageless about the main street and the sidewalks stretching beside it as they continued on past the boarding house to the railroad station, where they stopped. The greenest lawn and some of the brightest flowers in town grew there, but perhaps they were so colorful only in contrast to the drabness of the worn path behind the station that led to the Quarters.

The entire Nigra population of Bay Harbor lived beyond the railroad tracks in its own dusty little town. For the most part, the houses were small and unpainted, looking as though they were part of the earth beneath them. A few had somehow gotten painted, and one even had a white picket fence, but these were jammed in between their sorrier neighbors as if they were all the same. They lined either side of soft, powdery streets that were the color of gray dog ticks. These fed into their unpaved main street, which sported a few stores and a juke or two, owned and run by men from town who'd eat dust all day if there was a dollar in it. The rest of the main street was given to vacant lots covered with weeds that were sometimes cleared away to make room for a peanut stand.

They were kept separated from town and yet were a part of us, were so like Bay Harbor, for it was a quiet place and friendly. People didn't lock their doors at night. Even the air was still. Taking a deep breath in any direction, you could tell what the neighbors were having for supper.

But being a city, Bay Harbor was progressive. The first sign of progress I remember was the picture show. It seemed like nothing exciting had ever happened in Bay Harbor until they built the picture show. After that we had a rash of revival meetings, and the Ku Klux Klan burned crosses occasionally. That's the only thing the Klan ever did in Bay Harbor, burn crosses across the street from the picture show. Sometimes they'd even burn them during their lunch hour to keep from going out in the evening. They didn't stop anybody from going to the show, though. An ordinary movie could become quite exciting if a charred cross lay smoldering on the grass when you walked outside. Daddy said it was better advertising than the show owners could have bought. A lot of people had to see a picture twice just to find out what was wrong with it. In the face of such competition, Malone's Furniture had to lower the price of radios.

The newness still hadn't worn off the picture show when the posters about Mr. Magic began to appear. We'd never had a magic show in Bay Harbor before. I thought it must be something pretty wonderful, a special kind of show that couldn't be held in the outdoor tents where we'd watched dancing girls in filmy dresses. Because Daddy was the deputy sheriff, Mama and I could go to the tent shows without paying. Daddy didn't pay, either, but then he was working. He couldn't sit down with

Mama and me but stood in the back of the tent and watched from there.

If any doubted this was work, he proved them wrong the night he stopped the show. A lady on the stage was dancing around in a thin green dress when I noticed Daddy out of the corner of my eye. He was striding down the grassy aisle toward the stage, and even in the dim light of the tent I could see the sharp creases Mama had so carefully pressed into his pants. As Daddy walked in front of all those people, advancing on the stage, I knew she was glad she'd polished his shoes that morning, too. Not the least bit embarrassed, he walked right out on the stage and stood with his hands clasped behind him until the lady quit dancing. It wasn't a long wait. Then he walked around behind her and marched her off the stage just as though he'd been doing that sort of thing every day of his life. Mama wouldn't say what had been wrong. She promised to tell me when I was older, but I knew she'd forget.

Far beyond any of the traveling shows that came to Bay Harbor, the Magic Show was no more suited to the school auditorium, where the Grand Old Opry had been held, than it was to an outdoor tent. It was clear to me that the magician had waited for the proper setting—our new picture show with its red velvet curtains and popsicle-colored lights along the walls.

I studied the cardboard posters carefully. It was March and apt to be windy, so they were nailed securely to telephone poles or faced the sidewalk from inside grocery store windows. Mr. Magic had a great deal of blue wavy hair. In spite of the unnatural coloring, he looked a lot like Brother Palmer, the Baptist minister, but I tried to keep that from bothering me too much. I could talk of nothing but the Magic Show. The thought of having to wait two weeks to see Mr. Magic was almost unbearable. A lot could happen in two weeks.

I didn't worry that the war might keep Mr. Magic from coming to Bay Harbor. World War II was only news on the radio and a shortage of candy and chewing gum. My biggest dread was that the end of the world would come before he arrived.

Our next door neighbor, Miss Red, knew all the signs from the Book of Revelation and thought the end of the world was coming at most any time. When the picture show was completed, she was certain the end couldn't be far off. It pained her terribly to see people drawn to a place of sin, especially young people.

Living so close to Miss Red made it pretty hard on me at times. Nearly every Saturday it was the same thing. I'd dress with special care, and when it was time to leave for the picture show, I'd clutch a quarter tightly in my hand, eager to join the line waiting for the double feature to begin. But then I'd stop and look out the side window. Miss Red would be waiting for me on her front porch. There was no chance of my missing her by leaving early. Not even bothering to finish her meal, she'd come out and wait for me with a glass of iced tea in her hand. I'd stand for a minute with my hands against the screen door; then I'd fling it open and race across the porch and down the steps as fast as I could. I'd pretend I didn't see her, but she'd holler anyway.

"Hey there, Anna Lee Owens, how'd you like to be in the picture show when Jesus comes?"

I'd often wondered how she was so sure Jesus would pick Bay Harbor for His Second Coming, but I never asked her about it.

"This just might be the day, you know. He'll come like a thief in the night. Now think, Anna Lee, think how you'd feel if He found you in the picture show!"

She always spoiled a little of the show for me. Sometimes in the middle of the picture, I'd hear noises from the street and think the world really was coming to an end. I could almost see Jesus standing in front waiting for me to come out.

It was mainly because Miss Red was such a good cook that she kept such a strong hold on all the children in the neighborhood. We'd sit around her kitchen table with the oilcloth on it and listen to her talk about the Bible as long as the cookies held out. Little children were always taking her the stuff they made in Bible school because that meant extra cookies. She had quite a collection of macaroni necklaces, painted seashells, and brightly colored Bible pictures.

Except for an occasional serving of canned peach halves and store-bought pound cake, we didn't have dessert except on Sundays and holidays. But Miss Red had dessert every day of the week. Every day! And she wasn't fat, either. Of course, it was hard to say what Miss Red looked like, since so little of her showed beneath the long print dresses and black cotton stockings she wore summer and winter. Her hair was gray, but it was dark like the clothes she wore and pulled back into a knot at the nape of her neck. She had to be very old, but her body looked as smooth and unbending as a block of stove wood. And her face wasn't wrinkled with countless wandering lines. There were lines, but deep ones that divided her face into smooth little islands separated like chunks of floating clabber.

I'd had ample time to study Miss Red as I'd wait for her to make chocolate pudding. She had a way with chocolate pudding that made my mouth water just to think about it. The meringue was always high and billowy, with brown-tipped peaks and little yellow drops here and there like spilled beads. There were never any beads on Mama's meringues. She said there wouldn't have been any on Miss Red's if she'd known how to make one properly, but I was convinced there wasn't anything Miss Red couldn't cook properly if she wanted to. I don't suppose Miss Red ever made a chocolate pudding without giving me some because she knew I liked it so much. I always felt that I could eat the whole bowl of pudding instead of the single serving all wobbly and warm in the dish she'd set before me. I never found out if I could or not, though. Miss Red never offered me a whole bowl, and Mama wouldn't make one for me.

Every Sunday for what seemed the better part of a year, Mama specialized in banana puddings. One week there'd be bits of cherries tucked in among the bananas, and the next there'd be pecan halves. There was always something, but they were never as good as Miss Red's chocolate pudding, and Mama knew it. Not that I ever told her so; I just never showed any desire to eat the whole bowl. I was very careful when I talked to Mama about Miss Red's cooking because Mama wanted to be the best cook in all of Bay Harbor.

Once Miss Red sent over a jar of bread and butter pickles, and Daddy said he hadn't had any so good since his mother died. The very next day Mama went out and bought a half bushel of cucumbers. She took down the *Household Searchlight Recipe Book* Uncle Johnn had given her and blew the dust off it. Mama never used recipes, but Uncle Johnn had given her the cookbook before he knew that. She never measured anything, either, having taught herself to cook long before she'd learned how to read. Living alone with her daddy, she'd stood on a box in order to reach the stove.

It was a hot day, and Mama really worked over those pickles, wiping her face with a towel and blinking back moisture from her eyes to see the pages of the cookbook. I'd never had a particular fondness for pickles, but when they were ready she insisted I sample them for her. I could see Mama's eyes starting to glow with pride as I lifted the pickle to my mouth. I didn't see the light fade. The inside of my mouth seemed to draw together, trying to meet in the middle, and my tongue wanted to roll up like a piece of new linoleum. When she was sure I wasn't going to choke to death, she said in a low voice barely above a whisper, "Don't you ever breathe a word of this to anybody, you hear?"

I hadn't seen her so upset since the time I swallowed the asafoetida bag she'd hung around my neck to ward off disease. I nodded to her. I wasn't sure I'd ever be able to talk again.

People were used to burying things. Nigra maids buried stuff they stole from the houses where they worked, and people were still trying to dig up Spanish treasure rumored to be buried near Bay Harbor. It seemed impossible that a Spanish ship might lie beneath our town, something as big as a ship hidden under grass and trees and land where people walked without even getting their feet wet. Nevertheless, rumors persisted that a ship loaded with gold had foundered in a hurricane and sunk into the bay when it had extended miles inland around Bay Harbor. Mama insisted more money had been spent trying to locate that gold than it would be worth if they ever found it. From time to time, digging equipment and rigs were brought in, and iron jaws chewed away at the land. The only thing anybody ever got for their trouble was a bit of wood, thought to be from some wooden kegs carried on the ship. They may have even held the gold. The man who lost his money in the venture wasn't impressed with that bit of history, but one of the Nigra men who'd helped him with the digging gathered up all the bits and pieces and put them in a fruit jar, his toothless grin disappearing when the chief of police took it away from him to put on display at the police station. Daddy finally persuaded them to let the old man take the jar home. The police station was only a single room, hardly larger than an outhouse, and even something as small as a fruit jar took up valuable space.

Mama was one of the few people around who wasn't interested in buried treasure. But then Mama was a relative newcomer to Bay Harbor. A Georgia peach born and raised in Atlanta, she referred to Floridians as "crackers" and was very careful never to get involved with anything tacky. She considered treasure hunts tacky. Being unaccustomed, therefore, either to digging or to burying things, Mama probably went too deep and hit water. In the backyard near the steps, there appeared a slight mound that resembled a small grave, but I knew it was where Mama had buried those pickles. She'd become an unwilling participant in a Bay Harbor tradition. When I went out of my way at supper that night to tell her how much I loved her pickled peaches, she silenced me with a hidden kick beneath the table.

The closer the time came for the Magic Show, the more excited I became. I begged Mama to go with me, because that was the only way I'd get to wear a Sunday dress. She wouldn't go. She'd seen a magic show in New York City one time.

"If you've seen one," she said, "you've seen them all. The hand's quicker than the eye. That's all there is to it."

I didn't want tricks. I wanted real magic, hope for my dreams and promises beyond death. I didn't talk to her about it anymore. I was afraid she'd spoil it for me the way Miss Red spoiled the movies.

The world didn't come to an end. Saturday, March 27, 1943, finally arrived and with it Mr. Magic. He looked younger than his picture, and his youth was despised by the wives and mothers of absent soldiers. Whispers rose like dust in a sudden wind, and when Mr. Magic limped onto the stage of the Bay Harbor Theater, I knew it was a slight limp of the kind one could acquire from sticking a toe beneath a passing locomotive. His feet didn't concern me, however. I was determined to watch the hand that was quicker than my eye. If he held something in his right hand, I fastened my eyes on his left hand for one false move. I didn't see a thing to betray the magic and was finally able to settle back and enjoy the show.

In glittering clothes and polished tables, in endless boxes and trunks, magic had come to Bay Harbor. A lot of girls screamed when he started to cut the woman in half. She wore a pink-and-black-striped bathing suit and black stockings. I knew he wasn't about to cut her in half but was relieved nevertheless when she jumped out of the box, curtsied, and ran off stage. Next Mr. Magic pulled dozens of colored scarves out of his hat and laid them on the table. It was a thin little table, but Mama had warned me that it would have a false bottom in it. He pulled an egg out of the hat and placed it carefully on the table before he reached in again and pulled a white rabbit out by the ears. I heard him say, "Who'd like to have this rabbit? Would one of you fine boys or girls like to have this rabbit?"

I didn't even raise my hand. I hadn't lived nine years to be somebody's fool. He wouldn't give his rabbit away. That was just more magic. But he *was* giving it away! He pointed to Opal Sims and told her to come up on the stage. Too late, I raised my hand. He didn't give any more rabbits away. I'd been tricked after all. If only I had believed him, he might have given the rabbit to me. I could have walked past the velvet curtains and been close enough to touch Mr. Magic or the colored scarves. We might never see Mr. Magic again, and now he'd gone and left a little of himself behind with Opal Sims, the only albino in Bay Harbor.

Miss Red had a bowl of chocolate pudding waiting when I went to her house that afternoon. She wouldn't have asked if her life depended on it, but I knew she wanted me to tell her about Mr. Magic. She couldn't find any particular sin in listening.

"Well," she said to me, "I'm sure glad you didn't get that rabbit, Anna Lee. They're filthy things, rabbits. There's nothing magic about that filth. I knew a girl once that got ringworm from a rabbit. Got it all over her face. She was a pretty girl, too. I say *was*. Once she got that ringworm, her face was never fit to look at. Opal ain't the lucky one for getting that rabbit. No sir!"

I stood up suddenly, nearly overturning my chair. "Miss Red, you told me it was a cat that gave that girl ringworm. When I brought home those six kittens somebody tried to drown, you told Daddy it was a cat!"

"Cat. Rabbit. What difference does it make? They're all part and parcel of the same thing. They're all filth. And don't you ever forget, Anna Lee, that cleanliness is next to godliness. When you grow up and have a house and children of your own, you just remember that now, you hear?"

"Yes, ma'am, I hear."

I couldn't finish the rest of my pudding. I pushed my chair up to the table and told her I had to go.

I spent what was left of the afternoon at the drugstore with Uncle Johnn. I dusted the midnight blue bottles of Evening in Paris cologne and straightened the few funny books he could get during the war. The funny books were always a mess, but Uncle Johnn never said a word to the boys and girls who crowded around the stand reading them. He didn't mind that he sold so few of them, either. His only regret was that he couldn't provide real books for us to read. We had our schoolbooks and the teachers had books, but there was no library. To get a book you had to know somebody who owned one you could borrow.

By the time I had things in order, it was going on six o'clock, and when I felt a hand on my shoulder, I knew it was his. I touched his fingers lightly with my own, and his strong hand gripped mine and helped me to my feet. Walking home together, I told him the whole thing, every bit of it.

"And it wasn't a cat, Uncle Johnn. It was a rabbit. A rabbit gave that girl ringworm! I'll never go to Miss Red's house again as long as I live. Never! All those little kittens could have been mine!"

Miss Red, of all people, lying. Of course, her name was sort of a lie. Even though she'd been married once, she still went by her maiden name. But she wasn't deceiving us. We knew she'd been married, and she knew we knew it. Verna was living, breathing proof of Miss Red's marriage no matter what name they went by.

At least I felt better for having talked to Uncle Johnn. With Mama and Daddy I sometimes felt like an outsider, but never with Uncle Johnn. Having him for an uncle was as wonderful as knowing I wasn't a tourist or adopted or some other awful thing. With his strong, angular jaw, surprising in one so gentle, he was taller and more handsome than any man in town. So lean and straight, he gave his clothes the same quality Ashley Wilkes gave to his Confederate uniform in *Gone With the Wind*.

Maybe Mama and Helen were right when they declared *Gone With the Wind* to be the standard by which Southerners measured life. I liked Ashley better than Rhett Butler, Mama's favorite. She said Ashley was too weak to suit her, too much like Uncle Johnn. To me Ashley, like Uncle Johnn, was the strongest of them all, never pretending to be anything more than he was. And if, like Ashley, Uncle Johnn seemed preoccupied, almost sad at times, I had to remember that the burden of owning the only drugstore in town and filling all those prescriptions every day sometimes made him seem older than his thirty-one years. The most eligible bachelor in Bay Harbor, he was never a boisterous man, but oh, how he could curse. And it was so unlikely coming from him that it seemed all the more eloquent. He never raised his voice. He wouldn't call to you from another room, but curse words poured from his mouth as naturally as seaweed from the bay. He knew words people in Bay Harbor would never have dreamed of, each as vivid and brilliant as a sunset. Mama said that's what an education would do for you, but coming from Uncle Johnn, cursing wasn't dirty. It was an art. It was reserved for our family alone, though. Uncle Johnn cursed only at home.

Supper was already on the table when we walked into the house. Pie-shaped wedges of corn bread were stacked next to my plate, and the odor of collards filled the house. My favorite meal, and I didn't think I could swallow a mouthful. I picked at my food, and Mama was sure I'd eaten a whole bowl of Miss Red's chocolate pudding. As soon as we finished eating, she sent me to bed. If I had eaten all the pudding, going to bed was punishment; if I was truly sick, then I belonged in bed anyway. Daddy always said you had to get up early to get one on Mama.

It was still light outside when I lay down on my bed, and too much had happened for sleep to come easily, even as I watched the light beneath the window shades grow dimmer. I heard Uncle Johnn in the living room talking to Mama about the war news, and I thought back, remembering how he had come to live with us in Bay Harbor.

2

In the beginning Mama hadn't wanted him to live with us. I was only six years old when I watched her hold Uncle Johnn's letter above the steaming teakettle and then read and reseal it before Daddy came home. Her lips were set in a thin straight line, and she didn't say a word as Daddy read the letter and needlessly tore it into tiny pieces.

Holding his hand over his mouth the way he did when he was thinking about something, Daddy sat quietly for a few minutes and then cleared his throat.

"Well," he said, "Johnn would like to come live with us."

Mama hadn't budged an inch, intent on her crocheting, but Daddy held his hand up as though to stop her from saying anything. "Now, you know the drugstore's been for sale, Estelle, and you got to admit we need a good druggist, someone young enough to know about all the new medicines coming out and old enough to win people's confidence. Looks to me like Johnn could fill the bill. Johnn doesn't want to work for somebody else all his life. He's saved a little money aside and thinks it'd be a good buy."

"Saved, my foot!" Mama snorted. "Inherited, you mean. Money that should have been shared with you. I always wondered what kind of woman your grandmother was to leave all her money to him. I'm just glad I never knew her. He got the education. He got everything."

Daddy spoke quietly, maybe sadly. "That's water under the bridge, Estelle. It wasn't a lot of money, and anyway, he spent every night at her house for the last two years of her life. He was just a boy, and she was so old. He was all she lived for at the last."

15

Mama's eyes flashed. "Yes, that seems to be a peculiar talent of his!"

The color drained from Daddy's face. "So he has a way with women. There's no crime in that."

I thought Mama's hands trembled slightly when she stopped crocheting for a moment, but any movement was soon lost in the flashing of her fingers as they stabbed the crochet hook in and out of the thread.

Daddy spoke to Mama, but he stared out the window. "To my way of thinkin', he'd be helpin' us out. What's more, I don't know but what it'd be a good idea for us to put up part of the money for the drugstore. We're bound to get a good return on our investment. A deputy sheriff ain't never gone be rich. I'm thinkin' about you and Anna Lee, Stelle. It'd be better than any insurance policy I could buy."

"Who says you have to be a deputy all your life? I notice the sheriff lives in a fine house that never wants for a coat of paint, and he can afford to buy a piano for his living room when not a soul in the house can play it."

"I'm not gettin' involved in any popularity contest, Estelle. I'm happy with what I'm doing. When I walk down the street, I don't have to wonder if the man speakin' to me was a vote for or against me in the election. I don't envy Sheriff his money. He needs it. He don't see people out there. He sees votes."

Mama laughed nervously. "I sure didn't mean to open up any old wounds."

"You ain't opened any wounds of mine, Estelle. You're just tryin' to change the subject."

"Well, what do you expect me to do?" Mama asked in a high-pitched, tight voice, and I wondered if she was going to cry.

I wanted Uncle Johnn to come live with us. No more of the breathless, hurried visits. Uncle Johnn one of us.

Mama laid her crocheting down and leveled her gaze at Daddy. "I think you're risking a lot, Robert, for a bit of insurance. I can't imagine what you're thinking of to want him living here in the house with us, here with your wife, just like . . ." Her voice trailed off into nothingness, and she jerked a length of crochet thread from the ball in her lap. "Next thing I know, you'll be wanting Henry and Wilda to move in with us, too. We can all be crowded in here like common trash."

"Now, you know there ain't no way we'd ever have Henry or Wilda, either one, live here. Henry's blood, but he's not my brother. Don't go trying to muddy the waters, Estelle. Henry's got no place in this conversation, and you know it."

Daddy squatted on the floor in front of me.

"How'd you like to have your Uncle Johnn live here with us, Anna Lee?"

I looked beyond Daddy's back to Mama, and she quietly shook her head from side to side. I looked back at Daddy.

"All the time?"

He nodded.

"I'd love it," I said, and jumped up and down clapping my hands so I didn't have to see Mama's face very clearly.

Mama hadn't opened her mouth, so Daddy said, "Well, we'll talk about it later. You go on out and play now, Anna Lee."

I left by the front door and continued down the side of the house to the backyard where I could see through the screen door to the living room. Like shadows I watched Mama and Daddy pass through the dining room and into the hall leading to their bedroom. Crossing to the other side of the house, I walked toward the front yard but stopped close to the house, outside their bedroom window. The shades were pulled, but the windows weren't closed all the way. I could hear sounds of voices but couldn't make out any words until I stood on a log that bordered one of the flower beds and brought me closer to the window. Their voices were still muffled, and I missed a lot, but Daddy's voice was clearer than Mama's.

"This is an entirely different situation, Estelle, and you know it. And furthermore, when he's visited here, it's always been fine. He's never said or done anythin' out of the way, has he? Haven't we all gotten along just fine?"

Mama had to know we had. She never had anything nice to say about Uncle Johnn beforehand, but once he arrived for a visit she always appeared to enjoy his company.

Mama said something about someone named Grace, and a faint remembrance of something unpleasant tried to surface as I listened to Daddy hammering his point home. "Are you gone let some old gossip stand between us and our future? I thought we had that settled in your mind years ago. If I'd ever thought for a minute we hadn't . . ." His voice dropped lower, and I couldn't hear the rest of what he said, but then he walked closer to the window and I heard him say, "Johnn knows how things stand, Stelle, and if he makes his home with us, well, that's just further insurance for us. You don't think he's gone do anything to make himself unwelcome, do you? I mean, be reasonable! And he loves Anna Lee. You know he'd never say or do anythin' that might hurt her. Just put all that nonsense out of your head, because you know that's all it is. Do you think I'd have him here in the house for a visit, much less live with us, if I didn't think that it was? Use your head, woman!"

"With him here, we won't be a family anymore!" Mama shouted.

Daddy sounded determined and a bit mad. "Oh yes, Estelle, we'll be a family all right. God knows he's peculiar even if he is my brother, but if things get any tighter, we're gone be takin' us in a roomer. Is that what you want? Some stranger in the room next to us?"

Ants crawled down inside my shoes, and I danced off the log without knowing if Uncle Johnn would be living with us or not.

I wondered if Daddy meant it about taking in a roomer. Mama must have believed him. It wasn't long before they were fixing up a room for Uncle Johnn. By the time everything was settled and he arrived to stay, it was my seventh birthday. Mama went so far as to order a bakery cake special for the occasion. It came twenty-seven miles on the bread truck to the grocery store, and not a bit of the icing was mashed. But that was only the beginning of all the wonderful things that were to follow.

Mama said two families couldn't live under the same roof without problems, but Uncle Johnn was as much a part of us as if he'd always been there. Things worked out so well, Mama acted as though it had been her idea to have him live with us in the first place. After Uncle Johnn came we moved up in the world. Or so I thought. We stayed in the white frame house that didn't boast so much as a shutter at the dark-screened windows or a porch big enough to support a row of white rockers, but things were brighter, and people treated us with more respect. Mama sold our cool white wicker settee and chairs, replacing them with a studio couch and round-armed velvety upholstered pieces on which we sweated heavily but which she felt were more suited to a living room. We even hired a maid.

I was taken with the very idea. We'd never had anyone to wait on us before. A maid seemed a natural part of the excitement that came from having Uncle Johnn with us, but I never for one minute doubted that Edith was a price Daddy paid for that excitement. A maid, Mama said often enough, could be had for thirty cents a day if you trained her yourself, but as Mama didn't have to do that, our maid earned a slightly higher wage. It wasn't long, though, before I ceased thinking of Edith as a maid. Like Uncle Johnn, she was a part of the family. Of course, Daddy had been very careful in selecting her. He didn't rush out and bring in the first colored girl off the sidewalk. Mama fretted over the delay. With every passing day, she seemed more and more in need of a maid, but, as in most things, Daddy was deliberate and slow. "For God's sake, Robert," Mama complained, "it's not like we're planning to adopt her."

"Estelle," Daddy threatened, "you best be careful."

"I just need some help."

"Don't worry about it none, Estelle. I told you you'd have a maid by the time Johnn gets here. I'm a man of my word," he emphasized and hitched his pants up like he was going out of the house right then to hire somebody. His work, of course, took him to the Quarters often enough for him to know the ones who knew their place. Daddy didn't hate anything worse than an uppity nigger, but he was willing to admit there were good ones. They were the ones who knew their place. It seemed to me they'd have had to be blind not to know it. Not a one was allowed to live outside the Quarters.

Edith must have known her place very well because Daddy spent weeks talking to girls and to the people they'd worked for before selecting her from all the rest. Edith wasn't as young as some of the maids I knew, and she didn't look strange like the skinny, bulging-eyed Pansy. I tried hard not to stare at Pansy, but she was so ugly it was a real temptation to study her. Daddy even talked to her, but she wouldn't think that strange, not in his line of work. I'd never seen a Nigra refuse to speak to Daddy, which was a relief. In addition to the gun he always wore, he carried a blackjack in his back pocket and a nightstick in the car. He said at the dinner table one day that Pansy's eyes had been as normal as his when she went to work at the funeral home. "In fact," he said, leaning his head forward and looking at each of us in turn, "her eyes might have even been set back a bit in her head. It seems as I remember they were. I guess if she works there much longer, they'll just fall right out of her head some day."

Daddy laughed, but Mama didn't think it was funny. "You don't deserve a child, Robert Owens. You ought to be ashamed of yourself. You'll scare the wits out of her."

Daddy didn't like it when Mama ruined his jokes, so he had to have the last word. "I don't think, Estelle, that Anna Lee ever plans on being no undertaker, so there ain't no reason for her to be scared for her eyes. Anyway, only a nigger's scared of dead people."

Edith didn't demand staring. She was ordinary in looks. Her black hair was as neat and smoothed as wool can be, and her clothes were clean and pressed. And she had no odor. I sat on her lap, closer to her than anybody. I drew deep breaths and knew she had no odor, but Daddy said she did. "All niggers smell," he said. He hauled them to jail in the back seat of our car, but I'd never smelled anything.

"I could pick out a nigger if I was blind," Daddy said one day while we ate dinner. "I wouldn't have to see him. All I'd have to do is smell him." Edith was in the kitchen and I wanted to die.

Mama hadn't forgotten Edith was there either, but she couldn't resist fighting fire with fire. Her eyes flashed and she said, "It must be a smell you like, then, seeings how you can sit in a boat in the hot sun fishing all day with Fly."

Fly ran a fish bait stand, and Daddy, who over the years seemed to have less and less time to grub worms, was a frequent customer. More often than not, Fly would close the stand and the two of them would go off fishing together. Fly always rode in the back seat, of course, and Daddy acted as though he let him go along just to keep the boat bailed out, but Mama was unconvinced. She didn't care much for fishing herself. It took her away from her crocheting and radio stories. A bunch of gooey worms and struggling fish were no match for "Young Dr. Malone" and "Mary Noble, Backstage Wife," but Mama sure didn't like it when Daddy took Fly along.

If he had just kept quiet, Daddy could have saved himself a lot of grief, but he'd never been able to resist telling us something Fly had said or done.

Daddy ate another piece of corn bread and finished his iced tea before he answered Mama. He said wearily, "Estelle, I've told you and I've told you." He inclined his head in the direction of the kitchen as though he needed to remind Mama that Edith was there. "Them ain't just pleasure trips," he said in a hushed voice. "You better understand that once and for all. And don't they put food on the table?"

"And on Fly's," Mama countered.

"Well, he's got to eat, ain't he? Fly knows his place, which seems to be more'n I can say for you."

Daddy was mad, and Mama knew it.

Uncle Johnn coughed and started asking me how I was enjoying the book satchel he'd given me.

Daddy gave all his attention to the food Edith had cooked, looking up only once to say, "The truth never hurt nobody."

Mama didn't say another word. She didn't want to lose Edith. Heaven only knew how long it might take Daddy to find somebody else who knew her place.

It was nice to live in a house that didn't have squirrels' tails, as Edith called the dust under the beds, and Mama didn't have to rush each morning to get to the store. She lingered over her morning coffee as the heat built and the can of Pet milk began to sweat, drops of moisture rippling the paper like old skin. Later she would go the store for the day's meat and vegetables, but she could sit and crochet and listen to the radio while Edith cooked the noon meal. And after we finished eating and she had cleaned up the kitchen, there was always time for Edith to take me on her lap and read to me from the fairy-tale books Uncle Johnn had given me. Mama absolutely refused to read them. Nobody ever read to her, she said, and took that for reason enough not to read to me. Edith always brought me a little something, a stick of gum, a piece of suck candy, just some little something. Once she gave me some pennies tied into a knotted corner of a hand-kerchief. So proud, I showed Miss Red.

"Spend those pennies, Anna Lee, but I wouldn't be eating any of that candy and stuff she gives you. No telling what you're liable to get eating stuff she's had in her house. Why, you don't know what the inside of that house looks like. You can't be too careful, Anna Lee. I wouldn't have one in my house myself, but that's your mother's business, not mine."

I continued eating Edith's candy, never hinting that Miss Red had cautioned me against it. And each time I ate a piece, I chalked up a little victory for Edith. I offered Uncle Johnn a piece once, and when he ate it, it was a double victory. But Edith never knew about those victories. All she came to know was the hurt I brought to her.

I don't know if it was having a maid or having Uncle Johnn live with us that brought about the change in Mama. He hadn't been with us six months when Mama started going to church. Oh, not regularly, but once in a while. She joined the Missionary Society, and Uncle Johnn bought her a dress of dark blue sharkskin as a belated moving-in present. Though at times I still felt like an outsider, I was happier than I'd ever been in my life. The Missionary Society was to meet at our house! Edith did the cleaning, and Mama made lemon meringue pies. Edith could just as well have made them, but Mama wanted to show off her pies without any yellow beads on the meringue. We'd never had a meeting at our house before, and when I came home from school that day, the house smelled of furniture polish and newly varnished floors. I saw that Mama had finished her crocheted tablecloth. White as beach sand, it covered the dining room table like a frosting of sugar.

Afterward I could never think what made me do it. I didn't plan to do it, and at the time it didn't even seem wrong. I squatted underneath the dining room table, getting placed to watch the ladies come in. Staring ahead, squinting at the tiny holes in Mama's new tablecloth, I reached into my book satchel and took out a pair of small scissors. Carefully, following the circular pattern, I removed a perfect flower from my view. I had hardly gotten a good look at it before Mama saw what I had done. She had on the blue sharkskin dress and had fashioned her hair into long rolls that framed her face. Mama never hesitated to yell at me, but she must have been worried that some of the ladies would come in on her because her face changed, but she didn't yell. I don't suppose I'd ever seen her so mad. I thought she might kill me, but Edith was right there behind her.

"Why, Miss Anna Lee," Edith said softly, "what do you mean, cuttin' a hole in your mama's nice new cloth and her with company comin'? Lordy, Lordy, Miz Owens, I sure hopes you can fix that."

"Is this the way you're going to act when we have company, Anna Lee?" Mama hissed in a loud whisper. "What else have you got up your sleeve for today?" Her voice broke, and I thought she might cry. "What am I going to do with you? I can't turn my back on you, I guess."

As full awareness of what I'd done came to me, I burst into tears. All my excitement turned into tears and noisy sobs that only made Mama more nervous.

"Anna Lee, hush that racket. They'll be here any minute now."

I watched Edith take the cloth from the table and put up the ironing board to press an old one. I cried all the louder.

"My nerves just won't take this, Anna Lee," Mama pleaded. "People will think I'm beating you to death." But I couldn't stop crying. A few minutes later I felt a hand on my shoulder and looked around to see Edith with her hat on and her pocketbook slung over her arm.

"Come on, Miss Anna Lee, you're goin' home with me. Let's don't spoil your mama's party. Come on with Edith."

I was still crying as she led me out the back door and down the path beside our house. "You better hush now or somebody's gone think I'm kidnappin' you," she laughed, and my crying was reduced to jerking gasps.

It was early October and still warm as we walked slowly along the back side of town between the rows of houses to the railroad tracks, where we turned left and walked toward the depot. There we cut across the shiny, hot tracks and followed the path to the Quarters, past the church and the uneasy silence of their scarcely used school. Sad as death, idle swings hung limp beyond the vacant reflection of tightly closed windows. The cooks at the boarding house and most of the maids in town took their children to work with them, where they waited outside all day, never causing any trouble or darkening the schoolhouse door.

Edith's house was small and hot and smelled of kerosene. She had an old wood stove and kerosene lamps, and a wonderful hand pump at her kitchen sink. Paper pictures were fastened to the walls with straight pins, and screen wire had been nailed over all the windows, but there was no glass, just rough wooden shutters to push shut and latch from the outside. I quickly noted that I'd be able to tell Miss Red how clean everything was.

Edith went to the ice box and chipped at the small piece of ice with the ice pick. Without asking me what I wanted, she made each of us a glass of lemonade. We sat at the kitchen table, and Edith seemed at a loss for words. "I reckon it'd be okay to take you home pretty soon now," she said finally.

But she wasn't to take me home. We were still at the table looking at pictures in a Sears 'n Roebuck catalog when a car came flying down the road and stopped in front of her house in a cloud of dust. We walked to the front door, only a few steps really, and there was Daddy striding across Edith's yard. Mama had told him about the tablecloth! His face was white with rage. My heart started pounding loudly in my chest, and I knew it was more than the tablecloth.

"It's okay, honey," Edith said softly, but I knew it wasn't.

"Get in the car, Anna Lee," Daddy ordered. He didn't even thank Edith for having me over, and I was scared to do anything but run to the car. I could see people standing in their yards and on their porches watching us, and I wanted to die.

Edith walked out to the car after Daddy. "Mr. Owens?" she began hesitantly.

"I ain't blamin' you, Edith," Daddy said before he turned and got in the car. He started the motor but sat for a moment with his arms rigid, both hands grasping the steering wheel. He spoke out the window to Edith. "We won't be needin' you anymore."

Edith never moved. She just stood there, frozen. Daddy turned the car around in the middle of the road and, driving too fast, left Edith swallowed in dust.

Looking back at her, I quit worrying about the spanking I'd get. How could Daddy treat Edith that way?

Mama was cleaning up when we walked in the house. She came to the door of the kitchen and appeared stunned to see me with Daddy. "Why Robert, I . . ."

"My youngun," Daddy interrupted, "ain't never to go to the nigger quarters. A deputy sheriff's youngun in a nigger's house! Make me a laughingstock, will you? When the three o'clock shift let out at the mill, all them men going home saw 'em crossin' the railroad tracks. First thing I hear when I get back to the station is some fat ass asking me if Anna Lee is over in the Quarters interviewing for a new maid. Now, Estelle, how do you expect me to do my job if I don't have people's respect? They've got to respect me or I'm not one iota of good at what I'm doing. Robert Owens has got to be respected whether you have a maid or not. Have you lost your mind?"

At that Mama's face drained of color. "No, but I've obviously lost my maid."

Daddy held his hand up in the stop position, and he stopped her all right. "Now, I've never laid a hand on you, and I don't want to. I've been good to you, Estelle. I've been good to Anna Lee. We agreed to certain things before Anna Lee—"

Mama came back to life. "That's enough! Stop right there before you say something you're going to regret. You've scared Anna Lee half to death as it is. She's white as a sheet."

We were all white as sheets, all the whiter because I kept remembering Edith's darkness caught in the swirling dust.

Mama and Daddy reached some kind of understanding. He didn't lay a hand on her or on me, either. Mama repaired the tablecloth so well that afterwards I never could locate the spot, but she decided she didn't have time for the Missionary Society. If she thought that would bother Daddy though, she was mistaken. Daddy didn't see that respect had anything to do with the Missionary Society.

If only Mama could have crocheted Edith back into the fabric of our lives. I seldom saw her after that. She came by the house on my birthday once and brought me a present. Occasionally I would see her in a store, and when no one was looking, she'd squeeze my hand, but they were never good times. I was always too afraid of doing something more to hurt her.

I wondered if Mama could give me up as easily as she had the Missionary Society. Mama didn't have time for lots of things, especially me, and after Uncle Johnn came to live with us I confided in him and not her or Daddy. Mama knew this. She was always sneaking around when I was with Uncle Johnn, peeking into a room or slipping in quietly in hopes of hearing what we were saying. I'd stop talking in midsentence when she did that, taking a certain satisfaction in paying her back for all the times she'd done the same thing to me. Some of my earliest memories were of Mama's sudden silences when I walked into a room. In the hushed stillness, heavy with something that made me afraid, people would turn and look at me inquiringly, as though I were some stranger, some outsider.

It was never easy to talk to Mama. I would stand before her with some problem, watching her fingers fly as she forced the length of crochet thread into knots and loops that magically turned into flowers and pineapples and leaves. She would hardly look up, answering me in a measured voice as if she were no more than counting a chain stitch.

"Sticks and stones may break your bones, Anna Lee, but words will never harm you."

Did she really believe that? Did it say so in her pattern book? Didn't she know my hurt would still fester long after a bone had healed?

Uncle Johnn not only listened to me, he understood. That undoubtedly accounted for some of the ugly things Mama and Daddy said and the way they made fun of him behind his back. I would have been the first to admit he was different. I had never seen anyone else who looked or acted the way he did, but I hated the things Mama and Daddy said, for I loved him more than anyone in all the world.

"Anna Lee sure does love her Uncle Johnn." People were always saying that. I hoped Uncle Johnn heard them, but then I supposed he knew, the same as they did, how I felt. Mama said there were all kinds of love, but I thought the best love of all was what I felt for Uncle Johnn. I thought every man should want to be like my Uncle Johnn, but Mama and Daddy felt otherwise. They loved him, they said, but they were embarrassed because he wasn't like other men. Mama even felt his clothes were too showy, him being the only man in Bay Harbor walking the streets in a suit and tie. In the summer he wore straw hats and white suits, but Mama said he might as well have left his hat at home because he took it off to every woman he passed on the street. "Why, he'll get a sunstroke some day just from taking that hat off so much."

I loved his being different, but I couldn't help but wonder if there wasn't some place, a place unlike Bay Harbor, where all the men wore straw hats and he'd fit in with everybody else.

Mama, on the other hand, couldn't stand his difference and said he stuck out like a sore thumb.

"It's none of my business, Johnn, how you spend your money," she'd say to him. "If you want to put it all into clothes, that's all right with me. It surely does seem a waste, though. The minute you get to the drugstore, you put on that cotton work coat. All day long you're filling prescriptions, and people don't see a thing but that starched coat and an occasional glimpse of your pants."

Uncle Johnn always agreed with her. "You're absolutely right, Estelle. Yes, you are."

"Well, I thought you'd see it my way, Johnn. I treat you the same as if you were my own brother." Of course, Mama didn't have a brother, so how would she know how she'd have treated one?

Uncle Johnn would thank her for being so helpful, and it'd be some time before she'd realize he'd gone right on dressing the way he always had.

But in spite of all Mama's objections to Uncle Johnn's clothes, she was always ready to admit that he was a gentleman. Maybe he was the only gentleman in Bay Harbor. I knew, too, that he was a gentle man, but for a long time he carried a knife. Most men did. Daddy had a knife with him all the time. I don't suppose a day passed that he didn't use it for something. Daddy's thin, hard little knife looked mean to me.

"That's the silliest thing I ever heard of," Mama said. "You ought to be ashamed of yourself, saying that your own daddy's knife looks mean like he was a criminal or something. I'll be sure and tell him not to peel any more oranges for you with that mean knife of his."

The knife had saved me many a sore thumbnail, but I'd seen the same knife split the skin of a squirrel.

"Don't you hate to shoot them, Daddy?" I asked him once. "They're so cute. They don't hurt anybody."

He stood on the squirrel's tail and pulled the stiff pink body from its hairy covering.

"I've never noticed it botherin' you none to eat them when they're all cut up and fried for your supper. You can eat more squirrel brains and grits than I can. Good Lord, Anna Lee, people have got to eat. It don't bother me none to kill somethin' that'll keep my belly from growling." I'd also watched the fish scales fly in front of the blade and stared at the bright unseeing eyes on the fish heads. The scales would stick to my face and hair, and the knife would stink.

But Uncle Johnn's never did. His was a small, gold knife he wore on his watch chain. I'd never seen him use it. As far as I could see, it was just a means of identification, with a beautifully engraved "O" framed on the front. I'd been fascinated by the knife from the first time I saw it.

"Isn't it beautiful?" I'd said to Mama. "It's just like Uncle Johnn, isn't it?"

"That's the God's truth if you ever said it, Anna Lee. Your Uncle Johnn is just about as handy as that knife."

"I didn't mean it that way. It is like him, but not the way you say. You know what I mean." There was a swelling in my throat, and I swallowed hard.

"Don't start, young lady. Where your Uncle Johnn's concerned, you've got a way of closing your eyes to anything you don't want to see. The truth never hurt anybody. Just remember, 'All that shines isn't gold, and all that glitters isn't diamonds.' Just remember that, you hear?"

She surely pointed out to me often enough all the things Uncle Johnn couldn't do. They were always ordinary, insignificant things. He didn't know how to drive a car, and he'd never learned to light the kerosene stove in the kitchen properly. Mama had to heat the coffee herself to keep him from getting the pot smutty and maybe setting the house on fire. She didn't complain so much after he surprised her with a fancy glass dripolator. Mama never complained when Uncle Johnn gave her presents, but what she never seemed to understand was that most anybody could light a stove. Uncle Johnn knew about important things, like how to keep me from scratching when I had the measles.

It was right after he came to live with us that I caught them and was so terribly sick. Mama kept all the shades pulled down as far as they'd go, and the heat made the itching almost unbearable, but she refused to raise them even an inch. She said I might go blind if she did. Measles had almost killed Uncle Johnn. That's when they discovered he'd been born with a damaged heart. It didn't make him an invalid, but it was enough to keep him out of the war, at home with us.

Every night he came into that miserable room and talked to me. Once he caught me scratching and without a moment's hesitation, slipped the little gold knife from his watch chain. "Here, honey, you can have this if you'll promise Uncle Johnn you won't scratch anymore." Mama threatened me with scarring. Uncle Johnn offered me gold.

He offered me gold, and he talked to me about the past. Mama talked mainly of the future. Everything was in the future. "When my ship comes in," she'd say, or "When you're older, Anna Lee," or "When the war's over," but if I ever asked her a question about some distant event, it was always the same answer. "I might be dead and buried by then," she'd say, drawing a picture I couldn't bear to see.

Daddy didn't talk about the past or the future. He was a man of action, a man of few words. Daddy was for doing and not talking about it, and if it was done, you didn't look back. But Uncle Johnn did.

The nights of measles were endless, and another time Uncle Johnn told me about a ghostly space framed by giant oaks where once had stood the unpainted house he and Daddy still called home. "My mother," he told me, "came to that house a bride. She had bedroom eyes," he began, coughed and looked embarrassed. "I mean, she had that dreamy-eyed look common among girls with poor vision. How she did hate glasses! She hid her need for them the way I've known some women to hide a weakness for cigarettes. The stories her own mother would tell about her pretense at being able to see things! Mama swore her family to secrecy, though, and when she and Papa were married, she said he'd never catch her in glasses. Grandmother claimed Mama threw them in the weeds one time when Papa came home before she expected him. They were married ten years before Robert and Earl were born, and ten more before she was frightened into wearing them." He touched my nose playfully with his forefinger. "She fell down the steps with me in her arms. I was three weeks old, and my name was already in the family Bible.

She never would explain the second *n* she added to my name."
He laughed. "But would a woman that vain admit to a mistake?"

It rankled him, I think—not that he minded the second *n*, but
that his mother wouldn't tell him the reason for it. After all it was
his name. And in spite of the fact that Mama poked fun at the
spelling, she seemed to take it as a sign of favoritism and resented
the fact that Daddy had been christened Robert with only one *t*.
The fact that there had been two daddies didn't cut any ice with
Mama. The twin boys hadn't even been given rhyming names.
James Robert and Malcolm Earl they were called. Uncle Earl had
been killed in a hunting accident before I was born, but Uncle
Johnn said he would have been a mirror image of Daddy except
that he was so much the taller of the two. That shouldn't have
been possible for identical twins, Uncle Johnn told me, but it
happened.

"Uncle Johnn," I asked, "why doesn't Daddy ever talk about
Uncle Earl? They were twins, but he hardly ever mentions him."

"Because your daddy won't ever quit missing Earl. It was like
they didn't need anybody else. Earl was big, but he was so gentle.
He wouldn't hurt a fly. Being that big, I guess he could afford to
be gentle, but your daddy was always having to scrap with
somebody. It wasn't easy for Robert, I tell you, but I envied them
having each other. They were so close. I didn't think they'd either
one marry."

I'd never seen a picture of Uncle Earl, or my grandmother,
either, for that matter. Uncle Johnn said there had been some,
but no one seemed to know what had become of them. I'd seen
some pictures once. When Uncle Johnn came to live with us he'd
brought some snapshots in a small wooden chest. The ones on
top were of a woman, and the name *Grace* was written on the
back. I had hardly begun to look at them when Mama walked in.
She was so mad she was shaking. She jerked the picture from my
hand and told me I must never look at them again.

"You must never," she said, "be going through your Uncle
Johnn's things. Do you think he'd stay here five minutes? Five
minutes," she asked, "if he thought you were going to be
snooping in his things? We just won't ever mention that this

happened, and you stay out of his room now, you hear? If I ever catch you in here again, I'll spank you so hard you won't sit down for a week."

I wouldn't have done anything to make Uncle Johnn unhappy with us, so I never said anything, and the wooden chest vanished, too.

From beginning to end, it was eight long days and nights before I'd fully recovered from the measles. I wasn't scarred, and I had a gold knife to boot. So proud, I showed the knife to Daddy and told him Uncle Johnn had given it to me, but he only laughed. "You call that thing a knife? That's just a play pretty, Anna Lee, nothin' but a play pretty."

It might have been a play pretty to Daddy, but for a brief period of time following the measles, it was my most prized possession.

3

Having had a magic show on Saturday made Sunday duller than ever, but I went to Sunday school anyway. Nobody made me go, but the church was close by, and if I didn't miss Sunday school for an entire year, I'd get a copy of *Little Women*. Miss Red said that sounded just like something a Methodist church would do. The Baptists gave out Bibles, not novels. That was one more reason to be glad I was a Methodist. But the Methodists taught me there was something worse than sin. They never talked much about sin. Mostly they talked about hiding your light under a bushel. I was never sure if I was sinning, but I knew I was hiding my light under a bushel. Worse still, I was afraid there was no light. Our Sunday school teachers assured us everyone had a light, and I worried what mine might be. If I didn't know what it was, how could I help but hide it? Other girls could sing or dance, play musical instruments or recite poetry, but since there was nothing I could do, I was never totally comfortable, even as a Methodist. Thinking about *Little Women* made it easier to bear the discomfort, but even the Methodists didn't give books to people who stayed for church every Sunday, so as soon as Sunday school was over, I ambled leisurely in the direction of the railroad station to see if the Bullet was in.

I knew Bay Harbor from one end to the other. I was free to go just about anyplace I wanted, anytime I wanted, provided it wasn't during school hours or after dark. I wasn't allowed this freedom because I was brave but because Mama and Daddy believed me to be a coward. Fine-boned and thin, they couldn't imagine I'd be otherwise. I knew I wasn't a coward. But I wasn't a fool, either. In all of Bay Harbor there was only one place I knew better by car than by foot. Daddy had never come right out and told me not to go to the Quarters. Unable to bury the memory of the dust swirling around Edith, of Daddy's too-white face, or of my misery and shame, there was never any need for him to tell me that I could go only as far as the railroad tracks, that forever after, like the main street, that's where I had to stop.

I knew the Quarters by car because Daddy, Mama was fond of saying, loved boiled peanuts better than a hog loved slop. When the weed-filled lots made way for a peanut stand, a fire was built beneath a black Annie, or if the cast-iron caldron was needed for boiling clothes instead, then a metal drum cut in half would hold the boiling, salted water. Inside, hundreds of peanuts would bob up and down like a bunch of drowning tourists. Worried about what had been in the pot before the peanuts went in, Mama refused to eat them, but many a Sunday I rode with Daddy to the Quarters where we gorged ourselves on the blackeyed pea taste of soggy peanuts.

The peanut stand came and went with the seasons but not the church, and as I neared the railroad station, I could hear the swell of singing from the faithful. Shading my eyes from the sun, I saw that the Bullet, our only train, was parked in front, waiting. It wasn't called the Bullet for any feats of speed but for its dull, slate color. I'd ridden on it once, not quite a year ago, but I hadn't gone anyplace, just to the end of the line and back. That trip had been my ninth birthday present from Uncle Johnn, and Mama was still fuming because I hadn't asked for the heart-shaped gold stretch bracelet she'd picked out for me. She didn't like it that I had nothing to show for my birthday, and as I had ambled uneasily from the steps of the Bullet, I had thought it best not to tell her I'd spent most of time in the bathroom peering down the toilet seat, fascinated by the fact that there was absolutely nothing to separate me from the ground that passed so swiftly below. I came out at every stop though. I didn't want the conductor to think I was dumb enough to use the bathroom on somebody's main street.

I walked alongside the Bullet now, touching it here and there with my hand. Helen and Chester would be boarding the train

just before noon, and they were going further than the end of the
line. They would change trains and go on to New Orleans. They
were to spend almost two weeks in New Orleans, and I knew
Helen would leave Bay Harbor looking like a queen.

Mama said Helen gave me that impression only because she
wore a strong corset and carried herself well, but then Mama was
probably mad because I'd never said she looked like a queen. I
couldn't really say what Mama looked like. She was my mother,
but I couldn't see her the way I saw Helen. Mama went on diets,
but she wasn't fat, and she was neither short nor tall, but she said
I'd eat apples off her head someday. She wore rouge and lipstick
and nail polish. She was older than Helen and the mothers of
most of my friends, but she liked pretty dresses and curly hair. I
could never put it all together and describe her, though. Far more
familiar to me than Mama's face were her hands, the way they
looked and smelled and felt. Like Scarlett's following the war,
they weren't a queen's hands, but Helen's were. Hers were
smooth and white because she didn't have to do housework.
There were maids to clean the rooms and cooks to prepare the
food for her dining room. My only regret where Helen was
concerned was that she wasn't a relative. To say that she was a
friend, even a close friend, didn't explain the way I felt about her.

She was a large, handsome woman with long golden hair and
smooth, flawless skin. Tall and broad-shouldered, she might
have been descended from kings.

Though she seldom talked about her life before coming to Bay
Harbor, she did tell us that her first husband had been good-
looking, a giant of a man fond of practical jokes and rich food. It
had been his idea to move to Bay Harbor and buy the boarding
house. Helen seemed to look backward, beyond us, as she
described his happiness as the proprietor of such an important
establishment. Going to wake him for breakfast one morning,
she found him sitting propped up in bed, his hands behind his
head. Standing quietly just inside the door, she envisioned him
savoring the moment, anticipating the big breakfast waiting for
him in the kitchen. When she had to call him several times, she
thought this was only another joke. But if it was, the joke was on

him. He'd died with a smile on his face and the smell of country sausage in his nose. Helen had been overwhelmed with grief and the responsibility of the boarding house. Chester, a childhood friend, appeared at the funeral and couldn't do enough to console the grieving widow. She didn't offer it as an excuse, but there had to be some reason for her to have married him. But he was no longer consoling. They hadn't been married long when he'd burned every picture she had of her first husband. She'd been hurt but flattered, too, that he was so jealous. Mama said Chester was like a mole on Helen's backside. She didn't like having it there, but she was afraid to have it removed.

Chester worked on a dredge called the *Blackwater,* a common scavenger, a catfish that crawled along sucking up the filth and mud of the river bottom, and Bay Harbor was a better place because he was away on that dredge for weeks at a time. The direct opposite of Helen, there was nothing royal about him. As appealing as a bad case of worms, he was a mean, skinny hound dog of a man. A spray of freckles arched like whiskers from either side of his peeling, sunburned nose, and grooves plowed with a pocket comb were a permanent pattern in his brilliantined hair. I hated the way he made over me and patted my rear end with his big, calloused hand. He did it openly, but something in his touch told me it was wrong. I didn't even like taking money from Chester, but he was forever trying to force nickels and dimes on me. I wondered if they were rich. They were the only people I knew who took out-of-town vacations. Once they had gone to the state fair in Tampa, and I waited for their return in much the same way Miss Red waited for me to come home from the picture show. All through the winter months, Helen recounted that trip for me.

"Anna Lee, some day you really must see the state fair," she told me. "Why, you couldn't believe all the things just hearing me tell about them. There was a building bigger than this boarding house filled with flowers and displays the like you've never seen. It smelled so sweet and wild in there. And oh, the rides, Anna Lee. It was like a fairyland! They ran them all the time, and at night they were lit up like Christmas trees. There were so many, I can't even remember the names. Can you imagine that, Anna Lee? Here in Bay Harbor you get a merry-go-round once a year, and that's all you get, a merry-go-round."

"What's it like riding them?" I asked. "Were you afraid?"

"Oh, why, honey, I never rode any of them personally. I just looked, but you'll ride them some day. I know you will. You'll see it all, just like I did. It's like being in another world. I walked up and down in that dust looking and learning, just taking it all in. I watched an old man rolling cigars, and I saw the fattest women in the world. They can't even buy clothes to fit her. They buy whole bolts of cloth and wrap it around her. She has a special bed and everything. She has to lay down a lot. Her feet just won't support all that weight."

"It'd be awful to be that big and have people look at you all the time."

"I think it'd be a lot worse to be that big and have to live like everybody else, but, honey, she's like a queen up there on that stage. She travels all over and is well cared for. No, I don't feel sorry for her, Anna Lee, not a bit."

Souvenirs Helen brought back from their trips lined the shelves of a bookcase that stood in the corner of her living room, and the year she returned from the fair Helen added a Kewpie doll and a cigar to her collection. How I loved to smell that cigar! It wasn't just the tobacco. It smelled like a fair. I hoped that if I smelled it often enough, Helen would give it to me. Maybe she would have if Chester hadn't smoked it. I wanted to cry when he struck a match to that hand-made cigar, but I didn't. He squinted his eyes at me over the smoke, and I looked at Helen and said, "It stinks." She only laughed and didn't say a word about him burning up one of her souvenirs.

Already I was wondering what Helen would bring back from New Orleans, but I'd rather she not bring anything back than have Chester destroy it.

People were beginning to drift toward the station, and by the time Helen and Chester arrived, there was a small crowd to see them off. Helen was too rushed to stop and talk, but she saw me and waved. Chester didn't wave to anybody but just strutted around with all the grace of a wharf rat, his freckles standing out like beads of sweat in the sunlight. Pausing there in front of the Bullet, Helen rubbed a gloved finger over the crystal of her watch, and the striped hatbox hanging from her arm swayed with the motion. The sun's rays glinted off her glasses, casting up little stars all around her eyes. She did look like a queen! If only she'd had a king instead of that rawboned, freckled Chester to follow her up the steps of the train. They were the only passengers when the Bullet pulled and jerked its way out of Bay Harbor. It might have been their own private train, parked there for no other purpose than to take them away.

Turning to leave, I saw a dark figure coming rapidly up the path from the Quarters. I knew immediately it was Fly. I'd seen that shape etched like a dark shadow on our back screen door too many times not to recognize him a mile away. I knew he was headed for our house. I could never recall just when the fishing trips had been extended to visits to the house, and it had taken me a long time to figure out why he always came on Sunday. He wasn't as apt to be seen on Sunday because most of the Nigras were in church. Was Fly part of Daddy's success as a deputy sheriff? Or did they all have their informers? Was there one for the police chief, one for the sheriff — how did it work? I couldn't stand Fly. I asked Daddy one time how he could like somebody who betrayed his own people.

"I don't look at it that way, Anna Lee," he'd told me. "I have to do my job, and I try to do a good job. It's not like Fly is a-tellin' somethin' on somebody. He wants to do what's right, and he don't think it's right to break the law. All he's doing is tryin' to uphold the law — for everybody, whites and niggers alike. Do you think we could win this war if we didn't have spies? They'll be heroes when the war's over, not cause they told on somebody but because they upheld something they believed in."

"That's different. And it's important."

"You don't think this is important? It's important to me, and it sure ought to be important to you. It's my job you're talkin' about. And Fly does a lot of good, too. Them niggers will be grateful to him some day. He's kept many a black buck out of the penitentiary. Catch 'em doin' something the first time they do it and nine times out of ten, they'll mend their ways. But let 'em keep on doin' it and doin' it and gettin' away with it and, first thing you know, they're into the big time. No driving them to the county seat to jail then. They do something big and it's Raiford and the road gang."

I still couldn't think well of Fly for what he was doing and didn't believe the Nigras could either, but maybe he got away with being an informer because he was a celebrity in the Quarters. Even so, it made me mad that Daddy liked him. Fly was as black as the ace of spades, but he was all right in Daddy's book. Whenever Daddy spoke to Fly, he was serious, almost respectful. I asked Mama once if she'd ever noticed the special way Daddy had of talking to Fly.

"Yes," she said, "and it's no small feat considering Fly's reputation."

His full name, or all that I knew, was Fly Swatter, so called not from killing so many flies but from the way he did it. His technique, as Daddy called it, was to kill flies in flight. "Anybody can swat a fly that's lit," Daddy told us, "but Fly catches 'em in midair and slams 'em against the wall with such force it knocks 'em dead. Wham! Wham! Wham! Faster than I can fire my gun, he's slammin' 'em against the wall."

Nothing Fly did impressed Mama, and after Daddy fired Edith she liked him even less. "Some law enforcement we've got here in Bay Harbor," she was always saying. "A bunch of grown men standing around watching a Nigra kill flies." She'd shake her head in disbelief and laugh.

Daddy answered her only once that I knew of. "He does a lot more'n kill flies, and you better not ever forget it." She didn't, but it was the "lot more" that rankled Mama.

As I headed for home, I slowed my pace, but Fly's aim must have been a lot quicker than his mouth. He was just leaving our backyard and starting up the path when I crossed the street. I looked straight ahead and pretended I didn't see him. When I opened the front door, dinner was already on the table, and Mama was upset that the food was getting cold.

"Why'd you go ahead and put it on the table?" Daddy was asking. "You saw me and Fly a-talkin'. You could of waited till he left."

"Why couldn't he be the one to wait, I want to know?" Mama asked. "You go fishing often enough. I'd think you could get your talking done then. I think he just waits till mealtime. Maybe he expects us to invite him in. It wouldn't surprise me a bit if you did it. First thing I know you'll be wanting me to cook up a possum."

Daddy half chuckled. "That'd be the day. It was a month before you thought you'd washed the smell of bear meat off your hands. I doubt you could put the soap down long enough to cook a possum."

"Well, just hurry up and sit down. I don't suppose the butter will melt on the biscuits now. Johnn, come on. Anna Lee, wash your hands and get in here."

Uncle Johnn mumbled a hurried blessing, but Mama couldn't let it go. We hardly had our eyes open when she said, "Start the chicken, Johnn," and turned to Daddy. "I really don't know, Robert, why a celebrity such as Fly should be hidden away here in Bay Harbor. Fly ought to have his own road show. You men could fix him up with his own special wagon and paint it all white inside so everybody could get a good look at those flies. And Fly, too, of course. Why should we keep all that talent to ourselves?"

Daddy never spoke jokingly of Fly the way he might of other Nigras, and he didn't appreciate it when Mama did either. He hadn't eaten a bite but wiped his mouth with his napkin and said in a low voice, "I always felt bad, Estelle, about your mama runnin' off with that other man and leavin' you and your daddy alone to fend for yourselves. I always thought that was awful sad, but sometimes I can't help but wonder if she didn't have her reasons. Maybe your daddy was so damned mean she just couldn't stand it no longer."

Mama gasped. "Robert Owens! How could you? Papa was as fine a man as ever walked the face of this earth. Nobody could be better to me, not even you. Certainly not you," she amended.

"He was both mother and father to me. I couldn't have had a better bringing up. In Georgia we know better than to speak disrespectfully of the dead." Her voice broke as though she might cry, but she didn't.

"Okay, Estelle, let's just forget it."

"No, I'm not just forgetting it, not until you take back what you said about Papa."

"I'm sorry. I didn't mean it."

"Well, I should hope not. I don't know what you're thinking of to talk in front of Anna Lee that way."

Uncle Johnn hadn't said a word. I looked up at him, and he winked. There might have been just the two of us at the table. I thought I would burst with love for him.

4

When the school year had begun the previous September and I walked innocently into the fourth grade, I hadn't known that in some ways I was beginning a new way of life. We'd grown comfortable because Bay Harbor was unchanging. And then it seemed there was nothing but change. The month wasn't out before gas was rationed, and soon people pasted letters on their windshields. Like report cards in reverse, those with black *A*'s got the least amount of gas — three gallons a week — and if we hadn't known it already, the *A* announced that those people didn't hold defense jobs or jobs necessary to the war effort. For me, though, the biggest change was in the people. After the war started, there were more new people in Bay Harbor than I thought we'd ever get used to, and when school had started there was a new fourth-grade teacher. Her husband was stationed at the army base near Bay Harbor.

Mrs. Striker was the neatest, cleanest person I'd ever known, looking for all the world like freshly starched linen. From the individual Betty Grable curls on top of her head to the polished pumps on her trim little feet, there wasn't a wrinkle on her or a hair out of place. Partial to jumpers and white blouses, she never wore jewelry. She wore handkerchiefs. Every day there would be a hankerchief, fanned like an errant butterfly, near her left shoulder. Those handkerchiefs were the most artistic creations ever to hit Bay Harbor, perched on her jumpers in a never-ending assortment of shapes and colors. I wondered how long it took her to get ready for school. Surely every corkscrew curl was done fresh each morning. She wouldn't dare come to school in something she'd slept in because she told us often enough that we shouldn't sleep in our underclothes. "If you do," she said, "I can smell you," and her tiny white nose would draw together as she appeared to pull our scent toward her. Whenever I saw her nose start to move, I held my breath in an effort to hold my odor tight to my body. I begged Mama not to make me sleep in my slip, but even when I didn't sleep in it, I worried that Mrs. Striker might smell me. On hot days she cautioned us against running on the playground at recess. "You children get so hot," she told us, "you smell like a bunch of little dogs."

As the school year advanced, I had more to worry about than how I smelled. Learning the multiplication tables became an all-consuming task. Mrs. Striker printed them neatly across the blackboard, where, like tiny soldiers, they seemed to march forever. The sheer numbers of them broke me out in a sweat Mrs. Striker's nose couldn't have missed. No matter how desperately I tried, I couldn't remember those tables. The only thing I was learning in the fourth grade was that I smelled.

When I confided to Uncle Johnn how much trouble I was having, he urged me to be calm and use my time wisely. I gave up going to the picture show for a time and, using his system, was up to my sevens one night when Miss Red came over to our house and saw me kneeling beside my bed.

"Suffer the little children," I heard her say to Mama.

I suffered all right. I closed my eyes tighter and whispered, "Seven times six is forty-two." Miss Red had told me that one's last thought at night should be of God, but I got more immediate results from the multiplication tables.

I hadn't been to Miss Red's since the Magic Show, and with Helen in New Orleans the hours dragged. I spent more and more time at the beach walking among the rolling dunes where the sand, brushed by the wind, lay in undisturbed ripples. Below the dunes I watched the water move back and forth over the sand like a nervous dancer, leaving its dampness behind in the sea-weed and shells along the shore. It was my own special place, and the calling of the sea gulls and the lapping water might be the only sounds for hours. Perhaps Mama noticed the white sand that clung to my shoes or that I wasn't going to the house next door, but she didn't say anything — not that she would have cared anyway. If it hadn't been for Miss Red, I might have liked banana pudding better. But if not another soul noticed, I was so conscious of staying away that I thought of little else and hoped that every hour without my presence made Miss Red more miserable. Should I ever weaken and go to see her again, she'd be so glad to see me she'd think twice before telling me any more lies. But I suffered the greater punishment. I missed seeing her, and I found myself hard put to stay away. I'd liked her too long to stay mad and too, she lent a certain amount of prestige to the neighborhood by renting rooms to schoolteachers. Having Uncle Johnn live with us and schoolteachers for neighbors gave me a rather special standing in the community. They were always young and pretty, the teachers who lived at Miss Red's, and like Uncle Johnn they walked in a world apart, not quite belonging to Bay Harbor. This helped to make up for the fact that Hazel Sawyer lived across the street.

Hazel was a tiny little thing, every inch of her pure meanness. She bragged that she was half-French, and she was boy crazy. Everybody in town knew it. Not that Hazel cared. She advertised the fact as boldly as if she'd worn a sign across her chest. Nearly all I knew of hatred came from what I felt for Hazel, but I could never figure out what I'd done to make her dislike me so. She'd been real nice to me at first. I'd hardly been aware of her existence until I had the measles. I thought the gold knife beneath my pillow had brought me luck when Hazel walked into that hot, miserable room where I lay willing myself not to scratch. Mama explained that Hazel had already had the measles and said what a nice girl she was to come cheer me up. I don't suppose anyone could ever know how glad I was to see her. She told me a story about a little lame prince. I loved hearing her tell it and almost forgot about being so sick and not liking the way food tasted. Hazel promised to come again the following day, and true to her word, she came and told me the story a second time.

After that she came over every afternoon until I was well. Waiting for her visits helped to pass those stifling days that were trapped by the cracked and yellowed shades at my bedroom windows. Every day I thanked her for being so nice, but she'd only smile and not say anything. I felt she expected something more, but I didn't know what it could be. I tried so hard to please her. I showed her where I kept Uncle Johnn's knife and told her about my grandmother. I tried to describe my love for Uncle Johnn, but I couldn't, not the way I wanted to. I didn't even know the language. It was probably just as well. Later I remembered that Hazel's daddy was dead. I couldn't recall him, but Mama said he'd run a fruit and vegetable stand on the beach road. Returning with a load of produce one day, his truck had over-turned, killing him and Hazel's younger sister. Afterward Mrs. Sawyer had to give up the large downstairs apartment and move to one of the hotter but cheaper ones upstairs.

Although Hazel was nearly seven years older than me, she kept on coming to see me after I was well. Not too much bigger than I was, she even played dolls with me. Mama said Hazel probably missed her sister and was lonesome since her mother worked all the time.

Maybe it was just part of a plan she had, or maybe she didn't have a plan at all, but I couldn't understand what I'd done to her. It was just little things at first. She left my house one day and came back later with an older girl, some friend of hers from school. She ignored me completely and went to Mama and told her I had stolen a gold safety pin her favorite aunt had given her. She said it right in front of her girlfriend. There was a brass pin in the back of my doll's dress, but I hadn't taken it from Hazel. I brought the doll and showed them. Hazel said she knew brass when she saw it. She wanted to know where I'd hidden the gold pin. I cried then. I couldn't help it. And all the while I was crying, I knew the girlfriend really believed I'd taken the pin. Mama believed me, but the girl didn't. I wondered if they really made gold safety pins.

It wasn't until they were gone that I discovered my gold knife was missing. The instant I looked under my pillow, I knew Hazel had taken it, but I was afraid to tell anybody. She quit coming to my house. She told people I stole things from her.

"Just ignore her, Anna Lee," Mama advised. "People will judge you by your actions, not by what Hazel Sawyer tells them." But I kept right on feeling bad. I couldn't stop feeling guilty even though I knew I'd never taken a thing that belonged to Hazel and she had my knife. I wished I had stolen from her. It was worse somehow to feel guilty for something I hadn't done.

For a time Hazel left me alone, and I figured maybe it'd just been my gold knife she was after. I found out how wrong I was when a new family was moving into the downstairs portion of the Sawyers' house and I went over to see what their furniture looked like. I had just walked onto the back porch when Hazel came bounding down the back stairs with her long pageboy flying. She stopped at the landing, her pale eyes narrowed, and I thought how much she looked like our old cat that went crazy. I never hurt that cat, just eased it away from the door with my foot, and it jumped me. Eyes narrowed and hair standing out, it clung to my leg with its claws digging deep into my skin. I screamed and tried to run, but it was kind of hard to do with a cat between my legs. Mama ran out after us, and he finally fell off, but he kept after me anyway, running and making flying leaps in my direction. His claws slicing through the fabric of my skirt tore it to shreds. Somebody came out and handed Mama a broom, and after she whacked him good, he ran off into some bushes and snarled at us. Later we gave him to an old man who couldn't afford food for a watchdog.

Neither Hazel nor I had moved. "What do you think you're doing in my house?" she demanded.

"I'm not in your house," I said in the tone of voice I used for sassing Mama.

She kept coming down the stairs, slowly now, with smoldering eyes and her hair a dark blot melting down her shoulders. She knew very well how scared I was of her or I'd have gotten my knife back.

"Well," she said, "you have to walk through the door and across the porch where I walk, and I don't ever want you anyplace where I have to be."

I didn't know what she'd do to me. I kept thinking the new people would come out, and when they didn't I started running fast, back toward home. I hadn't gone far when a big piece of stove wood whizzed past my head.

From that day on I was more afraid of Hazel than ever and went to great lengths to avoid seeing her. She always found me, though. She was like a spider waiting to pounce when I'd least expect her. I never knew what form her torment would take, and I was never sure I was rid of her for good. Where Hazel was concerned, I couldn't let my guard down a minute. I learned that the day I carelessly crossed the street and started down the sidewalk that ran in front of her garage. I'd barely started past when I saw Hazel. She stood just inside the door. I hadn't noticed her or I wouldn't have been walking down her side of the sidewalk. She called to me in a real nice voice, though, and smiled. Her face looked so sweet when she smiled — something she'd learned, I supposed, from chasing boys. Her voice sounded the way it had when she told me about the little lame prince. She asked me to come into the garage with her, but I didn't move. I could see the soft dirt floor, and it was awfully dark inside.

"Oh, come on," she said and laughed. "Don't be a fraidy cat. I've got a little tabby kitten in here, and I want to show it to you."

If I'd had good sense, I would have told her to bring it out in the light so I could see it better, but I didn't think at all. I just walked right in to see that kitten.

"It's over there in the corner," she said.

When I walked to the back of the garage to look for it, she slammed the door shut. She wouldn't have had to do another thing to scare me. I thought that being there in the dark alone with Hazel was the worst thing that could happen to me.

"Where's the kitten?" I asked.

"Didn't you see it? Why, it must have disappeared. Maybe it's like the ghost that's in here with us. You can't see it, but it's here just the same."

I loved "Inner Sanctum." I'd sit by the radio with all the lights off listening and loving being scared. That may have been why it was so easy for me to believe her. Or maybe Hazel and the ghost merged into one fear.

"Sam Jones's ghost is standing there behind you."

I whirled around, and she laughed.

Sam had cut a boy's throat with a Gillette razor blade during recess one day. Casting a pall on a favorite game, he'd done it, center stage, on the hard-packed circle of dirt where the boys shot marbles. Gene had taunted Sam for as long as anyone could remember, and people were always saying Gene would get what was coming to him some day. They hadn't thought it'd be a cut throat, but he'd taunted Sam once too often. He was still laughing when Sam carved the U-shaped grin on his neck.

Hazel had some dishes and stuff in the garage. All the while she was scooping up sand and mixing it with water and other things she had on a table, she kept telling me about the ghost.

"Sam was my friend, Anna Lee. *Was*. Did you know your daddy sent him to reform school and he died there? Did you know that? Your daddy's a murderer. Maybe you noticed that strange smell in here. That's the death stench Sam brought with him."

"Smells more like dogs have been in here to me."

"That's 'cause you don't know much, Anna Lee. You don't know much at all." She told me she was mixing up something real special for me. All I had to do was drink it and the ghost would disappear.

"If you don't drink it" — she kept right on mixing and stirring as she talked — "Sam's ghost will go home with you. He'll follow you everyplace. I wonder what your folks would think if you brought home a ghost like Sam. I wouldn't be a bit surprised if your daddy went mad. He'd see Sam's ghost if nobody else did." She laughed, but I didn't say a word. I knew she was going to make me drink that stuff, and all the while I thought I could see a shape in the darkness, a shape that was the ghost, but I knew I'd drink the slimy brew to get rid of Hazel. I'd drink it so she'd open the door and let me out.

She picked up a little pan and pulled me by the arm over to the door. Her hands were icy cold. The sun filtered in between the

hinges of the door, and she held the pan so I could see what she'd
made for me. It was black and dirty. Bits of grass floated around
popping little bubbles. She handed it to me and told me to drink
it. Already reading my mind, she added, "And don't you tell or
there'll be something worse waiting for you."

I didn't think I could, and she pushed the pan against my
mouth. I could feel sand on my lips, and my throat tightened.
"Drink it," she hissed. I took a sip, and it was worse than
anything I could imagine, worse even than the taste in my mouth
after I'd had my tonsils out. "I said drink it!" and I could feel her
breath on my ear. I swallowed again and again, and when she
took the pan and pushed me outside, I kept on swallowing,
choking the swelling in my throat as I ran home, past Mama to
the bathroom. I flushed the toilet to hide the sound, and it came
up every bit as vile as it went down.

I prayed earnestly that Hazel would die. I laid awake nights
plotting my revenge, being a lot bolder and smarter than I ever
could be when daylight came. I wished on her my most secret
dread, envisioning her crumpled face when Mrs. Sawyer told her
she was adopted, the child of a common slut. She was so mean, it
was some comfort to think it might really be true. But when
sleep came, Hazel had the upper hand. She was always after me,
my screams wedged in my throat and my legs too leaden to run.
Even when she started chasing boys, I was afraid she might still
chase me.

5

Thanks to a dry spell, I stayed away from Miss Red's for nearly
two weeks, but on a warm Friday afternoon when rain was in the
air, I gave up the fight and followed the worn path to her back
door. Just as though I'd never stayed away, she nodded her head as
I walked in, and I knew she'd been expecting me all along.
Neither of us mentioned the cat incident as we sat at her kitchen
table waiting for Mark.

Mark was my best friend. I couldn't be best friends with a girl,
not after Hazel. Boys were more open, less spiteful. Mark and I
didn't spend a lot of time together but were best friends because
we told one another secrets we wouldn't tell anyone else. I knew
that Mark's grandmother licked the knife and put it back in the
mayonnaise jar and that he believed his daddy thought he was a
sissy because Mark read books all the time. And Mark knew all
about Hazel, every bit of it. But our special bond was the ritual
we'd made of sharing rainy days together at Miss Red's. Most
often the rains came in the afternoon, with the sky gradually
deepening in color. Sometimes it would be an hour or better
before it turned black. That's when I'd go to Miss Red's, knowing
it wouldn't be long until Mark would be there, too.

It seemed an eternity before I heard the rapid thudding of
Mark's shoes as he came up the steps. The back door slammed,
and Miss Red closed her eyes briefly, but she didn't say anything.
Rainy days were special to her, too. Mark stood beside the table
breathing hard and grinning. His dark curly hair was moist and
flat against his head.

Mark was the signal for Miss Red to get the coffeepot, and she
left the table to rummage in the cabinet, searching for the

separate pieces. She kept them spread out in the cabinet so they'd stay dry and not attract roaches.

With a deep sigh, Mark reached for a chair and dropped into it. His shirt stuck to his back, and I could see beads of sweat on his forehead. He'd had to run a ways to get that hot. I wondered if he'd been down inside the old tar-lined box we'd found abandoned in a field. It was pitch black and hot inside, but a lot of girls and boys went in there to kiss. Mark was a tall, quiet boy, more interested in books than girls, but I wondered if he'd been in there kissing, too. I looked more closely at his smooth skin and eyelashes that were longer and thicker than mine. Who in the world had he been kissing!

We sat quietly, the only sound coming from the wind outside and the water filling the coffeepot. Because the rain brought a chill to the air, Miss Red always made coffee. The teachers who lived with her might get wet on the way home from school and need something warm to drink. They got their meals in town; food and drink were forbidden in their rooms.

She turned from lighting the stove and looked at us. "If I have it waiting for them, they won't be apt to sneak hot plates into their rooms. First it'd be something to drink, then there'd be food, and the end result would be roaches."

Next to sin, Miss Red hated roaches more than anything in the world, and she'd go to any lengths — even providing free coffee for the teachers — in order to be rid of them. That's what she always said, but we knew that Miss Red wouldn't touch coffee after breakfast except on rainy days. At other times she contented herself with a mixture she called silver tea. I liked the thought of drinking silver tea, but it was really nothing more than saccharin and hot water. Whether the cup of coffee she drank after eight in the morning really kept her awake all night the way she claimed, or if she drank silver tea because coffee was rationed, we never knew. But just as the rain drew us to her house, it drew her to coffee.

Leaning our arms on the cool oilcloth that covered the square kitchen table, Mark and I watch hypnotically as the water rushed to the glass knob on the lid of the coffeepot. Each time, the water grew a little darker in color, until Miss Red took it off the kerosene burner.

The first heavy drops of rain on the tin roof sent echoes through the big old house. The kitchen grew dark, and the bulb over the sink looked dim and far away. We watched Miss Red get down the metal box she used for storing oatmeal cookies. Like the coffee, they were a special treat, and she saved them for rainy afternoons when we could be together. She made them from a secret recipe and said they had to age to be good.

Sitting around the table, we listened to the storm and waited for the teachers. The pounding sheets of rain on the hot tin roof made a kind of thunder all its own, quite apart from the deafening claps that followed the jagged lightning as it reached for earth. It was a very private thunder that existed only inside Miss Red's house. We could smell the coffee and the sour odor that becomes part of a kitchen after years of baking. I could look to the side through Miss Red's kitchen window or straight ahead through the door to the living room windows and see flashes of lightning.

Strangely silent, Miss Red rubbed her right hand over the yellow and red flowered oilcloth in a rhythmic motion as if to push some crumbs aside or to smooth a wrinkle. The rain shutting us off from everything always did something to Miss Red.

Having finished their day at school, the teachers joined us, and as we sat at the table in the deafening darkness, Miss Red was like a different person. Her voice lost its urgency and flowed as gently as a stream over worn rocks. She began telling us things she'd done as a young girl. But mostly she talked about her hair.

"A girl's hair," she said, "is her crowning glory." Hers, she told us, had been auburn, thick and rich in color.

I found it hard to believe that Miss Red's dark gray hair had ever been any other color. None of us said we didn't believe her, but she must have sensed our doubt because she stood up from the table and motioned us to follow her. We didn't say a word as we walked behind her. It was an eerie feeling, as though the storm led the way from room to room, darkening each as we approached. Her bedroom, where we stopped, seemed the darkest of all the rooms, and it smelled old, like the inside of a cedar chest.

She pulled a fringed shawl from the top of a high-domed trunk and got down on her knees to lift the lid. Kneeling before the trunk, we watched her take out a box wrapped in white tissue paper. She stared at it for a moment before opening the box to reveal what she'd saved. It was filled with thick auburn hair, so beautiful it was like a living thing. Hesitantly, the way one might reach out to stroke a baby's soft cheek, she touched the hair gently with her fingertips.

"My youth," she said, "locked up in an old trunk." I looked from the hair to Miss Red. It seemed more impossible than ever that it had been hers. The hair belonged to someone young. I wanted to stop her as she began framing some of it around her face, but I couldn't utter a word. I was frightened by the hair and by the way Miss Red looked. Her eyes appeared glazed, and her face, lifted to us, was that of a stranger. I turned and went back to the kitchen even as she knelt there on the floor, the overhead light casting ugly shadows that made the hair grow darker yet.

Later, when the rain let up and the sun pierced the clouds, the spell was broken. Miss Red straightened her shoulders and became herself again, that strong and yet rather frail and withered messenger of God. We couldn't be rude and leave her then. She always had to atone and do her part for Jesus. That too was part of the ritual.

She looked at Mark and me with misty eyes and said, "Suffer the little children." I wanted to run every time she said that, but we all sat there, respectful but hesitant, as though we'd stolen something.

"It's not an easy path," she said, "not for any of you. But you, you teachers, set the example for the youth of Bay Harbor. Don't ever forget that. Going to picture shows, drinking whiskey, or dancing — that's no example to set for the young people who look to you for guidance. No sir!" Caught up in what she was saying, she began shaking her finger at us. "And while you may say that one drink of whiskey might not hurt you, just stop to think that some little child seeing you might be started on the path to his downfall." She slapped the table with the palm of her hand. "If it don't hurt you, it could hurt somebody else."

Miss Red didn't say anything we hadn't heard before. We'd listened to her so often we could have said it for her, but Miss Cason was another matter. Nobody challenged Miss Red, especially if they'd been served oatmeal cookies and hot coffee. But Miss Cason couldn't keep still. Usually shy and soft-spoken, she had the quietest class in school. If it hadn't been, nobody could have heard a word she said. She cleared her throat, and her face flushed pink as she spoke.

"But Miss Red, we can't give up everything. We're young ourselves, and we want to have fun. Life's too short . . ."

Miss Red interrupted her before she finished. "You said it right! Life is too short. It's too short for all this sin. And believe me, what you're talking about is sin, not fun. Why, Christians can have fun. A Christian don't need worldly things to enjoy himself."

Miss Cason spread her hands in a gesture of defeat and let them drop to her lap. Almost under her breath she said, "Maybe there are degrees of heaven. Hell, too."

As quietly as she spoke, Miss Red heard her. Pale and stony-faced, she stood up from the table. She spoke in a low voice also, almost threateningly.

"Well, I don't want any degree of hell, not any degree of it. And I don't plan to go to heaven empty-handed, either. Anna Lee, your mother's calling you."

I opened my mouth to contradict her and then realized she'd given me a welcome excuse to leave, but I couldn't help wondering if Miss Cason would have a room at Miss Red's for the next school year.

Mama was in the kitchen cutting up a chicken when I walked in the back door. She looked over at me critically. "Well, have you managed to spoil your supper?"

"No, ma'am." I hesitated, thinking about the mass of beautiful hair in the old trunk. "We were just talking to the teachers."

"Well, that's good. Maybe you'll learn something."

"Did anybody in our family ever teach school?"

Mama let the chicken drop into the sink and turned and looked at me kind of funny. "What makes you ask that?"

"I just wondered if there were any schoolteachers in our family. I thought it'd be kind of nice."

"Schoolteachers are no better than anybody else. They're just people."

"Nobody in our family was ever a teacher?"

"I didn't say that. You're liable to find most anything in your daddy's family."

"Maybe I'll be a teacher when I grow up."

"That's news to me. Your Uncle Johnn putting ideas in your head?"

"No, ma'am. I just thought of it. Did you ever want to be a teacher when you were a little girl?"

"I never had time to think about what I wanted to be. I wasn't lazy like you. I had to work. And then after my daddy died, well, there would have been no way I could have been a teacher. I was a telephone operator before your daddy and me got married. It wasn't an easy job, I tell you. It wasn't like teaching school. Those headsets were heavy, and sometimes every light on the board would seem to come on at once. It was a lot of responsibility, and I was sure tired when I went home at night. You're a mighty lucky little girl, Anna Lee, to have a home and family and not have to work so hard."

"I guess so."

"You better know so!"

"Did Daddy and Uncle Johnn have to work hard when they were little?"

"Life's never easy on a farm, Anna Lee, though I must admit it strains the imagination to think of your Uncle Johnn doing physical labor."

"Was Uncle Earl a farmer?"

"Now, Anna Lee, you know we don't talk about your Uncle Earl. I don't know what's got into you today, asking so many questions. You know your Daddy can't stand to have Uncle Earl's name mentioned."

"Daddy's not here now."

"Don't you think I know that? It's best not to get in the habit of doing something behind somebody's back."

"Where's his wife?"

"Whose wife?"

"Uncle Earl's."

Mama's face drained perfectly white, and her eyes hardened. I knew better than to ask questions. I'd pushed her too far.

"Curiosity killed the cat, Anna Lee. Just remember that, you hear? She's dead. Now just drop the subject and go set the table for me. Make yourself useful."

I went to the drawer and began counting silverware.

"Did she die of a broken heart?" When she didn't answer, I kept on talking. "I saw a show the other day, and this woman died of a broken heart."

"People in a moving picture can do that. In real life people get sick and die. Grace got sick and died, and that's all there is to it. And I don't ever want the subject brought up again, do you hear me? You're getting on my nerves now, so just hush, you hear?"

I didn't ask any further questions, able now to quit thinking about Miss Red's hair. Where had I heard the name *Grace*, and why was it as disturbing somehow as Miss Red's hair?

6

Nearly every day after school, I walked to the post office for the mail. Seven to the right twice, twenty to the left twice, back to the right, and the box would open. We didn't receive many letters, but my pleasure came from opening the box. Because of the rain and going to Miss Red's, I hadn't gone to town after school on Friday, so Uncle Johnn went to the Post Office instead. Mama had thought he was going to be late for supper, and even though he wasn't, her eyes still snapped and her voice was sharp as she said, "You missed the news."

"Is that right, Estelle?" Uncle Johnn said pleasantly. "Well, I'm certainly sorry to be late."

Mama's eyes darkened and snapped. "Well, you should be. You really missed it. The Nazis have come out in favor of the Japanese's execution of those flyers!"

"The ones captured in the Doolittle raid on Tokyo last year?"

"The very ones. God only knows what those poor boys suffered before they were killed."

Uncle Johnn shook his head slowly from side to side. "I agree with President Roosevelt. It's barbaric, just barbaric."

"Damn yellowbellies," Daddy offered. "They'll be crawling soon. Mind what I tell you."

We could mind it all we wanted, but the war was a long way from Bay Harbor, and our supper was only a few steps away and getting cold fast. Mama was hurrying us around so, we were halfway through the meal before Uncle Johnn remembered to give her the mail. Excusing himself, he went to his room for his coat, and returned with a picture postcard from Helen. It showed

57

Canal Street in New Orleans, and Helen had circled one of the windows in a tall hotel building.

"Very colorful," she wrote. "Arrive home Saturday afternoon."

"She's surely mighty stingy with words," Mama complained. "She must have thought she was sending us a telegram."

A telegram, however, would have been very plain and measured, and Helen's writing was beautiful. The letters sprawled across the card, so curved and scrolled it was hard to believe it was only writing.

I could barely wait until the next day so that I could see Helen and the souvenirs she'd bring back from New Orleans. The minute the show was over on Saturday afternoon, I headed for the boarding house. I started up the front stairs as usual, but just as I pushed open the swinging doors that hung about a quarter of the way up the stairwell, I heard a noise that made me shudder. I stood frozen in my tracks, hearing a cracking sound again and again, knowing that it came from Helen's bedroom. Helen had said she was afraid of Chester. I'd heard her telling Mama the things he'd do. Standing there, I remembered every word she'd said.

"He comes in late at night sometimes when I'm already in bed. He'll take his hunting knife off his belt and put it on the bedside table. Then he'll stand over me, just daring me to move. 'If I see you breathe,' he'll say, 'I'll kill you right here and now.' He'll do it some day, too. He'll come in smelling like a brewery some night and kill me."

I listened to the rhythmic rise and fall and knew it was Chester's belt. My first thought was to turn and run, but I wanted to help Helen. I knew people could hear him. It was a warm, still day, and the cracking of the belt reverberated like gun shots. Why didn't somebody help her? All those boarders . . . Why didn't somebody stop him? And then I heard one of the cooks. I recognized Ruby's voice and could tell she was standing somewhere on the back stairs that led to the dining room.

"Miz Armstrong? Miz Armstrong?" she called.

And then I heard Helen answer her just as sweetly. "Yoohoo?" she called. She made it sound like she was sitting in a rocker on the front porch rocking and didn't want to turn around. She didn't sound a bit like she was being beaten. But the belt kept on hitting her, and Ruby didn't call again.

I waited a little longer, hoping he'd stop, but when he didn't, I pushed through the doors and ran up the stairs and across the big living room to their bedroom door. I beat on the door with both my fists. *"Helen! Helen!"* She didn't answer me, but I continued banging on the door until he quit.

I kept telling myself that he wouldn't hurt me. He knew better than to lay a hand on me. My fist was still raised when the door finally opened. Chester stood in the doorway, but I managed to get a glimpse of Helen. She was turned on her side, lying across the bed, and there were dark red streaks over her bare white shoulders and back. Tears smarted in my eyes as I slowly shifted my gaze to look at Chester. He didn't have on a shirt, and because he held the notched black belt in his hand, his pants sagged below his navel. For a moment I forgot all about the beating. I was stunned just looking at him. His skin was pale as the underside of a fish, and there were no freckles on his body. No hair either. He didn't have a hair on him, not on his chest or anyplace. He was smooth as a woman. Moving my gaze slowly up, I faced him. Beads of sweat stood out on his forehead, and his face was flushed. He didn't say a word but just stood there breathing hard through his mouth. Wire-like nerves flicked sickeningly up either side of my tongue as I realized he enjoyed having me look at him. I lowered my eyes to his bare, bony feet. Sometimes, Helen had told Mama, he'd make her wash them, a tense prelude to the beatings.

It seemed forever before I could move. When I did, I ran screaming back across the room. Above my screams I could hear him laughing as he followed me over to the stairs. He laughed all the louder as I stumbled down the stairs and out the door into the blinding sunlight.

A block away I thought I could still hear his laughter, and it was somehow more terrible than the sound of his belt. Though my legs were weak and I was trembling inside, I didn't think I could ever stop running. But I did. I stopped short at the water's edge and, hugging my aching sides, sat on some boards that had washed up along the shore.

I closed my eyes and tried to visualize a blackout shade inside my head that I could pull down to make my mind go blank. Hard as I tried, I could never get it all the way down. Straining, I willed it down, but it only flew back up tighter and higher than ever, and Chester stood in its place. I finally gave up and stared at several small boats tied up down the beach. They moved about in the shallow water, bumping together, and I knew that each time they touched, they made a soft, thudding noise.

The afternoon sun cast a glare on the still surface of the bay that stretched as far as I could see, water that touched the Gulf of Mexico and kept on going, going even to New Orleans. I'd always thought of the water as moving away and taking a part of me with it, but as I sat there, I realized it also kept me in Bay Harbor. I looked toward the pier and saw a soldier and a girl in shorts jump over one of the gaps where the plank floor had rotted away. Servicemen were always walking girls out to the end of the pier. There it was covered over with a roof, and they could sit and kiss without being so easily seen. Hazel had probably been there plenty of times.

When the aching left my sides, I walked along the beach past the pier, down an endless white avenue that stretched between the bay on my right and the higher ground on my left, where grass and trees grew above the beach. There were places where, during hurricanes, water had washed the sand away and left open caves beneath the trees, their naked roots dangling uselessly, exposed to the salt air. I peered closer into one of the caves that went deeper than the rest and gasped with fright. A bearded, dirty old tramp lay there asleep. I quickly retraced my steps, but I knew better than to tell anybody. One word and I'd not be allowed on the beach anymore. I hoped Helen wouldn't tell Mama what had happened that afternoon or I might not be allowed at the boarding house either.

For about as long as I could remember, Mama and Daddy and Uncle Johnn had gone out on Saturday night. Separately. After closing the drugstore, Uncle Johnn played pool in the back of

O'Kelly's Bar. He was good, too, but Mama made light of the talk and the bets. She thought he'd get a reputation, but Uncle Johnn already had a reputation and played pool far more often than she suspected. I'd walked slowly past the rusty screen door of the bar and peeked inside. I could hear the click of hard balls and smell the strange, heavy odor that seeped through the door and over the sidewalk. Inside on the wall was a special cue stick that no one but Uncle Johnn was allowed to use, and the men in the bar treated him with a different respect than they used in the drugstore. They slapped him on the back and cursed him fondly. He was one of them and at the same time better than they were. When Uncle Johnn rolled up his sleeves to reveal surprising muscles, there was nothing soft or of the gentleman about him. He was tough, a skilled hunter loose in the woods. Money changed hands, and I knew Uncle Johnn was a gambling man.

Any nightly outings Daddy had were seasonal. Daddy never went after pleasure idly but was grim and determined, and he always had something to show for his efforts. There were evenings of frog gigging, trips to the oyster bar, or overnight hunting and fishing trips, but for Mama and me Saturday nights seldom varied. They generally found us with Helen, sitting on the big screened upstairs porch in the summer and in her living room in the winter.

This was one Saturday night Mama missed, however, and she didn't miss many. She hadn't been to the boarding house since before Helen left for her vacation, and I knew she wanted to hear about the New Orleans trip, too, but I couldn't go back there, not yet, anyway. Mumps were going around, so after supper I ate a pickle and pretended to have some pain. First things first; I was sent to take a bath. Mama had two fears. One was of being in a car wreck with ragged underwear on, and the other was of having to call the doctor in the middle of the night when you hadn't taken a bath. Manners were equally important to Mama, of course, but there she had no fear. She never worried that I might slip up and embarrass her by whistling at the table or by forgetting to say "ma'am" and "sir." Manners were drilled into me day after day and came as natural as breathing. My insides stiffened and froze if I heard some smart-aleck boy answer with a plain "yes" or "no." Of course, this was something one didn't often hear except from tourists and Yankees.

After I was clean, I prayed long and earnestly that I'd wake up with the mumps. I might as well have said my multiplication tables. I wasn't at all surprised the next morning when I was perfectly healthy. I'd never yet had a prayer answered. I told Mama it must have been a toothache. I knew she was mad that it hadn't been the mumps, and I decided it'd be to my advantage to come straight home after Sunday school. I might just as well have stayed for church. That was the Sunday Mohammed came to Bay Harbor.

Brother Palmer was the only minister in Bay Harbor who had a two-story brick church. It was considered by many, especially Miss Red, to be the only sure door to heaven. With that sort of backing, Brother Palmer felt free to do anything in his power to bring sinners to Jesus. Having a flair for language, he didn't put it so simply.

"If the mountain won't come to Mohammed, Mohammed will go to the mountain." That was the way he expressed it. His version of Mohammed took the form of giant speakers installed on the roof of the Baptist church.

We'd all seen the men scurrying around on top of the church, and we'd seen the speakers, four of them, installed back-to-back, but it wasn't until eleven o'clock Sunday morning that we realized what we were in for. It was fantastic, as though the Baptist church had just swallowed Bay Harbor. No sinner sleeping late or lingering over the morning paper would miss the word of God anymore. Brother Palmer's preaching could be heard from any corner of town. From our front porch I could see, one by one, the windows of the Methodist church being closed.

An hour later I knew it was about over. "Yes sir, sisters and brothers," Brother Palmer was saying, "it's red, it's on fire with the word of God." I'd been to church with Miss Red and knew that at this point he'd be holding the red Bible over his head. That red Bible was his calling card. "Come touch it," he pleaded, "and your body will never be cold again. Let Jesus take care of that body. He wants to. It's His. He's only lent it to you. Yes, it's red. It's bright. You can all see it." He was beginning to shout. I figured they didn't have speakers inside the church. "Oh, let it be your light. Come give your life to Jesus." At this point the choir began singing softly, though loud enough to be picked up over the speakers, "Oh, Why Not Tonight." It didn't matter that it was still morning. They never lacked for people who wanted to repent or be saved. Brother Palmer claimed to feel the Spirit moving inside him when somebody who wanted to be saved held back. He'd keep the choir singing until somebody got tired enough or hungry enough to come forward. They used a kind of honor system and took turns being saved again and again.

Brother Palmer never seemed tired or hungry. He was relentless in his search for sinners. Plenty of times I'd seen him standing in the doorway of the picture show with his Bible tucked under his arm. Thrusting his head into the false night of the picture show, he'd pause while his eyes adjusted to the dark. People who thought he paused longer than was necessary were of the opinion that he was really watching the movie. After a time he'd lay a piece of paper on top of his Bible and start writing down the names of any Baptists he saw in the show. On Sunday he'd call their names out in church. Now we'd all be able to hear them over the speakers.

Uncle Johnn was mad. When Mama called him to dinner, he shook the newspaper to straighten it and tore it right in half, reminding me of the muscles beneath the soft fabric of his shirt. Uncle Johnn wasn't angry because he wanted to sleep late. He just didn't think people should have things forced on them, not even the word of God. He wasn't about to seek Brother Palmer out about it, though. Mama said it might be bad for business if he did, but Uncle Johnn told her that was beside the point.

"Business," Mama replied primly as she pulled her chair closer to the table, "is never beside the point."

Uncle Johnn ignored her. "I won't," he said, "force my opinions on that — that . . . man any more than I want his forced on me."

"Religion," Daddy said, inclining his head in the direction of Miss Red's, "will drive you crazy."

In the winter, when the windows were closed, Miss Red was a frequent topic of conversation at our dining room table, but as it wasn't winter now, Daddy spoke softly. "You quit spending so much time with Miss Red, Anna Lee. Be respectful and all, but watch out." Pushing food to one side of his mouth, he gestured with his fork. "I know people who are in the state hospital in Chattahoochee today, insane because of religion. Got to be regular fanatics. Too much religion will drive you crazy, Anna Lee. Just remember what I'm a-tellin' you, you hear?" He waved his fork at me, and I nodded my head.

Daddy had been telling me that for years. Unlike Mama, whose main concern with religion was that I not talk or look behind me to see who was coming into church, Daddy had very strong feelings about religion, the strongest being that the hypocrites were the ones who went to church. God was far more lenient with Daddy than He was with Miss Red. Daddy never worried about whether or not he was saved, certain he'd be taken to heaven with just a word and nothing more.

There was no way Mama could wait until the following Saturday to hear about Helen's trip. Instead of going for a short ride along the beach as she and Daddy sometimes did on Sunday, she changed clothes as soon as we'd cleaned up the kitchen, and we went to the boarding house. It being a Sunday, I thought Chester might be hanging around the police station bragging about his vacation, but he wasn't. He and Helen both acted like this was the first they'd seen of me, and I was so fascinated by the lovebirds Helen had brought back from New Orleans that I was almost able to forget about Chester.

"My living souvenirs," Helen called them. She hung the cage in the living room, and the boarders seemed to get no end of pleasure from watching them kiss.

"Was New Orleans as wonderful as the state fair?" I asked.

Helen hesitated before answering. "It was different, Anna Lee. Oh, it was wonderful. I saw strange and beautiful things. It was an education in itself, but I'd never want to go again. It's no place for a child."

"But why?" I started, and then stopped when I noticed Mama signaling me to be quiet.

Helen walked over to the bird cage. I'd never seen her so taken with anything as she was those birds. "I can hardly wait until the little female starts laying," she said and stood there making soft cooing noises to the birds. Nobody seemed to make anything of it but Chester. Right in front of everybody, he said, "You're makin' a damn fool of yourself, Helen, talkin' to them birds." And then he laughed, pulling his upper lip tight over his teeth. "They can't hear you. Don't you know they ain't got any ears?" He waved his arm around the room. "Now tell me, has anybody here seen any ears on them damn birds?"

Embarrassed, everybody laughed, and Helen walked away from the cage and sat down, curling her hands palm up in her lap like something dying.

Chester started down the hall toward the bathrooms and then stopped and turned around.

"I'll tell you somethin' else, too. That female ain't gonna lay no eggs, 'cause that ain't no female. Them's two boys sittin' in there kissin'. I don't know why you expected any different, gettin' 'em where you did."

The boarders began talking among themselves and saying that Chester could be right. Instead of being fascinated by the way the birds kissed and played together, they avoided looking at them altogether.

I followed Mama and Helen to the porch, where they settled themselves into rockers.

"They're still at it," Mama said, referring to the singing coming from the Quarters.

"Darkies are the happiest people in the world," Helen said dreamily, tapping time with her foot.

I thought of Edith and felt a great sense of relief. "Are they really, Helen?"

"Why, of course, sugar. They'd have to be to put up with so much and still be able to sing."

That wasn't at all what I'd hoped to hear, so I went back inside and walked over to the bird cage. I peered at the birds' downy backsides. Chester didn't know what he was talking about. Maybe they were boys, but he had no way of knowing if they were or not. I jumped and hit my head on the cage when Chester walked up behind me.

"There, sugar," he consoled, and pulled me close against him. "Chester didn't mean to scare you none." He patted my bottom in the same old way, and I pulled loose from him and went back to the porch. There wasn't anything Chester couldn't spoil.

7

Even though Mama and Miss Red held entirely different views on life, they had lived side by side for years without so much as a cross word. Of course, they could talk knowingly to each other about the war news or Ma Perkins, and they frequently exchanged box tops or ration stamps, but I felt that the smooth- ness of their relationship had to be due in part to the fact that I understood their separate views and behaved accordingly. Mama, I knew, was not so much concerned with what I did as with how I did it, whereas Miss Red took politeness and respect for granted. She could not, however, take sin for granted and was very much concerned with everything I did — with what every- body did. She was even worse when Verna was home because her only child kept sin fresh in Miss Red's mind at all times.

I'd managed for years to keep everybody's views neatly sorted inside my head, never saying the wrong thing to anybody, and could have gotten along this way indefinitely if Miss Red hadn't started saying ugly things about Uncle Johnn. Brother Palmer was the cause of it all when he tried to save Uncle Johnn. It was only a couple of weeks after the speakers had been installed on the church. Uncle Johnn came home at noon one day and told us all about it over dinner.

It was to Uncle Johnn's credit, I thought, that Brother Palmer had waited so long before approaching him. He'd tried convert- ing the only Jewish couple in Bay Harbor before he took on Uncle Johnn, but Mama figured Miss Red was behind the Weinberg business. She'd been almost fanatical about Jews ever since Verna had nearly eloped with the Weinberg boy. Miss Red insisted it was only puppy love, but everyone else seemed to think

67

otherwise. Daddy told us in hushed tones that Verna might be a bitch but she was sure no puppy.

Brother Palmer couldn't very well save Uncle Johnn until he found a sin, and the Baptists searched for sin the way the Methodists hunted for talent. Daddy said the sin Brother Palmer uncovered was drinking, but the rest of us thought it must have been pool. The only drinking Uncle Johnn did was in the privacy of our home, so it was doubtful Brother Palmer knew about that or his cursing, but Uncle Johnn never tried to hide his pool playing. He was uncommonly good at it, and pool was also one of the few entertainments he found in Bay Harbor.

Uncle Johnn had a good business going that day, and right in front of all those people Brother Palmer came in and started preaching to him about the sinful life he was leading and how he ought to give his life to Jesus.

"I didn't shout," Uncle Johnn said, "and I didn't raise my voice or order him out of the store."

Mama's eyes grew wide. "You didn't let him save you!"

Uncle Johnn smiled. "I just talked to him in language he could understand."

"You did?" Mama was visibly impressed. "What was that?"

"Nothing very original, I'm afraid. I just walked up to him and said, very politely, Estelle, 'You goddamned son of a bitch, I'll break a cue stick over your head if you ever come in here again.' He hiked his Bible under his arm and walked out of there like the floor was covered with hot coals.

"Excuse me, Anna Lee, Estelle," Uncle Johnn apologized before he continued eating. Uncle Johnn really was a gentleman. He had never once forgotten to apologize to Mama and me when he cursed in front of us. Cursing, Mama told me, was the other side of the gentleman in Uncle Johnn, even if he did apologize afterwards.

We didn't have a loudspeaker, but I was sure Miss Red heard every word Uncle Johnn said. No doubt that she'd heard him curse before. Our houses were so close we could almost raise each other's windows. He cursed mostly at mealtime, and his big armchair at the head of the table was right next to the windows, but in all the years he'd lived with us Miss Red had never said a word about it. Of course, she had to keep in mind the fact that Uncle Johnn gave her a discount on all the medicine she bought from the drugstore. He was that kind of person. But she couldn't stand it when he cursed Brother Palmer.

Later that same afternoon, after I got home from school, Mama and I were sitting on the front porch, and I saw Brother Palmer's car drive up to Miss Red's house. Grinning from ear to ear, he got out of the car and walked with short, rapid steps to her front door. That grin was proof that Christians were happy, but he didn't even look in our direction. I wanted to holler at him real loud, hoping maybe he'd drop his Bible, but I contented myself with only thinking about it.

Miss Red was almost sickening the way she simpered when she came to the door and saw him standing there.

"I'll bet she gives him oatmeal cookies," I said, "and it's not even raining. I hope he chokes."

"I'd love to know what she uses for ration stamps," Mama said. "How in the world she gets enough sugar for all that baking, I don't know."

Brother Palmer stayed long enough to have eaten all the cookies, and it'd take weeks for more to age. When he and Miss Red finally walked to the front porch together, they stood and talked some more. The whole time he stood there, Brother Palmer kept stroking a big green fern with his thin, white hand. Miss Red never let anybody touch her ferns, but she didn't say a word to him. When he finally turned to go, leaving the fern to turn brown, he was still grinning, but his eyes passed over our house as if it were no more than a vacant field.

The very next time Mark and I were at Miss Red's, she started in on Uncle Johnn. It was pouring rain in great silvery sheets that covered the windows, and it felt close inside the kitchen. The smell of coffee hung like a cloud over the room, and my arms stuck to the oilcloth. Hollowed from the storm, Miss Red's voice seemed to reach me from a dream, and I was slow to realize she was hinting that something was going on between Uncle Johnn and Miss Amy Walker.

"I never noticed Amy being so friendly to y'all till Dr. Owens moved in. Amy's a good-lookin' woman, warm-blooded and after a man, and did she ever set foot inside your house till he come here?" Talking to herself as much as to us, she answered her own question. "Course she didn't."

Her voice droned on, but my mind was working, and the sound dissolved with the rain. There was no getting around the fact that Miss Amy was pretty. With her creamy skin and green eyes she was, I knew, every bit as pretty as Uncle Johnn was handsome, but I couldn't let myself believe they'd ever be more than merely friends, that she might ever take him away from us. How could Miss Red be so hateful!

"Uncle Johnn is a good man," I said between clenched teeth, thankful that the teachers weren't around to hear the things Miss Red was saying.

"He sure is," Mark said, "to everybody. Why, even when a shipment of candy comes to the drugstore, he makes it his business to see that everybody gets a share. He could just give it all to Anna Lee."

"And look how many times I've had to share my candy when somebody was overlooked, Miss Red."

"Well, I should hope so, Anna Lee. Dr. Owens knows you get enough to eat at my house to satisfy your sweet tooth."

I knew she was right, but I wished I could explain to her the longing for things that weren't there because of the war, for an icy cold Coca-Cola fizzing with salty peanuts poured inside, the yearning for even a sucker when all you had was a memory of sweetness that melted from the hard, glassy surface as it rubbed against your mouth and made soft clicking noises along the back of your teeth. And, oh, the grainy give of sweet, pink bubble gum. Once I'd spit a piece in the dirt and watched a girl come along, pick it up, and chew it. How could Miss Red, with all her sugar, ever understand? When a shipment of candy and gum arrived, boys and girls marched through town like an army of ants, and by afternoon the shelves would be bare again.

Miss Red looked at us, shaking her head from side to side, and laughed. "I'm talking about sin, not candy!"

I took a deep breath to stop the trembling inside me.

"Look how good Dr. Owens is to the poor," Mark said.

"That's right, Miss Red, you know he doesn't charge poor people for their medicine."

Miss Red knew all about the stuff on our front porch. More than once we'd found a bushel of pears or a basket of roasting ears when we'd go out in the morning and known it was somebody's way of paying Uncle Johnn. Only the day before, we'd found a mound of real butter someone had made, and with summer coming there'd soon be watermelons. At least once a week in the summer we'd find a big striped watermelon. Miss Red never minded our sharing any of it with her. She appeared thoughtful, and I hoped she was remembering the stuff on our porch, but she wasn't.

"You're so young, Anna Lee," she said. "Maybe when you're older you'll understand and believe what I tell you. Just remember that there's a big difference between being morally good and being spiritually good. I'll be the first to admit that in most ways Dr. Owens is morally good, but his spiritual goodness is quite another matter. You can't get into heaven on moral goodness alone!"

I couldn't have been more stunned if she'd hit me with the back of her hand. That she could say something like that about Uncle Johnn! That she thought Uncle Johnn couldn't go to heaven! Thoughts rushed through my head like swirling water, but I was unable to tell her that Uncle Johnn knew God as surely as she did. His God wasn't like hers or Daddy's or Mama's. When I was finally able to talk again, I didn't mention God at all.

"Well, Miss Red, I know a lot of people who are in Chattahoochee today just because they went crazy over religion."

She answered me as though she'd known all along that's what I'd say. She lowered her wrinkled lids over watery blue eyes and said primly, "That's mighty interestin', Anna Lee, mighty interestin', but I'll tell you this, if I have to go crazy over something, I'd rather it be religion than anything else."

I opened my mouth wide to answer her but closed it and looked at Mark instead.

As casually as if we'd just been passing the time of day, he asked, "Heard the news today, Miss Red?"

She seemed more surprised by his question than by what I'd said to her. Only the unpatriotic didn't listen to the news and Kate Smith. In a tone that told us how ridiculous the question was, she countered with "Will General MacArthur return to the Philippines? Of course I've heard the news!" She stood up and turned on the little radio that sat on a shelf above the kitchen table. "I'm not crazy, despite what some people might think. I keep up with things." She kept turning the dial on the radio while she talked, but she was turning it too fast to pick up anything but static and turned it off. "Have I heard the news!"

Mark cleared his throat nervously and tried again. "What I really meant to ask was what you thought of the news. Do you think things look any better, Miss Red?"

"What do I think, Mark? I think it's awful, you hear? That's what I think. People getting killed. It's awful, just awful. Why can't people live in peace, I want to know. My own son-in-law killed. I know my poor Verna is about crazy with grief." She sank slowly into her chair as though suddenly overcome with sorrow herself.

Verna had been living in Chicago ever since she'd married. I found it hard to imagine Verna grieving over anybody, even the Jewish boy her mother prevented her from marrying. That's what I should have told her. People who live in glass houses shouldn't throw stones!

As though to get our attention, she tapped the table with the sides of her hands and started talking about the war again. "Don't ever let anybody try to tell you children that the Germans are smart. People go on and on about the Germans having such brilliant scientists and all, but don't you believe it, you hear? You know why? If those people are so smart, why are they listening to the maniacal ravings of a paperhanger or artist or whatever he is? Can you imagine a whole nation of people following a paperhanger — or artist, either, for that matter!" She shook her head from side to side and laughed at the mere thought of it.

In the same way that he raised uncomfortable questions in the classroom at school, Mark said, "Being a paperhanger has nothing to do with it, Miss Red. Christ was only a carpenter, and look at His following."

I don't think he said it to offend her or to make her forget about being mad at Uncle Johnn. Mark always seemed not only to know more but to think about things differently than the rest of us. Of course, everybody expected him to be smarter, his mother being a schoolteacher and all. Maybe he did get his ideas from all the books his mother had at home, but I liked to think they were original with him.

Apparently, Miss Red thought this one was his. She was so horrified she gasped and started choking. I wished to goodness I'd said it.

She raised clenched fists above her head and said hoarsely, "To think that talk like this would come in my house from someone I've sheltered and fed." Lowering her arms, she clasped her hands, and a blue vein throbbed in her temple. "Oh, sweet Jesus," she pleaded, "forgive them, they know not what they do."

After a minute her eyes narrowed, and she stood up from the table. A fleck of foam glistened in the corner of her mouth. "You're being sacrilegious, young man, and don't think your mother won't hear about this!" She slapped the table so hard I jumped.

My best friend lowered his eyes, and I knew I couldn't leave him out there alone. "His mother knows Christ was a carpenter, Miss Red." I swallowed hard. Dear God in heaven, Mark had only thrown off on Jesus. I'd sassed Miss Red. Mama would kill me for sure.

Shaking her finger and gradually her whole arm at me she said, "Just hold your tongue! Oh, how sharper than a serpent's tooth," she moaned. "I don't want to hear another word from either of you. You don't go around comparing our sweet Jesus to the likes of Hitler. All these years I've given to you children and told you about Jesus, and all for what? You never even heard me!" Her voice shook, and her right hand clutched at the pocket of her dress. "Why, the very idea! Just leave. The both of you, get out!"

We were glad to leave, yet we hesitated, knowing that we'd gone too far, that we'd never have rainy days together at Miss Red's again.

Her back steps were still wet from the rain, and I watched the chinaberry tree shed water like tears. Pretending for a moment that everything was all right, that nothing had changed, I stared at the remaining clusters of lavender blossoms, faded to near white in the brilliant jungle of fern-like leaves. Mark, his eyes riveted, like mine, on the chinaberry tree, said nothing. Finally, he turned and walked away from me, beneath the fading blossoms, across the backyard to his house.

I was as shaky as if I'd been treated for hookworms and dosed with Epsom salts. I went straight to my room and sat at the desk Daddy had built from the discarded wood of an old piano. I stared at the desk, hating its silence and black ugliness. I was miserable, but my tears wouldn't come. Maybe I should never have been friends with Miss Red in the first place. Staying on the good side of her was a balancing act. There had always been little digs, little hints about Uncle Johnn that I'd tried to ignore because I liked her. But I didn't like the way she planted fear in me.

I heard a knocking at the back door and waited for Mama to come in and tell me to cut a switch. When she did come in, she was too mad to wait. She had a belt in her hand and began swinging before I could get up from my chair. She caught my legs again and again and my wrists when I tried to shield myself. I screamed and cried, knowing all the while Hazel could hear me plain as anything.

"Haven't I raised you better?" she yelled. "How could you embarrass me this way? How dare you sass your elders! Our own neighbor. A friend. I'll never live this down, not to my dying day. If this is what comes of being around Mark Thomas, you just stay away from him, you hear me? Just stay away from him! Hear me? Hear me?"

"I hear, Mama. I hear. Oh, please stop."

"Don't you tell me what to do, young lady. I'll stop when I feel good and like it." She gave me one more whack and stormed out of the room.

When Daddy got home that night, he wanted to spank me too, but Mama stopped him. "She's had enough, Robert. I took care of it."

In Daddy's book, being disrespectful was nearly as bad as going crazy over religion. My legs and arms were still stinging, and I avoided looking at Uncle Johnn as I endured the humiliation of Daddy's lecture.

"Now, Anna Lee," he said, "you and Mark have been a-goin' over there all these years, and she's been givin' you eats and all. She's an old woman. What good's it gone do you to go and hurt her? It sure don't speak well of Mark. Here his daddy's overseas some place, gettin' shot at every day most likely, and his only child can't stay out of trouble. Is that how me and your mama raised you, to thank people by turning on them? I can hardly believe you'd say something like that, a big girl like you. You're eight years old!"

"Nine, for God's sake," Mama said, shaking her head. "Nearly ten."

"Nine?" Daddy questioned in utter disbelief. "Nine? Well, that makes it all the worse. I really thought better of you than that, Anna Lee."

He waited, but I couldn't answer right away. I did feel bad, and it was all the worse because I wouldn't repeat to them the things Miss Red had said about Uncle Johnn, the things I knew she'd omitted from the version she gave Mama.

"Anyway," I said finally, "I told her about all the people who are in Chattahoochee today because they went crazy over religion, and do you know what she said? She said that if she was going crazy, she'd rather it be over religion than anything else."

Daddy was dipping a scallion into the little mound of salt he'd poured on Mama's clean white tablecloth. He tapped it on the side of his plate before he answered. He looked disbelieving. "Miss Red,"—he pointed the scallion in the direction of her house—"said that to you?" He spoke softly because the windows were open.

"Yes, sir."

He shook his head. "Well, she's a lot worse off than I ever thought she was. If she'd ever been to Chattahoochee and seen what it's like up there, I'll bet she wouldn't talk thata way."

For Daddy Chattahoochee conjured up all sorts of devils. The only part of his job he didn't like was having to drive old people there to have them committed. Chattahoochee. The word itself had a horrible ring to it, and children who moved to Bay Harbor from there were ashamed to admit it. I'd often wondered whether, if the state mental hospital hadn't been there, the name would still have sounded so awful, so crazy itself.

Finishing the scallion and putting the green top to one side of his plate, Daddy looked over at me again. "You quit spendin' so much time over there. A big girl like you don't have no business hanging around an old woman anyway, especially if you're gonna sass her. It's probably the best thing all the way around."

Mama and Mrs. Thomas talked it over and decided that Mark and I should go together and apologize to Miss Red but then we weren't to meet there together anymore. The next afternoon we knocked on her back door. She didn't invite us in but just stood there with her head none too steady as we told her how sorry we were.

The next time I went to the picture show, I came back to her house, just like always, but I felt somehow she didn't interrupt or criticize as much. Maybe I shouldn't have bothered. Neither of us could forget what had been said that day. Just as the hair seemed to live inside Miss Red's trunk, those invisible words were a very real presence in her house. We couldn't pretend they hadn't been said, and as time went on they seemed to grow in intensity, just as Miss Red's shorn hair appeared to grow darker when it was really Miss Red and not the hair that changed.

When I talked to Uncle Johnn about it, he didn't have much to say, for once seeming somehow preoccupied. "Miss Red's worried about her own shortcomings, Anna Lee. Nine times out of ten, people are concerned with themselves, not somebody else.

She's too old to change and too scared to think she might be wrong. There's no turning back for her."

Maybe Uncle Johnn was right. He usually was, but that didn't quiet the real real gnawing in my chest, my own failure to quiet my growing concern about Uncle Johnn and Miss Amy Walker.

8

Miss Amy was a Bay Harbor girl, and everyone in town knew her story by heart. It had been told so often, polished and improved, that it was like a glittering fairy tale filled with sadness and beautiful words. Miss Amy, of course, was the fairy princess, and in spite of everything she'd done, the town was proud of her.

The older people had watched her grow up in a big white house surrounded by giant oaks and crepe myrtle trees. There were even some, Miss Red among them, who prided themselves on remembering that her first formal had been ivory. Her parents went all the way to Atlanta to buy it, and the following Thursday there had been an editorial in the *Bay Harbor Times* urging people to support their local merchants.

It had been been a pretty dress, though, and all the neighbors watched as Miss Amy stood in the front yard holding a pink crepe myrtle blossom in her hand while she had her picture painted. The finished picture was beautiful, and there wasn't a frame in all of Bay Harbor big enough to hold it. They had to send away for one, probably to Atlanta. Miss Amy's father, Stanford Caldwell, died trying to get that picture out of their house the night it burned.

For me her story really was a fairy tale. I'd heard how Miss Amy had ridden on floats in Halloween parades and had always taken the prettiest box and the best fried chicken to the annual Fourth of July Box Suppers. She had made cakes for bake sales and sold poppies on street corners for the American Legion. By the time I could remember her, she was still beautiful, but she wasn't a girl anymore. She was a grown woman in her twenties who didn't ride on floats or go to box suppers, but she still sold poppies. Every year she sold her first poppy to Uncle Johnn. He might drop money in the cardboard lids the other ladies held out to him, but it was Miss Amy's poppy that stuck out of the lapel of his coat, and everybody knew it. They also knew it was Miss Amy's poppy that faded all over his white coat when he got caught in a sudden shower one day. The stain never did come out, though it lightened some the way water colors will on a seashell. Uncle Johnn didn't even get mad about it. He said that was a mighty small price to pay for one's country when so many young men were dying on the battlefields every day.

It never seemed to occur to Uncle Johnn that the other women in town might feel slighted because he wouldn't wear their poppies. He'd bought his first poppy from Miss Amy and, sort of absentmindedly, I thought, bought one from her each year after that. Maybe he even did it out of pity.

Miss Amy, at a very young age, became a widow of sorts. Fashionable as she was with her orange colored hair and green eyes, Mama said she had no right to call herself a widow.

"Grass widow," Mama called her. "She's a divorcée no matter what name she puts to it. She's just putting on airs because she doesn't want to say her husband's in Chattahoochee or wherever it is she's got him. Everybody in town knows he's not dead."

Neither could Mama forgive her for not having freckles. "She's the only redheaded woman I ever saw who wasn't freckled, and I've seen many a one in my day," Mama was always saying. "I sometimes wonder if that hair doesn't come out of a bottle!"

Everything else aside, Miss Amy's house was enough to set her apart from the rest of the town. It sat on top of the only hill in Bay Harbor, not counting the cemetery, giving her nice cool breezes and a lovely view of the water. In the beginning, Mama said, no one else would have had a house on that hill. Some claimed it was no more than an Indian mound, a mound filled with corpses whose ghosts had been the fear of young boys as they dug for arrowheads and buried treasure in the bright noonday sun.

When young W. T. Walker decided to build a house there, people thought he was crazy. Turned out later he was, but he'd made no mistake about the house. Old men stood around every day watching the house go up and getting in the workers' way. If anything haunted the hill, it was their own boyhood dreams, and W. T.'s house became a wall raised between them and the vision of their youth. They came to hate him for the injustice of it all, seizing that one spot out of all the town to claim as their own.

When he married Miss Amy, W. T. took her there to live, and in time it became the most desired location in all of Bay Harbor. People looking for new houses were hopeful of a hilltop home after Miss Amy had her husband committed.

"You should move down and take a small bungalow," they advised kindly. "Just you and that girl shouldn't be all alone up there."

That girl was Miss Amy's maid, Pearl, and people never completely forgave Miss Amy for taking her into court to testify against W. T. But when anybody said anything about Pearl to Miss Amy, she just smiled the way she did when people told her she should move down off the hill, and went on living the way that suited her.

She gave little afternoon bridge parties and wore nylon stockings that swished against her soft flowered dresses. She never perspired, even on the hottest day.

Mama said she'd heard of a woman who suffocated from sealing her body with deodorant, but as Miss Amy continued quite healthy, she apparently had no need to resort to such drastic measures. Oh, sometimes her nose might be a little shiny, but that was the only sign she ever gave of being bothered by the heat. This didn't exactly endear her to the women at her parties, neither those who perspired in the confining stockings they'd taken from fruit jars, where they were protected from ants and roaches, and smoothed over their legs with gloved hands, or those who'd applied bottled stockings to their legs and worried that they might "run" in the heat. But anyone invited to a party at Miss Amy's house was always glad to go. Their names would appear in the paper and sometimes even their pictures.

Miss Amy loved parties, and perhaps she also knew how much the women liked being invited to her house. For those who didn't play bridge — Mama had learned when she visited friends in New York City — there were sewing parties and garden parties. That way she got just about everybody, but not everybody could get her.

Ours was the only house she visited regularly. Mama may even have suspected that it had something to do with Uncle Johnn, but she wasn't worried. She never for one minute thought Uncle Johnn would be interested in Miss Amy. Some men were meant to be bachelors.

"Anyway, why would he want to marry," she'd said plenty of times, "when he has a home here with us? Johnn wasn't behind the door when the brains were passed out. He knows a good thing when he sees it. We couldn't treat him better if we tried, and Anna Lee worships the ground he walks on."

What's more, Mama was convinced that Uncle Johnn didn't even like Miss Amy. That made any hidden motives on Miss Amy's part all the easier for Mama to bear. Oh, she knew about the poppy business but considered that further evidence of the gentleman in Uncle Johnn. She took comfort in the fact that he didn't even talk to Miss Amy when she stopped by our house on Sunday afternoons.

Miss Red had been quick to point out to me that Miss Amy always waited until Uncle Johnn was home to pay her visits. The fact that it happened to be cooler in late afternoon and people were more likely to be up from their naps never seemed to occur to her.

On those still Sunday afternoons, Uncle Johnn and Miss Amy would sit as quiet and shy as a couple of strangers and appear intent on the dessert they spooned from Mama's best green dishes. It was a coincidence that those dishes were the very color of Miss Amy's eyes, making them seem more brilliant than ever, but if Mama was ever aware of this, she didn't say anything. She probably didn't notice because she was too busy enjoying her conviction that Uncle Johnn disliked Miss Amy for what she'd done to her husband. I'd heard her tell Helen that Miss Amy was wasting her time. "Johnn's got a peculiar streak in him," she'd said, "and from what I've seen, his taste runs to older women. I'd even go so far as to say he might be afraid of Amy, being the kind of man he is."

I'd seen their eyes meet, though, and I'd watched him staring at her rear end when she walked, giving it the same studied attention he gave the pool table as he chalked his cue stick. I knew he wasn't afraid of her. I wished he had been.

Mama clearly didn't want Uncle Johnn to get married. She wouldn't have admitted it, but she'd done more than get used to having Uncle Johnn around. She liked it. Unlike Daddy, Uncle Johnn was home most nights, and while Mama complained about having another mouth to feed and having to wait on him, she never complained about having somebody to talk to in the evenings. And despite all her objections to pool and pinball machines and other forms of gambling, she never hesitated to make bets with Uncle Johnn. Perhaps they didn't count because she thought they were patriotic. Their bets were always on the war or what move which general would make. When Uncle Johnn expressed a preference for General Eisenhower, his picture went up in the dining room. Mama preferred General Mac-Arthur, and the following week his picture was hung on the opposite wall. President Roosevelt had been there all the time.

Uncle Johnn wasn't dumb, and it took me a while to understand why he never won any bets. They started out small. He came home from the drugstore one night and handed Mama an enormous box. It was the biggest fancy box I'd ever seen, and I prayed it'd be candy. It wasn't. Mama raised her eyebrows, and Uncle Johnn said, "You won it fair and square, Estelle." The satin-lined box contained a dresser set. There was a mirror, a comb and a brush, all sorts of little jars and even a fingernail file. All sorts of thing. And every bit of it matched.

Daddy laughed. "You don't know much about women, Johnn. She'll spend all her time a-sittin' in front of the mirror now. First thing you know, she'll be wantin' us to eat sandwiches for supper."

"You know better than that, don't you, Johnn?" Mama still sat with the box on her lap, lifting up one piece and then another, rubbing her fingers over their smooth blue tops. "Why, I bet there's not another set like this in town." She stopped smiling and looked up at Uncle Johnn. "You didn't order more of these for the store, did you?"

"Why, Estelle, you like it, don't you?"

"Of course I like it. I love it. Thank you, Johnn."

"It might just be good for business, you know. Doesn't it stand to reason that other women in town might like them, too? We could turn a real profit."

"You're the businessman," Mama said, her lips tight. "You know what's good for business."

"I sure do," Uncle Johnn laughed. "And no, Estelle, I didn't order any more. As far as I know, you have the only one for a hundred miles around."

After that Mama seemed to take an added interest in the war news. No one dared talk in the evening when she listened to Lowell Thomas or Howard K. Smith. Uncle Johnn was at a disadvantage, I thought, because he couldn't always get away from work in time to listen to the news with us, but when I questioned Mama about her unfair advantage, she said, "Why, he's got a radio right there in the store, Anna Lee. There's nothing to keep him from listening to the news the same as me." The sound of Lowell Thomas's "So long until tomorrow" grew familiar, but it was Walter Winchell who excited me. When he addressed all the ships at sea, he transported us out of the living room and made us part of the war. Despite the fact that I was more interested in "Baby Snooks" or "Inner Sanctum" than I was in the war news, words like Luzon and Tunisia, and Corregidor grew familiar. We hated Hitler, Tojo, Mussolini, and Tokyo Rose, and Mama even hated the pope and Mrs. Roosevelt.

The war moved swiftly, faster than anything we'd ever known in Bay Harbor. Mama had barely grown accustomed to letting the dust settle on her new dresser set when Uncle Johnn paid his next bet with a flower vase and matching candlesticks. He bought them from the jewelry store, so Mama said they had to be good. If anything, she was even happier with them than she had been with the dresser set. She promptly arranged them on the dining room table beneath the gaze of President Roosevelt and his generals, and there they stayed except at mealtimes. She managed to have flowers in the vase most days, and although the candles were never lit, they did look impressive in their low-cut holders except on very hot days, when they would begin to melt and bend despite their cellophane wrappers.

Daddy never stooped to betting with Mama, but he wasn't to be outdone. He bought Mama a present, too. He came home for supper one night carrying a piece of pottery hidden by layers of paper I recognized from the butcher shop. When Mama unwrapped it, a huge green frog sat gaping, exposing the inside of its bright red mouth.

"Why, where in the world did you find that, Robert?" Mama asked. "I don't believe I've ever seen a frog as big as that."

Daddy wasn't used to giving gifts and was embarrassed by what he took for praise. He hooked his thumbs into the top of his belt and hitched his pants up a bit so that he appeared to be swaggering. "Some fella come through town sellin' 'em. I don't know if he sold many or not, but there might not be another one like it in town."

"We can hope, Robert," Mama said. "We can hope."

Before Mama could decide where to put it, Daddy took it over to the front door and set it down. "That'll make a fine doorstop," he said. "It'll take a strong wind to ever move that rascal."

We found out later that there was one more. Chester had bought one for Helen.

Daddy soon found out he was no match for Uncle Johnn though and dropped out of the competition. The war news threatened to replace "Ma Perkins" and "Helen Trent" in Mama's life. She and Uncle Johnn were into long-term bets, and the stakes were higher. When Malone's Furniture truck backed up to our front porch and we stared into the cave-like darkness of its back end, Mama was so excited she stood with her legs crossed, but she didn't let on that she hadn't been expecting the big Philco radio they carried into our living room.

"That is a beautiful piece of furniture," Mama said as Mr. Malone wiped it off and showed us how to turn it on and off and adjust the volume and most fascinating of all to me, the overseas bands. Mama could listen to the news if she wanted to; I could listen to the actual war!

When Mr. Malone left, Mama began arranging pictures on top of the radio. Stepping back to see how they looked, she said, "Your Uncle Johnn may not come from much, but he's a man of his word."

"Don't you like him better now, Mama?"

"I've never said I didn't like your Uncle Johnn, Anna Lee. I'm not blind to his faults, that's all. I don't owe him anything, Anna Lee, not anything. He's mighty lucky to be living here with us, mighty lucky, and he knows it. I admit he's pleasant, and he's generous" — she looked toward the radio — "but I deserve it."

When Uncle Johnn first came to Bay Harbor, he hadn't known a soul outside our family, so Mama had lost no time in trying to acquaint him with all the particulars — past, present, and future — of just about everybody in town. Miss Amy's story was not only the longest and most involved but the most exciting as well. I listened along with Uncle Johnn, and that may have been the first time I remembered hearing it.

I sat close to Uncle Johnn on the settee, and Mama leaned forward in the wicker rocker opposite as she told him that she remembered W. T. Walker very well. "He was the school principal when Robert and I moved here. Or was it the year after?" I was afraid she might get hung up right there, but finally she continued without figuring it out. "I do know," she assured Uncle Johnn, "that it was after we came here that he began courting Amy. Why, all of Bay Harbor was so pleased they became somewhat of a public pastime. W. T. was a nice-looking man. I can still see him as good as the back of my hand, but I don't know, he was kind of different-looking, sort of artistic-like. There was never an extra ounce of weight on him, and he had such pretty white teeth." Both of these things Mama found strange in light of the fact that he bragged of never having been to the dentist and had a particular fondness for sweets. Mama said

most every night she'd see him walking Miss Amy to the drugstore for a strawberry soda. "Sitting at the fountain, bent over
their striped straws," she said, "they looked like a couple of
children. At eighteen Amy was little more than a child, but W. T.
was older than her, by about six years, I believe. It seemed like a
perfect love match. He had brains, and she had money. But later,
things turning out the way they did, people blamed Amy for not
having listened to Carlotta.

"Now Carlotta, Johnn, that's another story! She came to Bay
Harbor as a fortune teller with a tent show long before the
picture show was built. She was dark and pretty for all that gypsy
look about her, and Donald Sneads, tall, shy Donald, who'd
never kissed a girl in his life, was so smitten that he had his palm
read every night!"

The way Mama told it, Carlotta had acquired quite a reputation by Saturday night when almost everybody in town was lined
up at her tent waiting to have their palms read, too. It took some
time for the word to reach those at the end of the line. The
fortune teller was gone. She and Donald had eloped! But even
then people were reluctant to give up their places in line, passing
comment back and forth along a human telephone line. Donald!
They could hardly believe it. Out of the darkness a woman's
voice offered an explanation they'd overlooked: "Still waters run
deep." But there had still been laughter, even in the disappointment of all those unread palms, for what in the world, they all
wondered, had Carlotta seen in Donald's future?

Later, when Donald and Carlotta returned to Bay Harbor to
settle down, people were of divided opinions on the matter.
Some questioned the honesty of Carlotta's talents, and others
doubted it was his palm she'd been reading behind the closed
flaps of her tent, for Donald returned to Bay Harbor a very
married man. With his new authority as her husband, he told
Carlotta she'd read her last palm. "I have to hand it to him,"
Mama said. "He tried very hard to make an everyday housewife
out of Carlotta." She smiled. "He never quite succeeded,
though. She just had to keep on reading and looking into the

future. She said it kept her alive, that and the goat milk she got from a little nanny penned up in their backyard."

More than once I'd heard Mama say Donald could have gotten rich if he'd bottled that goat milk and sold it. It was told about town that Carlotta not only drank the milk but bathed in it like a queen or something. I still remembered the way Mama laughed when she told Uncle Johnn, "If she wasn't an everyday house-wife, she wasn't an everyday gypsy, either!"

There had always been stories about Carlotta. Mama insisted she invited them by dressing in her loud clothes and walking the dark streets when Donald worked nights at the mill. On one of those nights, she wandered into the drugstore where W. T. and Miss Amy sat drinking their sodas. They thought it'd be a lark to let Carlotta read their palms and moved from their stools to a table in the back of the store. Even so, people heard most of what was said. Seeming rather nervous and giddy at first, Miss Amy laughed a lot, but when Carlotta said there was a black spot in W. T.'s future, she clamped her mouth shut and didn't utter another word.

"Bad blood," Carlotta kept repeating when she stood up, not indicating which of them she meant. But it didn't take a gypsy to figure that one out. People knew all about Miss Amy. She'd been born right there in Bay Harbor, but W. T. was, Mama whispered, "adopted." This was the part of the story I didn't like — to think of poor W. T. being adopted, never really knowing who he was.

The Walkers had been far from young when they left town one day and returned bringing a baby with them. "Just like that!" Mama said to Uncle Johnn and snapped her fingers. "The way I heard it, they never made any explanations to anybody and acted just like they'd had it themselves. Even that far back, adopting had been serious business in Bay Harbor, but the Walkers never appeared concerned about how somebody else's child might turn out. And as the years passed, people hadn't said much about W. T.'s having been adopted. He seemed okay and even grew up to favor Mr. Walker. When W. T. completed his education, came back as a schoolteacher, and went on to become the school principal, people were sure he was all right. The Walkers themselves probably couldn't have done any better.

Carlotta had been known to take to bed sick after a particularly disturbing reading, and, standing there in the drugstore, people noticed that even though the night was warm, a chill seemed to pass over her and she pulled her fringed shawl tight about her shoulders.

W. T. made a big show of not being worried, but the crowd in the drugstore knew better. He hadn't even finished his strawberry soda.

Carlotta had quite a following in Bay Harbor, and old doubts about W. T. were stirred up again, but Miss Amy only chalked them off as nonsense and proceeded to make wedding plans. For a time it looked as though Carlotta had been wrong after all. W. T. and Miss Amy were very happy and had such a lot going for them. The honeymoon was hardly over before a baby was on the way. The first suspicion anyone had that something was wrong was at the baby shower. Right in the middle of opening the gifts, Miss Amy broke down and started crying, and they had to call W. T. to come after her. They gave him some little cakes and nuts and told him not to worry. It was very natural for a woman in Miss Amy's condition to cry. It was generally agreed, however, that she'd picked a pretty poor time to do it.

Mama had been at the shower. She gave Miss Amy the same thing she'd made for every other baby in Bay Harbor — a little crocheted sweater set, but Miss Amy left without her gifts, and they were sent to her house the following day.

When the baby arrived, people took it to be the black spot Carlotta had seen in W. T.'s future. It was a blue baby, and Miss Amy never even saw it. The nurses said W. T. saw it, that he asked to be alone with his daughter, but for all that Miss Amy pleaded for one look at her baby girl, W. T. wouldn't hear of it, insisting he knew best. When she left the hospital, there was a tiny fresh grave in the cemetery. It wasn't the only small grave, but it was surely the only fresh one. The cemetery hadn't been used since Bay Harbor had buried its fever victims there in the 1800s. Everybody else used cemeteries further inland in neighboring towns, but not Miss Amy. W. T. not letting her see the baby and all, she'd been like something wild and insisted the baby be kept in Bay Harbor where it belonged. The cemetery was the only spot, other than her own backyard, that was high enough to bury somebody without drowning them at the same time. It was close enough that she could go there and look each day if she wanted to, but she could only imagine what lay inside. Maybe that's why the marble stone shaped like a tiny angel was blank, not a date or anything on it. No name, nothing, just always looking new, as though it had just been placed there. That's the way she'd always feel, she said — as though it had just been placed there.

I'd looked at it plenty of times myself, fascinated somehow by its smallness and the little white picket fence enclosing it. The whole cemetery was a fascination to me, though. With the exception of Miss Amy's baby's grave, which was kept tended and the fence freshly painted, the other graves had fallen to neglect. Tombstones were knocked over, and some of the larger elevated vaults had fallen into chunks of concrete and brick after vandals searched them for valuables, but the desecrated graves yielded no ghosts. Our cemetery was haunted by things far more terrible.

On bright sunny days when the stillness made you strain to hear some silent sound and your skin jerked with fear, or in the blowing rain or the darkest night, you wondered and were afraid. Could they possibly still be there, the deadly fever germs, sealed up all those years, or exposed, waiting in broken graves? The germs were a real fear, the thing that made going to the cemetery a breathtaking experience. In graves so old, the occupants were all strangers from the time when Bay Harbor had been a wicked city. And even though Bay Harbor was no longer wicked, I knew it wasn't perfect, either. If it had been, Daddy would have been out of a job. As would be expected, most of the problems Daddy ran into were in the Quarters. Oh, occasionally he would talk about trouble in town with drunks or soldiers and sailors, or there might be whispered conversations with Mama about seeing somebody's wife in the back seat of the wrong Studebaker on a dark night, and there was one girl in town who dressed like a boy. Daddy said she never bothered anybody, though, and it was his business to know if she did, so she couldn't be considered wicked.

All that was wicked had been washed white as snow with the giant tidal wave, and while the water may have lapped at its base, it had never reached the cemetery. High on that hill, the dead were the only ones safe. Even if He was God, I thought that was downright tacky. Still, I was glad the cemetery had been spared. There was much more of romance and mystery to it than sadness, the dead being more like characters in a book than real people. It took Miss Amy to put a baby there, a real baby. Some people would have timidly placed the grave at the outermost edge of the grounds, but not Miss Amy. Her baby was smack dab in the middle of the cemetery.

After the baby died, everyone had breathed easier. Carlotta's prediction had been realized and was out of the way. There could be other babies. W. T.'s trouble, then, came as a double shock. People had quit looking for bad news at the Walkers'. Oh, there'd been some talk, Mama said, when W. T. fainted in the school sickroom. It was good-natured talk, though. He'd gone in for some aspirin and saw the nurse cleaning out a wound on a boy's head. That he passed out at the sight of blood didn't surprise anybody. No one had ever accused a schoolteacher, or even a principal, of being strong. All that thinking didn't build muscles.

Had Miss Amy complained some at the time, people might have been more understanding later, but she hadn't said a word. She just sort of dropped out of sight for a while, and W. T. gave up his job at the school. She explained that he needed a rest, and she spent all her time taking care of him. She even cut his hair. They didn't go into town for anything. The young Nigra, Pearl, did all the shopping and lugged things back up the hill.

Miss Amy discouraged callers, and no one caught a glimpse of W. T. Mama said Miss Amy had looked bad, but everybody figured that being shut up all the time had just made her brood over the baby again. And then, out of the blue, she took W. T. to Chattahoochee.

"It was in the spring, maybe even summer," Mama told Uncle Johnn. "I know it was in '39. Just like that!" Mama snapped her fingers again to show Uncle Johnn how quick it'd been. "She said she wanted to talk to the doctors there. She even hired an ambulance for the trip so he'd be comfortable. She could have put him in a straitjacket, and she and Pearl could have taken him up in the car with Robert, but she never did have any trouble trying to figure out ways to spend money."

They hadn't been gone two weeks when Miss Amy showed up in town one day, picked up some of her clothes, and left again. That time she was gone for about six months, and when she returned a second time, she was alone. She'd had W. T. committed, not in Chattahoochee, she'd told people. She couldn't do that. He was in a private hospital. She wouldn't say where. His parents, like hers, were both dead, so there was no one she had to answer to if she didn't feel like it. And she didn't.

I couldn't visualize Miss Amy ever looking awful, but Mama said she had. She said she'd lost weight and was so thin her clothes just hung on her. "She looked hard," Mama said, drawing her lips into a tight line of disapproval. At that time, she pointed out, Miss Amy had been visiting W. T. regularly. Finally, though, the visits stopped.

"He doesn't even know me," she told people. "He doesn't know who I am. They say he never will."

Everybody felt sorry for her then, and for him, and talked about the thin line between genius and insanity. But any sympathy given to Miss Amy turned to shock and disbelief when she started talking about divorce. That she would think of her own freedom when he would never have his seemed unforgivable if not downright illegal.

Mama raised her eyebrows. "It wasn't too awful long before you came to live with us, Johnn, that there was a kind of trial at the county seat. Robert said Amy just kept repeating in a dazed fashion that W. T. didn't know her. But it was Pearl's testimony that got her the divorce. Pearl told it that W. T. had mistreated Amy before his breakdown, once almost choking her to death.

No, the ink wasn't dry on those papers when you got here, Johnn."

All the men in town were just as kind and gentle with Miss Amy as if she'd been a real widow, but nobody rushed up and proposed to her. It looked like she just might as well have saved herself the bother and expense of the divorce.

"She just looks soft and helpless," I heard Mama tell Helen. "A man would be afraid to marry a woman like that."

Uncle Johnn never seemed afraid of her. For a time I had the impression he'd never even noticed her, not the way other people did. But he had noticed her, in ways I'd never dreamed possible.

9

When the school year ended in May, I determined to put the fourth grade and Mr. Magic behind me forever. It had been the worst year I'd ever had, what with trying to learn the multiplication tables and worrying about how I smelled all the time. On that last day of the fourth grade and Mrs. Striker, I was delirious with joy. When the bell rang, I rushed to join my school friends as, shouting and shoving, we left behind the smells of chalk and paste and books. We burst from the dark halls into the sunlight, spilling down the steps and over the ground like a giant wave, drowning the call of sea gulls as they swooped over the school yard in search of scraps from discarded lunches. Freedom was at its sharpest as I raced past Mark and punched his shoulder. I didn't even go by home but headed instead for the drugstore and Uncle Johnn. Hardly pausing for breath, I ran all the way, not even slowing my pace as I entered the door and ran headlong into someone standing just inside. My nose stung from the impact, and I looked up to see Chester grinning down on me. I tried to go around him, but he grabbed my arm in his hand and pulled me to the pharmacy counter where Uncle Johnn stood working. Nobody seemed to think this looked a bit unusual. Mama and Helen were best friends.

"Looka here, Doc," he said, stretching my arm so hard I had to stand on tiptoe, "don't she look just like her daddy? Look at that arm. Robert Owens won't be dead as long as she's alive. She's the spittin' image of her daddy, ain't she?"

Uncle Johnn was busy, and a strange look came over his face, but he nodded rather absentmindedly. I didn't say a word. I just stood there with my arm held tightly in his grip. I hated him with all my being, but I didn't flinch or pull away. There'd be bruise marks on my arm, but something warned me not to let him know I was afraid. When he released my arm, I still didn't move but stood there as silent as Uncle Johnn. I hoped he felt uneasy because he adjusted the small holster that held his hunting knife, turned, and, without even buying anything, swaggered out the door.

I walked behind the counter with Uncle Johnn and sat down. My knees felt weak, and my heart was pounding.

"You're okay, aren't you, Anna Lee?" Uncle Johnn asked as he reached a big bottle of pills off the shelf. "Don't let Chester get under your skin. He can't help being such a clod."

He kept talking as he worked, but I hardly heard him. The joy of my freedom was tarnished. I could only be happy in the thought that in a world with people like Chester, Uncle Johnn was mine.

Finally I had to leave. Mama would wonder why I hadn't stopped by the house. I wanted to go to the beach, but there wasn't time. Mama wanted me home to help her get ready for Uncle Henry's visit.

Each year Uncle Henry came to Bay Harbor for a week's vacation with us. Mama would have preferred that he not come at all, but every year he came the same as if he'd been welcome. Daddy jokingly called Mama the unwelcome mat, apparently untroubled by her slights to his family. Other than Uncle Johnn, Uncle Henry was the only relative ever to stay overnight at our house, and I was at a loss to understand why he should be so privileged.

"Well, Anna Lee," Uncle Johnn attempted to explain one day, "Henry's your grandfather's baby brother, half brother actually, the closest link Robert and I have to Papa. Then, too, there's the matter of your mother not having any family of her own. She might feel put upon if your daddy and I had our people in and out of the house all the time. Estelle and Robert decided a long time ago to pull away from the rest and strike out by themselves with their own family here in Bay Harbor. I think it's mighty fine of Estelle to have made an exception where Henry is concerned, and me, too, of course. Robert and I think a lot of Henry, and I'm glad you have an opportunity to see how some of the rest of the family lives. Just thank your lucky stars you don't have to spend a week with your Aunt Wilda!"

Mama was not a religious person but called herself a Christian in spite of Brother Palmer's insistence that a Christian did more than just believe in God. Her own acknowledged connection with any deity — that's what people called God in New York City — was the cross she'd been sent to bear. Daddy's relatives were the cross, and Uncle Henry added an undue burden to its weight, not only because he visited us but because Aunt Wilda shared the space Mama had allotted him.

They didn't live in town the way we did, but out in the country in a house that was a stranger to paint. Uncle Henry even looked half related, and he was married to a woman who didn't believe in painted women any more than she believed in painted houses. Aunt Wilda was a stout white-haired woman who wore print dresses so obviously made from flour sacks that I always expected puffs of white mist to seep through the seams when she walked about or stooped over to take a pan of biscuits from her old wood stove.

Uncle Henry never brought Aunt Wilda when he came to see us. I never questioned his coming without her, though. It seemed a natural thing for him to do. She would have spoiled his vacation the way I'd always felt she'd spoiled his life. I wondered what made people get married and mess their lives up that way. Helen might look like a queen, but married to Chester she was no better off than poor Uncle Henry. I didn't even mind sleeping on the studio couch in the living room so that he could have my bed. I figured Uncle Henry lived all year long just for that week in Bay Harbor. He always found plenty to do, mostly in the way of visiting. He and Miss Red would sit under her chinaberry tree and talk, he'd spend hours at the boarding house talking to the boarders, and he got no end of pleasure from hanging around the police station with Daddy. And naturally Miss Amy had to get into the act. She'd invite us over for dessert or at least take Mama and Uncle Henry and me for a ride along the beach. Mama always insisted I go along. The one time I hadn't, Uncle Henry jumped in the front seat with Miss Amy, and Mama had to sit in the back by herself. Since Aunt Wilda never seemed to like it when Uncle Henry was enjoying himself, I couldn't understand why she didn't come with him to Bay Harbor and spoil his fun. She ended up telling me herself when we were visiting their house.

It was a hot day, and we were eating at the long table on their back porch when I heard Daddy tell Aunt Wilda that she should come to see us sometime. "No, Owens," she said. She always called him by his last name, as though he was a hired hand or something. "No, I won't be going to Bay Harbor. I know the kind of people that'd be there, so I'll just stay here on the place."

I marveled that Daddy could sit there smiling at his plate. We were the kind of people she'd find in Bay Harbor! Uncle Henry didn't say a word, and if he smiled, the big mustache concealed it. Knowing how Mama felt about Daddy's relatives, I was surprised that she hadn't been the least bit insulted by Aunt Wilda's crack about Bay Harbor. She told me later, "She wasn't talking about us, Anna Lee. Wilda doesn't have any use for your Uncle Johnn."

The entire house was cleaned, just as it had been every other year, and we settled back to wait for Uncle Henry. I was never given to quoting Scripture, but waiting for Uncle Henry always filled me with the urge to rush to the door when he arrived and shout, "Behold, the bridegroom cometh!" He surely didn't look like a bridegroom, but the preparation seemed to warrant one.

I went to bed thinking about Uncle Henry, but I dreamed it was Chester we were expecting. Uncle Johnn wasn't with us anymore, and Mama was letting Chester move into his room. I cried and begged her not to, but she kept on crocheting and wouldn't answer me. It was so real I woke up with a sense of dread, but when I realized it was only a dream, I took a renewed interest in the old man's arrival.

The bus arrived on schedule, but without a sign of Uncle Henry. Daddy walked the length of the bus, checking all the seats and looking along the floor as though he might find Uncle

Henry's toothbrush. Mama never found it amusing that Uncle
Henry traveled with his toothbrush, bristle side up, in his shirt
pocket, but even Mama was worried when Daddy told her Uncle
Henry hadn't been on the bus. I was sent to the post office to
check the mail. I didn't see any letters as I peered through the
tiny window of the mailbox, but I opened it anyway and was
about to slam the door when I noticed the letter lying thin and
flat on the floor of the box. It was addressed to Daddy, but I took
it home to Mama, knowing she'd open it anyway.

Aunt Wilda, Uncle Henry had written in an uncertain hand,
was terribly sick and needed to be in the hospital, but neither he
nor the doctor could get her there. She told them that when her
time was up, it was up, and there was nothing a hospital could do
about it.

Daddy said Mama could rise to any emergency, and feeling
the way she did, it was to her credit that she rose to this one.
Uncle Henry and Aunt Wilda had never had any children, and
since no one else had offered to go, Mama decided she'd have to
take care of Aunt Wilda herself.

The bus Mama and I took early the next morning had a big
sign on the side that read, "Is this trip necessary?" It surely was.
Much as I liked going places, I was far from happy at the prospect
of spending any part of my summer vacation with Aunt Wilda.
I'd always been afraid of her, and as we rode along on the bus, her
stern, unsmiling face kept floating up in front of me. It was so
natural to fear Aunt Wilda, it came to me that Uncle Henry
might be afraid of her, too.

She was a God-fearing, churchgoing woman. She did her best
to make Uncle Henry the same kind of person, but judging from
his weekday behavior, the only God Uncle Henry feared was the
one residing inside Aunt Wilda. If he didn't fear it, he seemed to
at least respect it because he did go to church with her every
Sunday. During the week, often as not, you'd find him sitting on
the front porch watching the cars pass on the highway that ran
close to their house.

"Hold her tight, boy," I'd hear him yell at the passing cars.
Uncle Henry seemed to get no end of pleasure from yelling at

the strangers who zoomed past his front yard. This was some-thing Aunt Wilda hadn't counted on. Who would have thought that a highway would be cut right through the farming country almost to their doorstep? She just couldn't stand Uncle Henry's yelling and slapping his leg, having so much fun. Aunt Wilda didn't have fun, and she must have felt that she lost a little of Uncle Henry in each of those passing cars. She'd walk to the porch with her plump white hands on her hips and stare at him.

"Henry!" Coming from her, that one word held a multitude of warning in it.

"Ah, Wilda," he'd say, running his forefinger under his nose and into the depths of the mustache, "they can't hear what I say. What harm can it do?"

"Whether they hear you or not is of no matter. It's the fact that you feel called upon to say it that bothers me. It's you I'm worried about."

But the minute she went back into the house, Uncle Henry would lean forward, straining to see another car in the distance.

It was a long ride. We went through Port St. Joe, where Mark's grandmother lived, and finally passed the clearing that had been home to Daddy and Uncle Johnn. A few miles further, the bus stopped along the highway to let Mama and me out, but no Uncle Henry sat on the front porch. We found him at Aunt Wilda's bedside.

As Mama and I stood at the foot of Aunt Wilda's bed, her eyes fluttered briefly. "Grace?" she whispered hoarsely.

"No, Wilda, it's Estelle," Mama replied loudly. "Estelle's come to take care of you." Turning to me, she said, "She's out of her head. Better find yourself something to do. Just stay out of my way."

Looking around, I wondered if there was anything duller than a Sunday in the country. Only the flies seemed busy. The flies and Mama. She changed her clothes and took command, but Uncle Henry didn't leave the bedroom until later in the after-noon when Mama asked him if there were any fresh vegetables for supper. I followed him to the garden, where I picked some snap beans and he dug around searching for potatoes left from his spring crop.

I looked back toward the house where death was expected and felt ashamed to feel the beauty of the still, warm afternoon. I moved down the row of beans, and Uncle Henry broke our silence.

"Careful of snakes, honey."

It was an ordinary thing to say, but Uncle Henry didn't often talk to me, and there was an unexpected tenderness to his tone.

"Yes, sir. Uncle Henry?"

"Uh huh?"

I drew a breath and asked what had been on my mind all afternoon. "Why did Aunt Wilda call Mama Grace?"

He leaned forward on his hands, resting on all fours. He turned to look at me but blinked against the sun and stared back at the ground instead. "She's lost in time, Anna Lee. I s'pose it's God way of being merciful when there's such a little bit of it left. Grace roomed with us the first year she taught school. Only woman I ever knew Wilda to get along with. Sure broke her up when Grace and Earl got married and moved away." His voice grew softer, and he seemed to forget me and be talking to himself. "Time flies by so. Faster than them cars out yonder on the highway. Faster'n you realize. Yep." He stopped and was still for a moment. Then he stood up and started brushing the dirt from his pant legs. "And we better be gettin' back." He cradled three good-sized potatoes in the crook of his arm as we started up the path to the house.

Cooking supper that night, Mama told me she didn't think we'd be there long. "She's sinking fast," she kept saying.

Before going to bed, I tiptoed to the open door of Aunt Wilda's bedroom. I stared at her as she lay on the big metal bed, and it looked to me as though her white hair and gown had, in fact, sunk into the bed and become part of the linen. Only her face was left on the pillow. A few mornings later I woke up and her face was gone, too.

Uncle Johnn stayed in Bay Harbor, but Daddy came right away to help with the funeral arrangements. My grandparents had come from large families, and in no time at all relatives were everywhere. Mama's eyes flashed and sparked. "For God's sake," she snapped at Daddy, "are they coming out of the woodwork? I never bargained for this! It's funny nobody could come when she was sick and there was work to be done, but they're all free now. They can't do her any good now that she's gone. The heathens!"

"They've come for Henry's sake, Estelle," Daddy said as he tried to calm her down, but the fact that he was enjoying himself with people he hadn't seen in years didn't improve her disposition any.

Aunt Wilda's casket was placed in the front room, and someone sat with her at all times. She was never alone now. Because the house was warm, windows were opened behind the casket, and with every breeze the curtains blew out over the open lid and covered Aunt Wilda's face. It gave the sitter something to do, to get up and move the curtains every now and then, until Mama tied them in a knot high above the casket.

Later, with so many people going in and out, a cat came in the house and walked along the edge of the casket, balancing carefully as it walked toward the open lid, and then dropped down onto Aunt Wilda's chest and started washing itself.

"Praise Jesus," someone said.

"It's a sign," somebody else added in a hushed tone.

"It sure is," Mama observed as nobody stirred to move the cat, which by now had washed all its paws and turned its neck around and was starting on its back. "It's the sign of a carnival, that's what!"

I'd heard her complaining to Daddy about all the laughing and joking going on. "No respect for the dead whatever," she'd said to him. But it was the poor cat that caught the force of her anger. As determinedly as she'd handled the curtains, she descended on the casket, jerked the cat up, and threw it out the front door as hard as she could. Daddy had told me a cat always landed on its feet. This one, I feared, would be the exception, and I ran out the front door after it. I wasn't all the way down the steps when a voice cut through the stunned silence Mama had created. "Isn't Anna Lee Grace's child?"

Grace's child? Grace's child? Pictures of a woman snatched from my hands. Not Aunt Grace, Grace's child! Not me. Hazel! I wasn't adopted. Oh, dear God, don't let me be adopted. Words throbbed inside my head until they became only words with no meaning. The day seemed suddenly black, and I stumbled in the direction of our car, climbed into the back seat, and lay there for the rest of the afternoon. It was hot and flies buzzed around me, but I didn't dare sit up because I didn't want to be seen. Later, I heard someone approaching the car.

"Oh, here you are. What in the world are you doing?"

I sat up and stretched, staring hard at the familiar face of a stranger called Mama. "I guess I fell asleep."

"Don't you want to come in now?"

"I'll be in later, in a little while. Just let me get good and awake first." I opened my mouth wide and pretended to yawn.

"I never sleep good in strange beds, either," she said. "I could use a nap myself."

I continued to stare as she turned to leave. The sudden silences, the broken conversations, so many things told me Mama's pain would be worse than mine if she found out what I had learned. It was up to me to see that she never knew. I must never let anyone speak out in my presence again. As for my own pain, I musn't know, either. A numbness settled like a headache inside my brain until all I remembered was that I didn't want to be with the relatives anymore.

Uncle Henry wore a black suit to the funeral, carried a black cane, and put a glass stickpin in his tie. It looked like a diamond, but Daddy said he didn't think it was real. I'd never seen him wear it before, and Daddy said that was because Aunt Wilda had thought it was a sin to wear jewelry.

We sat with Uncle Henry in one of the front pews marked off with black crepe paper. Uncle Henry sat very erect with his hands resting on top of the cane he held ramrod straight between his outstretched knees. He looked so like a picture, and the scene was spoiled only occasionally when he rubbed a freshly ironed handkerchief under his nose.

I could hear people whispering. "Henry's bearing up well," someone said. From the sidelong glances Mama sent his way, I judged he was bearing up too well.

The minister talked a long time about what a fine woman Aunt Wilda had been, but I didn't hear a great deal of what he said. I was more fascinated by his tic than by what he was saying. Every few minutes his head jerked to the left as though he expected Jesus to be sneaking up behind him. I'd counted the windows, the flowers, and half the timbers in the roof before he quit talking.

By the time we left the church and rode down the highway past Uncle Henry's house to follow a red clay road deeper into the woods to the cemetery, it began to look as though Aunt Wilda had died a lot quicker than we could bury her.

We rode in the head car, a long black Cadillac, with Uncle Henry. We sat in the back seat. Uncle Henry sat up front with the driver. He said he'd never ridden in a Cadillac before. He'd never owned a car, and at all the other funerals, he and Aunt Wilda had ridden with relatives in old Chevrolets or Fords, in the back seat, no doubt.

Still taking an interest in passing traffic, Uncle Henry shouted at the cars we passed. Of course, he did it in such a way as to show respect to Aunt Wilda, but this didn't pacify Mama any. "Hold on there, boy," he yelled. "Pull her over to the side of the road. This here is a funeral procession!"

From inside the car, there was room for doubt. Uncle Henry still sat proud and erect, and somewhere along the way he had acquired a pair of white gloves that covered his gnarled, splotchy hands as he gestured with all the emotion of a band director at the passing traffic. He even had a word for those who respected the dead enough to park their cars along the side of the highway as we passed. "That's right, boy, you'd better pull her over," he shouted. Uncle Henry made it sound as if we had to fight for our place on the road.

Mama sat with closed eyes until we finally arrived at the cemetery. I was sure people didn't act this way in New York City. Not until the driver went around to open the door for Uncle Henry did she break her silence. "I've never been so humiliated, so embarrassed in all my life!"

Uncle Henry didn't give any indication of having heard her and continued to sit statue-like, waiting for his door to be opened.

I thought the day would never end. Even after the striped canopy, the fake grass, and the folding chairs had been taken away, everybody stood around and talked. They talked about how the children had grown since the last funeral, and we stood back-to-back, embarrassed by the proximity of our growing behinds. Mostly, though, they talked about who would be next. Uncle Henry didn't seem to think it would be him. When he wasn't drinking coffee from a glass fruit jar, he was tearfully hugging all the better-looking female relatives.

I felt dreamlike and tired, disturbed by something unpleasant in the back of my mind that filled me with a vague sense of unease. Drifting away from the crowd, I went off by myself and sat under a tree until they called me back to the car.

Ignoring Mama's stony silence, Daddy insisted Uncle Henry come home with us. We'd been expecting him anyway, he pointed out.

Unmindful, for once, of the passing traffic, a tired Uncle Henry slept slumped over in the back seat all the way to Bay Harbor. I dozed and dreamed of a faceless woman in a small photograph.

10

During the course of his visit, it became more and more apparent that Uncle Henry wasn't exactly the same as before Aunt Wilda died. For one thing, his week was nearly up and he showed no sign of wanting to go home. And whereas before he'd never talked about her at all, now he was always telling us what a fine woman Aunt Wilda had been. He may have even found life a little dull, but he never fully escaped Aunt Wilda. He still whispered when he asked Daddy to give him a drink.

After Daddy and the sheriff broke up a still one time, he came home with two huge jugs of moonshine. He tipped one on its side, and the white liquid poured out on the ground gurgling the same way water would. When he'd finished, he put the clear blue-white jug in the garbage can and broke it with a hammer. Later that night, he brought the other jug inside the house and hid it in the back of the closet. After that, whenever Uncle Henry came to visit, Daddy always gave him a little something to drink. He knew Aunt Wilda never allowed him to have any alcohol on the place. The only difference now was that Uncle Henry whispered a little more often. He always said the same thing, almost as though he was trying to make it up to Aunt Wilda for taking a drink.

"Could I have a little Blood of the Jesus, Robert?" he'd ask. And then the clothes would be pushed aside, the jug dragged forward on the floor, and I'd hear the whine of the tight cork as Daddy twisted and pulled to release it. The white liquid sank to an all time low, and it soon became evident that Uncle Henry wasn't even bothering to ask for his drinks. He helped himself quite freely, grew confused, and started yelling at the cars that passed in front of our house. Mama didn't like it any more than Aunt Wilda had.

"Henry," she said, "it's all right for you to do that at home, but city people just don't go for that sort of thing."

Uncle Henry appeared thoughtful for a moment, and then, running his finger into the depths of his mustache, he stood up and told Mama he was going to the drugstore.

I went into the living room and began fooling with the overseas bands on the radio. I'd just pulled in some static and what may have been voices when I heard myself hollering, "Wait, Uncle Henry, and I'll go with you."

Mama looked a little surprised and said uncertainly, "What a thoughtful thing to do, Anna Lee." Never one to lose the advantage of an unexpected opportunity, she hesitated a minute before saying, "Just wait. I'll be right back." She went into the bedroom and came back with her black change purse. She handed me some money and said, "Take your Uncle Henry to the show, Anna Lee. I bet he's never seen a moving picture."

"But it's not time," I protested.

"When it is time, then, take him."

I was sure Uncle Henry had never been inside a picture show before, but he just stood there, silent and rheumy-eyed, not the least bit excited. He walked slowly and a bit unsteadily toward town, and when I suggested we go by the park and sit down until the show opened, he didn't protest. He followed me to one of the green benches, where we sat and stared at the bay.

I cleared my throat. "Uncle Henry, why did Aunt Wilda like Grace so much?"

"Huh? What?" He sounded startled, as though I had just awakened him. "Grace? Grace liked to go to church." He spoke brokenly, swallowing hard between each word. "You want to know about Grace, you better ask your Uncle Johnny. They were like two peas in a pod."

The drinking that had loosened his tongue had clouded his mind. "No, Uncle Henry. She was married to Earl, not Uncle Johnn."

He threw his shoulders back and sat up straighter on the bench, indignant. "I know she was married to Earl, but your Uncle Johnny never acted like he knew it."

I could feel a weakness seeping into my arms and legs, and my chest grew tighter with every breath. Crazy old fool. Filthy-mouthed drunk!

"Let's see if the show's open now," I said woodenly, and we continued toward town. I didn't even look to see what was playing as we bought our tickets and went to sit in the semi-darkness until it was time for the show to begin. It was a Bette Davis movie, but I never once looked at Uncle Henry to see what he thought of a moving picture. He sat silent and still beside me until someone, Bette Davis maybe, announced she was going to have a baby.

Suddenly he stood up and said in a loud voice, "I'm not watching that," and walked past me out of the theater. I didn't budge, caught somewhere between the movement on the screen and the aching numbness in my head.

After the show, I walked to the drugstore and lay down on some boxes in the back room. I stared unseeing at the ceiling. After a bit Uncle Johnn came in and stood over me. "Are you okay, Anna Lee? You look kind of pale."

In the summer everybody worried about infantile paralysis. Unlike my own problem, that was at least something I understood. Tears welled up in my eyes, but I nodded my head.

"You sure?" he asked, and I stood up and threw my arms around his waist, tighter and tighter. I never wanted to let him go.

"Why, Anna Lee, sweetheart, what's wrong? What's happened?"

I couldn't tell him. All I could do was cry and hold him.

"You're going to make yourself sick." He sat down and, pulling me to his lap, held my head against his chest with his soft, warm hand.

Quietly, not certain I wanted him to hear me, I spoke against his chest. "Uncle Johnn, did you love Aunt Grace?"

I imagined for a moment that his breathing stopped, but he continued holding me and asked quite casually, "What made you think of Grace?"

"I don't know. Just something Uncle Henry said, I guess."

"Just something, huh? Well, your Aunt Grace was a special person. We all loved her, but not everybody understood her. It isn't right to pass judgment on things you don't understand. If everybody learned that, the world would be a better place."

"Do people understand you, Uncle Johnn?"

"Me? God, no! I'm not sure I understand myself. But, Anna Lee, understand one thing. I'm an honorable person. Remember that, okay?"

I was at once relieved and disappointed. Twisted through my worry had been hope of something I couldn't name. And yet, wouldn't a gambling man lie?

Walking home, I tried to close my mind to the whole problem, to push it under the bushel with my light. By the time I reached the house, I'd forgotten all about Uncle Henry and was stunned when Mama called to me from the kitchen, "How'd y'all make out at the show?" She walked to the door of the dining room drying her hands on an apron.

I felt as though I'd left home weeks ago.

"Where's Henry?"

"He left before the show was over. He was embarrassed because somebody was going to have a baby."

"Well, I've never known him to miss a meal. I reckon he'll come along home with Johnn or your daddy."

But he didn't. When both Daddy and Uncle Johnn arrived home without Uncle Henry, we began to worry. Uncle Johnn appeared thoughtful, but Daddy was the one who was really troubled.

"Robert, you of all people," Mama fumed. "You're the law. I thought for sure you could keep track of your own kin. Doesn't say much for the rest of Bay Harbor if you can't."

"Now hold on a minute, Estelle. I wasn't told about no crisis. Nobody gave me a missing person on Henry. This here is the first I've heard of it."

"Well, all the same . . ." She stopped as we saw Miss Amy's car drive up in front of the house. Uncle Henry was sitting slumped sideways in the back seat. He was drunk as a coot, and I wasn't sure but what Mama wasn't going to faint dead away on the spot. She hadn't been so humiliated since the time I whistled at the dinner table. Miss Amy came inside the house with us while Daddy and Uncle Johnn struggled to get Uncle Henry out of the car. Mama kept looking out the window, relieved that none of the neighbors came out to watch.

"I'm so sorry," Miss Amy said. She looked it, too. She was the sorriest-looking thing I'd seen in a long time. Her eyes were all red and swollen, and her face was puffy. I couldn't imagine what in the world Uncle Henry could have done to reduce her to such a state. He was nothing but an old man, even if he was a drunk. While Mama and Daddy tried to get Uncle Henry to bed, Uncle Johnn asked Miss Amy to sit down. He didn't ask me, but I sat, too.

"Please accept our apologies, Amy. We never dreamed Henry would behave this way. Maybe with his wife dying and all, we can feel sorry for him, but that doesn't justify his abusing your hospitality."

Miss Amy closed her eyes a moment and sighed. "I do feel sorry for him, very much so. And I knew you'd be worried. I tried to get him here sooner, but he was so insistent." She hesitated a moment. "I don't know quite how to say this," she began, "but you see, he's asked me to marry him."

Uncle Johnn stood up suddenly and as quickly sat back down. "He what?"

Miss Amy just nodded her head and ran her fingers lightly across Mama's crocheted arm cover.

Maybe Miss Red was right. She sure had to be hinting. A proposal from Uncle Henry was no compliment.

"God!" Uncle Johnn leaned forward in his chair and took her hand in his. He didn't absently flex or form a bridge with his forefinger, giving all his attention to her. "He probably won't remember a thing tomorrow," Uncle Johnn consoled, "but it's different for you. I know the pain he must have brought you."

At that, Miss Amy drew a deep, gasping breath and burst into tears. Uncle Johnn moved from his chair and sat beside her on the couch. As though it was the most natural thing in the world to do, he put his arm around her shoulders and drew her closer to his side. For an instant I hated both of them, hated my Uncle Johnn where I'd never felt a thing but love before.

Uncle Johnn gave her his handkerchief and said soft things like "There, there." It was mighty convenient that by the time Mama and Daddy came back into the room, Miss Amy was beginning to get hold of herself. I was relieved once more to see how truly awful she looked. Even Uncle Johnn couldn't fail to notice that.

She tried to smile at Mama. "I don't like to bother friends with my problems, but I can't let you go on thinking it's Henry's fault. And too—" She stopped. "And, too, I have to talk to someone. I've received the most terrible news. It seems like a bad dream, too awful to be real." Her voice trailed off as if she was just too given out to talk anymore. Then she took a deep breath and continued.

"Dr. Lawrence, the psychiatrist at the hospital where W. T. . . ." She stopped again, swallowed hard, and said, "Dr. Lawrence called me today. It seems that, I mean, well, it's W. T. I mean, they were admitting a new patient, and somehow—I don't know how these things happen—he got away when there was some kind of disturbance in the lobby. There was a building outside where they stored gardening equipment and things like that. Some of the patients were being allowed to tend gardens—something new they were trying. A group of patients was inside the building getting their things, and this new man ran in there with them. Dr. Lawrence assured me there was an attendant with the men, but somehow the door was locked. They don't know what happened. Well," her voice quavered, "there—there was a fire. I can't even bear to think of it. They weren't sure at first who all had been in the building, and they couldn't, I mean, identification was—was . . ." She stopped talking again, and we waited for her to continue. "W. T., it seems, was one of the privileged patients who was allowed to garden. He was signed out for that activity. They know one man escaped, but they feel sure it was the new patient. They found the remains of W. T.'s ID bracelet just inside the door. I didn't realize they let him wear it. I suppose that was some small dignity they allowed him."

"Maybe that new man set the fire," I offered, and Mama silenced me with a glaring look.

"Perhaps," Miss Amy replied. "In all probability," she said, nodding her head. "Until they find him, they don't know anything certain. It's just that, well, in a way I always felt it would be kinder if W. T. were dead, if he would never be any better, but this is so horrible. It's so unfair! Dr. Lawrence said there had been improvement in W. T.'s condition. Improvement! They'd even let him have a garden. Why, he might have come home again. Oh, it's so unfair!" she said and began crying once more.

Uncle Johnn stood up. "Estelle, don't wait dinner for me."

He'd always said "supper" before. That was the kind of effect Miss Amy had on people. I wondered if she'd been that way with W. T., too.

"I'll see Amy home," Uncle Johnn continued, "and then I'm going for something to help her sleep. I may be late, so don't wait up for me."

"We're real sorry, Amy," Mama offered. "If we can do anything, anything at all, just let us know. I mean it now, you hear?" She patted Miss Amy's arm, but Miss Amy only nodded and walked out with Uncle Johnn following behind her.

"Do you reckon Uncle Johnn will drive her car home?" I ventured to ask.

"Good God, Anna Lee," Daddy answered. "Don't you think she's had enough shocks for one day? Johnn would be about as good at drivin' as your Uncle Henry is at drinkin'."

"If she divorced W. T.," I asked, "why's she so upset? It's not like she was still married to him."

"Mr. Walker to you, miss," Mama said. She chewed her lower lip a moment, appearing thoughtful. "Sometimes," she said, "it seems to me people almost ask for things to happen. Her calling herself a widow and all. Now she really is a widow, but poor W. T. had to pay the price to make her one. But then, Anna Lee, you've got to remember that W. T. was probably Amy's first love. You don't ever get over your first love. Your Uncle Johnn would do well to remember that, too."

"Yes, and you'd do well to get us something to eat," Daddy said sternly. "I'm not willin' to starve myself just because W. T. Walker's left us. Twice! Most people leave the world once, and now he's gone and done it twice. Guess we shouldn't of expected any less from a Walker, though."

"He wasn't really a Walker," Mama corrected.

Daddy sat down to the supper table. "That's right, he wasn't, was he? Huh!" he said, shaking his head with wonder. "Just goes to show you faith ain't always enough, is it? 'Specially not if you're a-borrowin' trouble."

"Well, let's talk about something pleasant," Mama said. "This is making my skin crawl. And now I suppose Henry will want a big breakfast in the morning. I can't see him waking up to eat anytime tonight. I want you to realize, Robert, that there are limits to what I'll put up with from your family."

"Time heals all wounds," Daddy said. I didn't know who he meant, but it sure couldn't heal them fast enough for me to get my mind off Uncle Johnn being alone with Miss Amy. I tried to concentrate on how awful she'd looked, but as the evening wore on, Uncle Johnn stayed far longer than seemed necessary. He came in late, smiling and smelling of honeysuckle. I started to follow him to his room, but Mama stopped me. "I don't think he's in any mood to talk tonight," she said, pulling out a long length of crochet thread.

I felt a chilling numbness inside me but went to bed without so much as a good night to Uncle Johnn.

If Uncle Henry remembered proposing to Miss Amy, he had the good sense not to mention it when he got up the next morning. He grew sober in mind and body—in body because Daddy carried the jug around in the car with him, and in mind because of Mama's stony silence. Nobody was surprised by his eagerness to leave. The sheriff allowed Daddy the use of some gas allotted to the station, and we drove Uncle Henry home the second Sunday in June, the same day Miss Amy was attending W. T.'s funeral in Georgia.

When we arrived at Uncle Henry's house, Mama handed him a packet of pictures she'd taken of Aunt Wilda in her casket and of the flower laden grave. "You'll appreciate these later," she said softly and patted him on the arm. Then she got busy and straightened up the house and aired everything out. She'd even taken a supply of groceries and cooked food to leave for him, but we knew it wasn't all charity on her part. The better Uncle Henry found things at home, the less likely we'd be to have him in Bay Harbor again soon.

She could have saved herself the trouble. Uncle Henry waved good-bye to us from the porch as we went to the car. He looked so small and alone standing there that Mama got out her handkerchief and blew her nose real hard. When Daddy backed the car around and eased toward the highway, we turned once more to wave, but Uncle Henry had already forgotten us. There he sat on his old cowhide chair, leaning forward, straining to see a car in the distance.

11

With Uncle Henry gone, things settled into a more normal routine. Saturday night came, and Mama couldn't wait to get to the boarding house. I asked if I could stay home.

"Of course you can't stay home. Just because you're going to be ten, don't think you're grown, young lady." Her eyes narrowed. "What are you up to? You've never minded going there before."

"It's Chester, Mama."

"Chester?" She looked at me suspiciously. "Has he bothered you any?"

"No, ma'am. Not really. He just scares me sometimes."

Relief flooded her face. "He's got rough ways, but I've always thought he cared about you, them not having any children of their own. He's no prize, that's for sure, but he's your elder, and you must be polite to him."

"But, Mama," I pleaded, before she cut me off.

"I don't want to hear any more about it. I think the world of Helen, and if I can put up with Chester, you can too." She was unwilling to discuss it any further, and a short time later we were sitting with Helen and the boarders on the big upstairs porch.

With the war on, the boarding house was more crowded than I'd ever seen it. Being so close to an army base had made Bay Harbor more of a tourist center than ever. There was seldom a vacant room, and most of the time there were cots on the front porch to take care of the overflow of soldiers and government workers.

All the men wanted someone to talk to them. There were happy men and sad men, mean ones and drunks. She got them all once the war started. And there were the liars, too. They all promised something, the liars did.

A row of wooden rockers stretched the length of the porch, and we all sat rocking and staring down at the busy Saturday night activity. The stores didn't close until nine o'clock on Saturday, and people came to town who didn't get there any other day of the week. The men stood in small groups on the sidewalk, and the women sat on wooden benches nursing their babies. They all wanted to be outside seeing the electric lights and watching the city folks moving around. And the city folks sat in parked cars watching the country folks. We saw them all from Helen's front porch.

"Yes sir, little lady," the red-faced man with the cigar was saying to me. "I'm going to bring you a real-to-God jackass. Straight from Mexico! That's where I'm going when I leave here." He leaned forward in his chair and covered part of his mouth with his hand. "Government business," he said seriously and settled back in his chair again. "Yep, sure as I'm living, I'm bringing you that Mexican jackass. You can hitch it up to a little cart, and it'll pull you all over town. Now, you be here the next time I come through town and I'll give it to you." He puffed harder on the cigar and blew smoke toward the screen. "Yes sir, I'm free as a bird and going to dear old Meh-he-co."

Helen stopped rocking and sat forward, looking at him. "Mr. Rollins, have you ever seen a bullfight?"

"Have I ever seen a bullfight?" he laughed. "That's like asking Jesus if He knows the way to heaven!" He jumped up, still holding the cigar, and poised one hand in front of him and one over his head, shouting, "Olé!"

Instinctively, we all leaned forward in our rockers and looked down. People on the sidewalk turned their heads upward trying to see us. Looking back at Mr. Rollins, we watched silently as cigar ashes dropped into his hair. They flared slightly, and he slapped his head with his left hand and sat down to smooth his hair with a pocket comb. Sitting back in his rocker, he hitched his right leg up and rested his ankle on his left knee. "Yes sir, only fourteen years old and hard and straight as an arrow. I thought of being a matador myself. All them snake-hipped greasers laughed at me 'cause of my red hair. I don't guess I really wanted to be one anyway or I'd have gone through with it, red hair or no red hair. As it is, I just sit in the stands and enjoy myself while they sweat it out with them bulls and them tight pants."

"I've always thought," Helen said, "that a bullfight would be the most beautiful sight in the world. That's something I want to see before I die."

"And it's something you should see, too. Yes sir, a woman of taste like you was meant to see the best life has to offer. Just say the word and I'll take you to see a bullfight." He glanced over his shoulder toward the living room door, and I knew he was looking to see if Chester was around.

I prayed that Chester wouldn't come out, but at the same time I worried that he'd be inside tormenting the poor little lovebirds. They were so frightened and skittish any more you couldn't get near the cage without them flying around and banging against the side until their feathers fell in soft green clouds to the floor. There was nothing Chester was above doing to those birds. Once he put one on a phonograph record, and while it sat there with its little chest heaving with fright, Chester turned the volume up real loud and started the record spinning. I thought Helen would never catch that bird and calm it down enough to put back inside the cage. I knew she was upset, but she hadn't said a word to him. It wouldn't have mattered if she had. She couldn't even keep him from beating her.

Helen appeared to consider Mr. Rollins's offer for a moment, and then she laughed, the sound of it floating out over the street and down on the people below. "I appreciate the offer, Mr. Rollins, I really do, but you know that it's out of the question."

"Well, it's an open offer. Anytime you reconsider, just say the word."

She was such a gentle person, I couldn't imagine her wanting to see a bullfight. "Helen?"

"Uh huh?"

"Don't you know they kill that bull? You don't want to see them kill a bull, do you?"

"Why, honey, they'd kill it whether I was there or not. I want to be a part of all that excitement. I want to feel that tension and see all that grace and beauty of movement." She rubbed her hands up and down her arms. "Why, it gives me chills just thinking about it."

A hand touched my shoulder, and I leaped straight up out of my chair. It was Chester. He laughed and reached inside his pocket. I could hear money jingling. He held a coin out to me.

I tried to control the quavering in my voice. "I don't need it," I said and inched back away from the line of rockers, stopping when I felt the screen behind me. It was rusty, and if I pressed against it, I might fall to the sidewalk below.

Quick as a wink, Mama spoke up, and I knew she was mad. "It's not a matter of need, Anna Lee. Chester's trying to be nice to you. Now thank him and take the money."

Still I hesitated, and Chester laughed and returned the money to his pocket. "She's nobody's dummy, Estelle. She's gettin' too big for small change all right." I could smell the bootleg liquor on his breath and heard the sound of his fingers working the billfold out of his back pocket. Nobody said a word and not a rocker moved as he turned and held the billfold out in front of him as though trying to catch the light from the living room to study its contents. He could see well enough. President Roosevelt gave us longer days when he declared wartime in 1942, but Chester was on stage, playing to the audience in rocking chairs. He moistened a finger with his tongue, carefully selected a bill, and returned the billfold to his pocket. Turning toward me once more, he reached forward and slowly and carefully tucked the money into the pocket of my blouse, his bony fingers working up and down against my breast as he did so. Then he patted my pocket and said, "Don't you lose that now, you hear?"

"Don't worry, Chester, she won't," Mama answered. "Say thank you, Anna Lee," she added sternly.

"Why, she thanked me already, ain't you, sugar?"

"Oh? I guess I didn't hear her," Mama said, knowing full well she didn't have a hearing problem.

Chester dropped into one of the rockers, and I could hear him breathing. It was a thin, raspy sound, as though his insides had rusted in the damp river air aboard the *Blackwater*. We were all quieter with him there. I was glad Mr. Rollins had slipped off to bed while Chester was forcing his money on me. The earlier a start he got, the sooner he'd be back with my donkey.

It was after eleven when we finally left Helen's, but I was too keyed up to be sleepy. I tried to concentrate on the donkey and forget the way Chester's fingers had felt moving sluggishly inside my pocket. Was it the liquor that made him move so slowly, or did it only seem that way because I hated his touch? A real donkey, I kept reminding myself. A real donkey.

"How much did he give you?" Mama asked.

"Ma'am?"

With a disgusted sigh she grabbed the money from my pocket. "Ten dollars," she exclaimed. "I always did say Chester had money. He'd have to for them to live like they do. You be nicer to him and maybe he'll leave it to you some day. I always said you were like their own youngun. I'll just keep this for you. Maybe I'll put it toward that gold stretch bracelet." She opened her purse and put the money inside, just like that. But I didn't care. I didn't want anything of Chester's, not even money to buy feed for a donkey.

Chester was slowly edging Hazel out of my nightmares, lurking in alleys and behind buildings, jumping out at me with a ten dollar bill in his oversized hand.

Much as I wanted to be the only person in Bay Harbor with a donkey, I wasn't sure it would set well with Daddy. Added to my discomfort was Mama's silence. She never mentioned the donkey or the ten dollars, and until she said something, I knew that I shouldn't either. Daddy might have thought ten dollars a bit generous, even for Chester, and he wouldn't know Mr. Rollins if he stepped on him. Would he think there was something odd about a strange man giving me a donkey from Mexico, something that had to do with Mama and the boarding house? What would he do to me if he found out, or, worse, to Mama?

Days passed, and my stomach grew warm with the fear of silence. And the longer I kept quiet, the more it seemed I was doing it to protect Mama. Helen didn't need protecting, so I finally talked to her about it.

"Do you really think he'll bring me a donkey?" I asked, but until she answered, I had never really doubted that he would.

She smiled. "Why, he said he would, didn't he? If he said so, he'll bring it, Anna Lee. Just remember, Mexico is a long way from Bay Harbor. It'll take time."

There was something so soft and dream-like about the way she talked. Maybe living in the boarding house, surrounded always by strangers, made her believe in things people said. The boarding house was real enough, but it wasn't the same as a home with grass and flowers and rooms that had the same people in them every day. When a boarder left with his pictures and shoes and suitcases, his room was cleaned, the straight chair pushed against the wall by the door, and the window shades raised exactly halfway. It looked like all the other empty rooms, and he might never have been there at all.

When I left Helen, I felt better than I had in weeks. Mama wasn't trying to hide anything; she hadn't told Daddy because she wasn't sure I'd ever get a donkey. I wasn't as certain, either, but all the joy and excitement of the anticipation had returned.

I went to Miss Red's, and, sitting at her kitchen table, my stomach fluttered with butterflies. What in the world would she say if she knew I was getting a donkey? If I'd planned it all, I didn't think I could have found a pet more acceptable to Miss Red. I felt perfectly safe, for who had ever heard of Jesus having ringworm!

In the yellow heat and stillness of summer, time dragged as I waited the long days for Mr. Rollins's return. I'd almost quit hoping when, near the end of July, he finally came back. He came in the night, like a thief, and I didn't even see him.

"He arrived late," I heard Helen say to Mama on Friday afternoon, "and he was off again early the next morning. Said he might not be back for a long time. I'll miss him. He's such an interesting man."

"He'll be back, Helen," Mama said. "He likes you too much to stay away. If you weren't married to Chester, you wouldn't be able to shake him off with a stick."

"Oh, don't say that, Miz Owens. I am married to Chester."

Like a queen, Helen was so formal, never even calling Mama by her first name.

Helen sighed. "Mr. Rollins just likes somebody to talk to him. It has nothing to do with me personally. He's just a nice, friendly man."

"That's just it. He is nice. And you don't have to be married to Chester Armstrong. There's no court in the country would make you put up with what you've been through."

"Oh, but there was a time when I felt such pity for Chester. He had a perfectly terrible childhood. I felt so sorry for him, but any more . . . " She looked at Mama and shook her head.

I could hardly breathe, waiting for her to say something to me. Was the donkey already out back? Was she waiting to surprise me? I imagined us walking down the back stairs like we were going for something to eat, and there'd be my donkey tied up at the back door.

"The donkey?" I asked. "What did he do with my donkey?"

Helen's eyes looked blank for a moment, and I bit my lower lip. "He didn't bring it, did he? He never meant to bring it at all."

"No, Anna Lee, he did get the donkey for you," she said gently, and I drew in a quick breath. "He told me he did, but it kicked out the window in the back of his station wagon so there was no way for him to get it back to Bay Harbor."

I just looked at her and wondered how she could believe that, much less repeat it to me. I wished I'd never seen Mr. Rollins. I'd never even wanted a donkey until he talked about it, and then it seemed I'd been waiting for one all my life. I hoped Mama was wrong. I hoped we never saw Mr. Rollins again.

I left Mama and Helen talking and walked along the beach. Feeling empty and drained, I was vaguely aware of walking past the pier, but I wasn't really paying any attention to where I was going. I should have remembered the tramp, but I wasn't thinking about anything but my donkey when something moved in one of the sand caves. Chester! I still believed it was better that I not let him know I was afraid. If he ever knew I was scared, I'd lost the ball game for sure. I started past him.

"Come here and sit with old Chester, Anna Lee."

"I can't. Mama wants me home."

"Just tell her you've been with Chester, and she won't care. For ten dollars you ought to be able to talk to me a little bit."

He moved faster than I ever thought he could. Before I could budge, he lunged sideways like a crab and grabbed my ankle. He was partially hidden by the cave, and no one down the beach would see him. I looked, hoping to see somebody, but only the white sand stretched beyond me in either direction. His grip tightened like a steel band, and as he tugged gently to keep me from falling, I walked into the cave and sat beside him.

"You sure must like water," I stated flatly in an attempt at conversation.

"Helen told me you was smart, Anna Lee." He laughed. "You don't think I work on that dredge 'cause I'm scared of water, do you?" He rested his long brown-flecked hand on my left leg, and I stiffened.

"Just relax. Chester ain't gonna hurt you."

"I know you're not," I said with as much confidence as I could muster.

"See there? You are smart. We understand each other, you and me, don't we, little Anna Lee?"

"I'm not little. I'm a lot bigger than you think."

He laughed again. "Sure you are, but you're little compared to Helen, now, ain't you? Why, beside of Helen, you're no more than a little souvenir." He turned slightly, leaning more on his right side. "That's what you are, Anna Lee, a souvenir, a regular little lovebird. You can be my lovebird, sugar, and you won't be all skittish and fly away, now, will you?"

My mouth was dry as a piece of flannel, and I shivered with cold against the warm white sand as he pushed my dress up.

"Why, you're cold. Here, let old Chester get you warm."

He started rubbing his hand up and down my thigh, squeezing, but not so hard as to make bruises this time. Up and down along my leg, and up and . . . I didn't think I could stand it, but I sat paralyzed, unable to draw a breath, when he pushed his hand between my legs.

"That feel good?" he asked in a low breathless voice, as though he actually thought it might.

I turned and faced him then, the nerves jerking and twisting in the sides of my tongue until I thought I'd scream. "I'll tell," I croaked, but it was little more than a whisper. "I'll tell," I quavered, louder.

"No. No, you ain't tellin' nothin', Anna Lee, 'cause you got alternatives. Your alternatives will keep you from tellin'."

He said it again and again, rolling my "alternatives" over and around his tongue like a piece of hard candy, never moving his hand.

"See here, if you tell your daddy, he's just liable to shoot me, but as I ain't really harmed you none, he'd go to prison. You want to send your poor old daddy to prison?"

My mind darted, trying to think of some out, but he had me fast. Daddy would shoot him all right.

"And then there's the matter of your Uncle Johnn. Maybe I don't like bein' shot at so much so I just say you're lyin' to cover up for the guilty party. It wasn't me at all, I'll say, it was you and your Uncle Johnn, just like a couple of lovebirds."

"But that's not true!"

"Now, who'd doubt me, sugar? There's not a soul in this town don't know how crazy you are about Doc Owens. Don't you think it looks kinda peculiar, him never marryin' and all, livin' there in the same house, sleepin' right next to you almost — never having any women friends or anything? But he's got to be human, ain't he? What's he do, sweat it out? You say one word, one word, and they won't put your Uncle Johnn in jail, they'll put him *under* the jail — and all because you don't want to be friendly to Chester."

I didn't answer. I couldn't. I saw someone walking onto the pier, but still I didn't move. They were a long way from us, but Chester pulled away from me and told me to go home. "I'm tired, Anna Lee, I better get me some shut-eye. I leave town on the risin' tide. Go on home now, you hear?"

My knees would hardly bend, and I walked home woodenly, as though Chester's hand still rested between my legs. I went straight to the bathroom and drew a tub of water. Mama was still at the boarding house, and my mind screamed with pain at my predicament. I cut my underwear into tiny pieces and flushed them down the toilet. I scrubbed myself until my skin was red and raw, and still I felt his hand between my legs.

When Mama came home I was sitting in her rocker wondering how long I could go on protecting everybody.

"You could have come back and helped me carry these groceries," she complained. "If this war's ever over, I'm going to see to it that your daddy buys me a car. Whenever I need the car, he's at work."

I didn't say a word, but my mind raced.

"Come help me put these things away, Anna Lee. You're on your first legs. I'm tired."

"Mama?"

"What is it?"

"Mama?"

"For God's sake, what's wrong with you?"

"Has Daddy ever killed anybody?"

"In the line of work your daddy's in, that sometimes happens. Why?"

"You mean he'd really kill somebody?"

"If he had to. You've been seeing too many shows about the war, that's what it is. You're always in that picture show. That's why you have all those bad dreams."

"But, Mama . . . "

"Anna Lee, you're making me nervous. Just hush, you hear? All this talk about killing. We've got enough killing with a war going on. You just be a good girl, and that'll be one less thing I have to worry about."

But how could I know if I was a good girl now?

12

Mama accused me of being sullen and unfriendly. I was, but there was so much to avoid. I couldn't even go to the drugstore. What if Uncle Johnn touched me and somebody saw and remembered it later? I spent hours hiding in the darkness behind the studio couch. Uncle Johnn knew something was wrong. I was behind the couch after dinner on Monday when I heard him talking to Mama about it.

"Estelle, have you noticed a change in Anna Lee lately? I don't mean to alarm you, but something isn't right. I'm afraid Henry may have said something to upset her. Don't you think she'd old enough that we should tell—"

"No!" Mama snapped. "It's probably that donkey, that's all," she added, admitting for the first time that she'd paid any attention to that conversation. "One of the men at the boarding house said he'd bring her a donkey back from Mexico. She got upset when he didn't come through with it." She didn't say any more. All I could hear was her counting lightly under her breath, "nine, ten, eleven," as she went on with her crocheting.

I was still behind the couch when Than Carter came to the door. Than and her son Clarence ran the telegraph office. At least Clarence thought he ran it. All he did was deliver telegrams after school and on weekends. Than seldom dropped by unless she had some good gossip. This time it was about Hazel. I didn't move a muscle as I listened to every word they said. How I loved knowing all of Hazel's secrets! When they left I eased myself from behind the couch and, trying to appear as calm as possible, walked across the street to Hazel's house. Stepping here and there on a patch of grass, I walked across her dusty yard, and up the front steps to the door that led to the Sawyers' apartment. The stairs were dark, and I walked slowly, enjoying every minute because I wasn't afraid. Hazel was upstairs in bed, so no one would be throwing a piece of stove wood at me. I heard footsteps and looked up. Mrs. Sawyer was leaning over the banister rail looking down at me.

I smiled. "I've come to see the baby."

She waited until I reached the landing, and I followed her into Hazel's bedroom. Hazel was propped up against a pillow with her black hair all spread out like she was expecting company. She wasn't expecting me, though. She wouldn't have bothered trying to look pretty for me — as if she could ever be pretty with her pinched, hard little face. If she was mad at me for coming, she didn't say anything. Maybe she kept quiet because her mother stayed in the room with us. I didn't say anything either but just stood there enjoying myself. I looked at the big vase of red roses by the bed and then over at the little basket all covered with bows where the baby was sleeping.

"What are you going to name the baby, Hazel?" I asked politely.

"I — well, we haven't decided yet."

"Does her daddy know she's born?"

"Oh, yes, he knows," she said smugly and picked up a piece of yellow paper. "This is a telegram from him telling me how sorry he is that he can't be here with us." She gestured with her left hand. "He had these beautiful roses sent to me."

I couldn't help smiling again. Maybe I wasn't old enough to be having a baby, but I was old enough to know what they were doing. I'd heard Than tell Mama that Mrs. Sawyer sent the telegram to try to make things look better for Hazel.

"Mrs. Sawyer is a good Christian woman," she'd said, "and I wouldn't be a bit surprised if Hazel hadn't put her up to it. Why, she even sent flowers and signed that boy's name to the card. I know that for a fact!"

I'd heard people talk often enough about the way Hazel was always waiting at the dock every time a boat full of sailors came to town. Whenever I'd see her walking real fast on her shapely paper-doll legs, I'd wonder if she was rushing down to meet a boat.

When her stomach first started swelling out, she said she had a tumor and might have to be operated on. Then a little later she claimed she'd been secretly married to a sailor named Clyde and how glad they were that it wasn't a tumor after all. A baby would keep her company while Clyde was away at war.

Lying there in bed, she was telling me how her little girl was going to have the best of everything there was, always. She'd see to that. And all the while she was saying it, I knew she was hating being tied down and not able to run to the docks every time a boat came in. I felt like jumping up and down laughing just looking at her. I remembered what she'd done to me that summer afternoon, and I pressed my tongue against my teeth, fighting the memory of the taste. But it was almost worth having drunk that hot, bubbly, muddy water just to see the fix she was in now. Still, even seeing her, it didn't seem possible that tiny little Hazel, who bragged that she could chew only half a stick of gum at a time, had a baby, that Hazel was a mother. A baby and Hazel just didn't go together. I watched her closely as Mrs. Sawyer laid the baby on the bed beside her. Hazel's face looked almost sweet as she pushed the blanket away and looked at her little girl. I couldn't help feeling sorry for the baby because I remembered how sweet her face had looked the day she'd waited for me in her garage. More than ever since that day, I'd made it a point never to be around where she was. At least I had until now, now that she had a baby. For that I wouldn't have missed being with Hazel for anything. I still had a doll with a brass pin in the back of its dress, but Hazel had a real baby to take care of all the time. She wouldn't even get to graduate from high school. I looked at her and hoped she knew what I was thinking. She looked me right in the eye. Hazel was like that, but this time I stared back, and I didn't turn away. Over and over I kept thinking to myself, You'll never catch me running down to meet a boat full of sailors. I'll graduate from high school too. I'll wear a white cap and gown and march down the aisle in white high heels like you'll never get to do. And I won't have a baby until it has a daddy to give it a name.

I didn't know how long I'd been standing there, but I figured it'd been long enough. I leaned over the bed and looked closer at the baby. "I'm real glad it's a girl, Hazel. When she's older, her hair will be long enough that no one will ever notice her ear is grown to her head that way."

She acted like it didn't bother her a bit. Real unconcerned and snippy, she said, "I just might have it operated on, too, you know."

"Well, I have to go now. The baby's real cute." I tried to appear happy as I walked out of the room and down the steps humming to myself. Hazel probably figured I'd slam the door at the foot of the stairs, and then she could say something ugly to her mother about how thoughtless I was. I turned the dented metal knob and closed the door softly, without a sound.

Outside again I squinted against the sunlight as I turned to look at the rambling stucco house where Hazel lived. Half Spanish, half bad taste, it had once been home to a retired banker but was later divided into three apartments. A strange-looking place, it never lacked for tenants, people moving in and out as regularly as the shifting tide. Once it had been painted a shocking pink, an event of such proportions that even two coats of white paint left it fused with the rosy glow of a tourist too long in the sun. Solid as a fortress, it cut off all our breeze from the bay. If Hazel had built it herself, she couldn't have done a better job of making our house hotter than hers. During the summer, nights were almost unbearable at times without a breeze. Too uncomfortable to sleep, I'd lie awake and listen to the fans whirring in the other bedrooms. Children weren't supposed to have trouble sleeping on hot nights, so I didn't have a fan. Daddy said it made his feet hurt anyway to have the air blowing on him all night that way. My feet didn't hurt, but the nightmares did. Sitting up in bed, my nightgown bunched around my waist, I'd see Chester lying beside me and leap out of bed and race down the hall away from my room. Mama always caught me before I got outside.

"What were you yelling, Anna Lee?" she asked every time.

"A donkey. I was dreaming about a donkey."

I started wearing underpants to bed, but still the nightmares didn't stop.

Happy as I was to have the tables turned on Hazel for a change, the whole thing left a bad taste in my mouth and reminded me uneasily of Chester. I shivered and headed for the beach. Chester was away on the dredge, and I made a game of my bravery, walking right up to the sand caves, just daring anything to happen. I walked farther than usual, past all the houses, almost to the seawall. This was the quietest part of the beach, nearly always deserted. There were no houses close by, no cars. The highway curved inland for a short distance here because the water sometimes went over the seawall in hurricane season. It might also be, I'd often thought, the one nearly undisturbed part of old Bay Harbor. I stood there thinking about the brick walks and wells some fishermen had said were out in the bay when I realized I'd been staring at something.

There were a lot of broken pieces of concrete on the north side of the seawall, but some of them looked different, more orderly, almost like a little stone fence in front of one of the sand caves. Puzzled, I walked closer and, dropping to my knees, looked inside. Way back in the shadows, I saw a foot. Too afraid to get up and run, I sat there trembling and crying. My terror eased some when I realized the foot hadn't moved. Wiping my nose on the sleeve of my dress, I backed out of the cave. Slowly, deliberately, I stood up, but I made no move to leave. As mindless as if I'd been cutting a hole in Mama's new tablecloth, I knelt and looked inside again. Sickeningly white against the shadows, the foot glistened like a skeleton. Was it a body? Or maybe — my hopes rose — I'd found a spy. Even before I started back inside the cave, I envisioned the movie they'd make of my life. I'd be a movie star, and Chester could never touch me again. I inched my way in slowly until I crawled alongside a man. He was barefooted and wearing a pair of ragged khaki pants and a white undershirt. I'd seen enough shows about the war to recognize death, and I saw it now. His head was at a funny angle and his mouth was slack. To be certain, though, that he wasn't just unconscious, I laid my hand on his chest to feel for a heartbeat. When he grabbed my wrist, fear stifled my scream, and I gasped and tried to pull away.

"No!"

That's all he said, but I thought his grip relaxed. My heart pounded, and an ocean seemed to roar inside my head.

"Sick."

"You're sick?" I whispered because he had.

"Yes."

"Maybe I can get you some medicine."

At that he made a low moaning sound.

"Let me go, and I'll get you some medicine. What do you need? We've got lots of medicine. Castoria, Musterole, castor oil, Groves Chill Tonic. What's wrong with you, anyway?" I waited, but he didn't answer. He began to cry instead. He cried quietly, and as I felt the jerking movement of his chest beneath my hand, I realized he no longer held me. His hand simply rested on mine. I'd never seen a man cry before, and pity mingled with my terrible fear, my need to escape. I eased my hand from beneath his, and with all the stealth my trembling body could muster, I backed out of the cave. He never moved, seeming to be asleep once more. I blinked at the sun and shivered, the way you do when somebody walks across your grave. I drew short, gasping breaths as I made my way home, no longer thinking about Hollywood. I thought only of the sick man crying in the cave.

When I walked into the house, Mama was sitting in the living room listening to the radio while she crocheted.

"Mama?" I ventured.

"Hush, Anna Lee, I'm counting."

I could see her lips moving, but the radio was on, and I had an idea she didn't want me to interrupt her story. The straight pin she used to mark her place stuck straight up out of the pattern book. There were so many holes in the page, it looked like a piece of braille. Sometimes I'd run my fingers over the pages, pretending to be blind. I leaned over and touched the page lightly with my finger. She straightened the book and said, "Stop that."

"But, Mama, please, this is —"

She didn't say a word, but she stopped crocheting. Leveling a gaze at me, she held her hands poised with the thread draped around her fingers and the crochet hook motionless. When Mama stopped crocheting, I was usually in trouble. I backed away until the crochet hook continued its dance, dipping and pulling, dipping and pulling.

"Mama?" The silver wand froze, and I continued hurriedly, "I have to tell you something."

With an exasperated "tsk" she dropped the crocheting into her lap. "What is it this time? If it's that donkey, Anna Lee, you might as well quit moping around about it. I never expected anything to come of that in the first place. And no, your daddy hasn't killed anybody today — yet."

Something froze inside me. What if I told her about the man in the cave, and when she told Daddy, he ran out and shot him, thinking he'd done something to me when he hadn't? I couldn't bear to think of it. I had to keep Daddy from killing a sick, crying man.

"Anna Lee!"

I jumped. "Ma'am?"

Sighing, she closed her eyes briefly. Danger wasn't only on the beach. "What is it you want, for God's sake?"

"I went to see Hazel's baby."

She eyed me suspiciously. "How'd you know about that?"

"I overheard somebody talking."

"Little pitchers have big ears. Well, that was nice of you anyway considering how you've always been so scared of her. Just shows you're made of better stuff than she is." She picked up the crocheting again and peered at the pattern book.

My mouth was so dry I could hardly swallow as I made my way to the kitchen. If only Mark hadn't been spending the summer with his grandmother, he'd know what to do. Not sure I was doing the right thing at all, I spooned some leftover chicken pie into a big old cup with a broken handle, grabbed a half-empty bottle of Grove's Chill Tonic, and eased out the back door. I ran around to the front of the house before I hollered, "Bye, Mama."

"Where you going?" she called absently, and I knew she was still sitting down.

"Just around. I don't know."

"Be home for supper, you hear?"

"Yes, ma'am."

I hadn't seen Miss Red on her front porch and was startled when she called to me.

"What you got there, Anna Lee? That's not a white kitten you're hiding, is it?"

"No, ma'am. I just got myself a drink of water in this cup." She said something else, but I was across the street and pretended not to hear.

By the time I reached the seawall, I was out of breath and courage as well. Trembling, I approached the crude fence and, kneeling in the sand, cautiously laid the food and medicine on one of the concrete slabs. Then I backed away from the wall and retreated to the wooded area a short distance above the beach. Hiding behind a large pine, I watched for any movement from the cave. It was a long time. I grew tired of waiting and was about to leave when I saw him. On all fours he crawled so slowly toward the food that it might have been nothing more than a mirage in the desert. It gave me a good feeling to know it wasn't, but without touching a thing he lay down in the sand and didn't move. If this was a trick to get me down there, I wasn't falling for it. I waited and finally he pulled himself up to a sitting position. Neat as a cat, he tried cleaning his hands off before he began eating. He looked around and scanned the woods, but I didn't move, hardly daring to breathe. When he finished eating he unscrewed the cap on the Chill Tonic and turned the bottle up and drank it. Knowing how it tasted, I grimaced.

"Hey, you," he called softly, but I knew he couldn't see me. I didn't leave until he crawled back inside the cave.

When I went home, Mama was busy in the kitchen and wanted me to set the table and help her carry supper in. Daddy and Fly had been fishing, and she fried bream and hush puppies, made coleslaw, and warmed the leftover chicken pie and rice. As soon as Uncle Johnn finished saying the blessing, I put a huge mound of rice on my plate and spooned some broth over the top, but I hardly touched it and only nibbled at the crunchy fish tail, leaving the rest on my plate.

"Eyes bigger than your stomach, Anna Lee?" Mama asked.

"Yes, ma'am. I guess so."

"That's why they're so pretty," Uncle Johnn said. "Because they're so big."

"Cat eyes!" Mama said to tease me, but all I could think of was the man in the cave.

When Mama went outside to shake the tablecloth after supper, I began scraping my rice into an old mayonnaise jar. She caught me before I was done.

"Okay, Anna Lee. What are you up to?"

I didn't hesitate a minute. "There's this cat, Mama, and I think she has kittens. She's in the woods over near the bay. Please, can I feed her? I promise I won't bring her home."

"Oh, all right. So long as you don't go bringing her or the kittens in here. Why don't you break up a little of that chicken meat? Be good for her."

"Yes, ma'am. And maybe she'd like a hush puppy."

Mama looked at me. "I don't think a cat would like a hush puppy. If you're still hungry, say so."

I smiled. "Maybe I'll just eat it on the way over there."

"Make sure you finish it. I don't want you eating anything after you touch a stray cat, now, you hear?"

"Yes, ma'am, I hear."

"You may as well take that fish you didn't finish too."

"Yes, ma'am, I will. Cats love fish."

I thought we'd never finish the dishes so I could get away. I was rushing so I nearly scalded Mama's hand when I poured boiling water over the dishes on the drainer.

"You burn me, Anna Lee, and you can forget about that cat. Now just settle down."

"I'm sorry, Mama. I didn't mean to burn you."

"You didn't burn me, but you better be more careful. Now get out of here. But be back before dark, you hear?"

"Yes, ma'am, I sure will!" I called as I ran down the back steps with the hush puppy and fish in one hand and the jar in the other.

When I reached the seawall, the sun was a deep red ball descending toward the bay. I stared at the fence in front of the cave and nearly lost my nerve. Carefully, quietly, my heels sinking into the soft white sand, I made my way down the slope from the woods. I cautiously approached the fence and had just deposited the food when he came running out of the cave. I screamed and ran in the direction of the woods, but he didn't follow, already sunk to his knees. "Don't tell," he called hoarsely and turned his attention to the food.

"Who are you?" I called softly from the safe distance of the woods.

"It's none of your business."

"I brought you food!"

"Nobody asked you to."

He didn't have any manners at all. But for the soft slurring of his words, I'd have taken him for a Yankee. He might have been about Uncle Johnn's age, but he hadn't shaved in a long time and looked ragged and thin. I continued through the woods toward home. He could get a lot thinner before I'd take him anything more to eat.

At home that night I was terrified by what I'd done. Why in the world had I gone back? I didn't know anything about him. He could be a spy or an escaped convict or another Chester, for all I knew.

"You're mighty quiet tonight, Anna Lee," Mama said, and I could hear her whispered counting beneath her breath.

"I'm thinking."

"Well, if you're trying to think of some way to bring that cat in here, forget it, you hear?"

"She's kind of wild. I won't bring her home."

"Just see that you don't."

Later, lying on my bed in the dark, I was afraid and sad all at the same time. I'd never seen a man cry before.

Mama made French toast for breakfast, and eating it I remembered how hungry Scarlett had been after the war, how ragged Ashley looked when he came home. I wrapped a piece in my napkin.

"You going to devote the rest of your summer to taking care of a stray cat?" Mama asked.

"No, ma'am. But I can just drop her off some food. I don't have anything else to do."

"That's the pity of it. When I was your age, I was taking . . . Well, never mind. Get your bed made and go feed the cat."

Grease had soaked through the napkin by the time I reached the seawall, and my dress stuck to my back. It was going to be hotter than the day before. My scalp felt tight, and I wiped my palms on my dress. I was afraid but at the same time filled with an overriding pity. And there was also the hope that things might work out so that I would be a celebrity. I didn't know quite how, but there was always the possibility of doing some good deed, a Hans Brinker kind of thing, so everybody would be grateful. Then I'd be rid of Chester because people would believe me and not him if he said things about Uncle Johnn. Daddy wouldn't have to shoot him after all.

I'd just put the toast down when I heard the sound coming from inside the cave. He was crying again. "Here's your breakfast," I called and ran. I went straight to the post office and checked every one of the "Wanted" pictures hanging on the wall. Satisfied, I went to the drugstore and asked Uncle Johnn if I could have some oil of citronella. He didn't ask for an explanation, but I found myself lying to him anyway. "There's lots of mosquitoes in the woods where I go to feed that cat."

"You be careful of snakes, Anna Lee. That cat'll find birds and mice in the woods. Maybe you'd better let it fend for itself."

"I don't go far into the woods, and I think she kind of expects me now."

"Still, be careful. Your life's more important than a cat's."

I looked at him and smiled. He really meant it, but I stepped back before he could touch me. The drugstore was filled with people.

I took the citronella bottle and started toward home to help Mama when I decided to go by the cave first so I didn't have to worry about her finding it. I started through the woods again and stopped. Just because his picture wasn't up in the post office . . . I turned back. Looking up in the distance, I could see shafts of silvery light bouncing off the polished surface of Miss Amy's bay window. Maybe she and Uncle Johnn stood there together looking out over the water. It was a disgusting thought, and I turned and continued through the woods to the beach.

I saw his head. He was lying on his stomach just inside the cave watching the fence. I didn't move. We just stared at each other. He'd plastered sand all over his body. He needed the citronella all right. I tossed him the bottle, and it landed a few feet from his head. He reached for it and said, "Thanks." He had some manners after all. He sat up, and I took a step backwards.

"Please, don't be so afraid." He spoke quietly, and I had trouble hearing him, but I kept my distance. "I wish you wouldn't come here."

"You're sick. You need help."

"You got any brothers or sisters?"

It sounded like his mouth was dry as cotton. I shook my head.

"You told anybody I'm here?"

I shook my head again.

"Why?"

"I'm afraid Daddy would shoot you."

"Why should you care?"

"You cried."

"Yeah. I've been sick. I've come a long way."

"Are you a soldier?"

"Huh? Yeah, I'm a soldier."

"Where are your dog tags?"

"What?"

"Soldiers wear dog tags." I tensed. "You're not a soldier." I backed away and moved nearer the water.

"Don't be so afraid," he snapped. "You calling me a liar?"

"No, sir."

I could see his tongue pass over his dry lips. "Do you want me to get you some water?"

He shook his head and crawled into the cave. Coming back to the entrance, he drank water from the mayonnaise jar.

"Where'd you get it?"

He pointed toward some houses up the beach near the highway.

I made a face. "It must taste awful."

"I've had worse."

"Do you know what town this is?"

He nodded.

"Lots of soldiers and sailors don't. They have to stop some-body on the street and ask where they are. Where are your dog tags?"

"I'm tired. I want to sleep now." He crawled back inside and left me standing there in the hot sun. I waited, though, to see if he'd cry again.

"It's about time you got here," Mama said as soon as I started up the front steps. "That must be some cat for you to be gone half the morning almost."

"It hasn't scratched me yet, anyway. I went to town, though. That's what took so long."

"Well, you'll have to shake a leg to get your work done before dinner."

I dust-mopped the bedrooms with special care and wiped all the furniture until it glistened and the house reeked with furni-ture polish. Under the pretext of cleaning Uncle Johnn's closet, I searched for the wooden box of pictures. I quit looking when a big spider crawled out. Mama always worried about snakes, but it was spiders that scared me. I leaped on top of a chair and called her to come kill it. Mama wasn't afraid of anything. She killed the spider and swept it out of the room, but still I hesitated to leave the chair.

Mama stuck her head in the door and laughed. "There's no more spiders, Anna Lee."

I kept a close eye out just to be sure as I continued helping her until it was time to go to the show. As I was leaving the house, I looked up and saw Hazel standing on her porch wearing a pink ruffly housecoat. Her hair hung loose, nearly covering her shoulders. I hollered up real loud, "How's the baby, Hazel?'

"Comin' along just fine," she said and walked back into the house the way she did every time I caught her on the porch.

I quit thinking about the spider when I got to the show, but I couldn't enjoy myself for thinking about the man in the cave. Why did I care that he was so sad? He wasn't my concern, and yet he was. He had to be lying about being a soldier, but there was something about him, a feeling, a closeness I couldn't describe. I wasn't even afraid of him, not the way I was of Chester.

After the show I decided to go by Miss Red's. She hadn't made chocolate pudding since our run-in about Jesus, but this just might be the day. It wasn't. She was taking a nap, and time hung heavy on my hands, my thoughts traveling to the stranger on the beach the way the tongue seeks the hollow of a missing tooth. I lived for mealtime and the thrill of taking food to him. This was a lot more fun than having a donkey.

After supper I began collecting food.

"What in the world do you think you're doing?" Mama asked. "No cat's going to eat a sweet potato."

"I thought I'd eat it."

"What was wrong with eating it at the table when we had supper?"

"I just didn't feel like it, I guess."

"I swear to goodness, Anna Lee. I don't know how you stay so thin. You must eat so much it makes you poor to carry it."

"That old cat's glad to get anything to eat. She still won't let me pet her though."

"Some cats never will tame down. You know that. I don't know why you're so bent on feeding her."

"I feel sorry for her. She's so sad-looking, and I still think she has kittens someplace, but I haven't found them yet."

"Well, if you're going to be rummaging around in those woods looking for kittens, I don't want you going over there. You're liable to step on a snake."

"I'm careful. I just call and listen to see if I can hear them crying."

"Well, so long as you don't do any more than that."

He was just inside the cave, hugging his skinny legs close to his chest. I put the food down, but he continued staring out at the bay, not even turning to look at me.

"Aren't you hungry?" I asked finally.

He turned then, and I saw tears streaking down his face, glistening in his beard like foam on seaweed.

"I brought you something to eat."

His voice had the hollow, uneven quality of choked-back tears. "You're going to tell, aren't you? This is just a game, and you'll tell."

"No, sir. I'd get in trouble if I told."

Disbelieving, he screwed his face up. "What?"

"I'm not supposed to talk to strangers."

"You're a little late to be thinking of that."

"Yes, sir. That's why I'd be in trouble. Mama thinks I'm feeding a cat up in the woods. I'd get it for lying, too."

"She doesn't spare the rod, huh?" He backed toward the cave with the food.

I walked around the fence until I faced the cave.

"You shouldn't talk to strangers," he said. "It's dangerous."

"Friends are sometimes dangerous, too."

"Yeah. Even friends. I won't harm you. You have no reason to believe me, but I won't harm you."

"You told me you were a soldier."

"Yeah?"

"You don't have any dog tags."

"Those damned dog tags again! I threw them away."

"A soldier would never do that."

"Even a soldier who'd deserted?"

"Deserted?"

"Yeah."

"But there's a war . . ."

"Yes, and there'll always be wars. What's your name?"

"Anna Lee."

"Annabelle Lee?"

"No, sir, Anna Lee Owens."

"Anna Lee Owens," he said thoughtfully. "Anna Lee Owens."

He wasn't going to get me off the track this time. "I've never known a deserter before."

"Well, you do now."

"But why?"

"Why? Well, I was sick, and I was scared. More scared than you are of me. I couldn't go on living in that hell, in that fear."

Like Scarlett squeezing red clay in her fist, he crushed one of Mama's biscuits in his hand and then stared at what he'd done with a puzzled look on his face.

Carefully picking the biscuit from his hand, he spoke my name as naturally as if he said it every day. "Anna Lee, I don't owe you an explanation. You don't have to come here. Just leave me alone. I've paid my dues. Just leave me alone." He twisted his flat palm back and forth on the sand. "I've paid. I paid, I paid," he sobbed.

I'd made him cry again. "Please, sir, don't cry. Please." I was crying too. "Please stop," I begged. "It's okay if you deserted. Really, it's okay."

He pulled his undershirt off and wiped his face. "No, it'll never be okay, but there's no turning back the clock. The moving finger . . ."

"The moving finger?"

"Nothing. I can't remember. So much I can't remember."

"Maybe when you're stronger."

"Yeah, sure. When I'm stronger."

"I have to go before dark."

"Go."

"Are you all right?"

"Sure. Sure I am. I'm okay, Anna Lee. Just do me one favor. Don't come here every day. Not every day, please."

"How will you eat?"

"I'll make out. I've come a long way without you."

The house was empty and dark. Mama had left the radio on, its dim light glowing like a distant star. I was sitting on the floor leaning against the couch when she came up the front steps calling my name.

"Why don't you turn on the lights? I'm liable to break my neck out here in the dark. You think we're having an air raid drill?"

"No, ma'am, I was just sitting here."

"Well, I'm sure glad you're home. You stay out after dark one time and there'll be no more feeding that cat. You ought not to be in those woods so much."

"Maybe I'll just go once in a while from now on."

"That's a switch. Knowing how you are about cats, I didn't expect you to give in so easy. Guess you're growing up. It'll be one less thing for me to worry about if you stay out of those woods." She picked up her crocheting and, as if she were reading from her pattern book, announced, "I went to see Hazel's baby."

"You did?"

"I was just being neighborly. I like Mrs. Sawyer. She's sure had a hard life, poor soul. And then to have a deformed grandchild. I hope to God there's nothing more than that ear wrong with it. You see that?"

"Yes, ma'am."

"Well, you didn't say anything about it to me. I nearly swallowed my teeth."

"Hazel says she might have it operated on."

"That right? Well, she should know a lot about operations after all her tumor trouble, but if that's punishment for Hazel, it might not be nearly enough."

"Mama, that's punishing the baby."

"Wait until you have children. Then you'll know how a mother suffers."

"Even Hazel?"

"She's a mother now, so she can't escape it. She's already suffering, though, just being shut up in the house with that baby. After all, she's been home almost a week now." Mama hesitated. "She's quitting school, of course, and Mrs. Sawyer told me Hazel's going to be working at the picture show as soon as she's able."

God was punishing me, too. "There's no chance she'll die?"

"What a thing to say!" Mama eyed me suspiciously. "What makes you think she'd die?"

"Don't women die having babies?"

Mama leaned forward and glared at me, her eyes as hard and unmoving as the holes in her pattern book. "Where'd you ever hear anything like that?"

"Isn't that what killed Melanie?"

"Oh," Mama said, leaning back in her chair, "sort of."

There was a stirring, though, some pinprick of memory I couldn't quite grasp, and I knew it had nothing to do with Melanie.

The following Wednesday I was waiting until it was time to go to the show when I saw Hazel leave her house and start walking toward town. She didn't look a bit different than she had before the baby was born. I'd heard Mama tell Than that, small as she was, Hazel wouldn't ever be skinny again, not the way she'd put on weight those last few months.

Than had laughed. "That was after she remembered she'd been married all that time."

She was, though. She was just as tiny as ever.

I stood at the screen door, hesitant, and said to Mama, "I guess Hazel's starting her job at the show."

"I wouldn't be a bit surprised. Get some money out of my change purse and go on. Don't worry about Hazel. If she's busy working, there's no reason for you to be scared of her, is there?"

"No, ma'am."

"Well, go on. It's about time for my story to come on."

I bought my ticket from Jessie and turned to go inside the show when I saw Hazel standing behind the candy counter. There was a long line of people waiting for popcorn, and I slowed my steps as I walked up the inclining floor. Going over to the wall opposite the candy counter, I studied the glittery framed pictures of movie stars and watched Hazel from the corner of my eye. I had to give her credit. She was smiling and didn't make any fuss about so many people wanting popcorn the way Jessie had sometimes done. Jessie thought she was the queen bee at the picture show. She sat in the little glass booth in front selling tickets, but she'd had to work behind the candy counter a long time before she was promoted.

There was only one person left in line when I finally mustered the courage to approach the candy counter. My palms were sweating, but Hazel treated me the same as if I was anybody else. Of course, a group of sailors had just come in, so Hazel would have smiled at a rattlesnake. They jostled each other and crowded around the candy counter, hanging on every word she said. Not one of them could buy anything without checking it three times over with Hazel. She couldn't have been happier if she'd been running a battleship.

Caught up in all the merriment, I called her name louder than I'd intended.

"Uh huh?" she inquired sweetly.

"Have you named the baby yet?"

Her smile froze, and she turned to the sailors, ignoring me completely.

13

The war came home to Bay Harbor in August. It began on Sunday with a telegram from the government. I was in church at the time and saw the whole thing. One of the deacons was dimming the overhead lights when I saw Sugar Lawson, a friend of Mrs. Sawyer's, tiptoeing up the church steps. It was a hot day, and the doors were propped open. There was a terrible glare out, and Sugar stood in the doorway for a minute blinking her eyes and looking around before she walked to the back of the church. She was breathing hard and walking on her toes. Every now and then the heel of her shoe hit the floor and made a loud noise. She stopped at the pew where Mrs. Sawyer was sitting and reached across several people to tap her on the arm. With a crooked finger she signaled Mrs. Sawyer to follow her and started back down the aisle. People began whispering behind their hands, but Brother Ryals went right on preaching the same as if we'd still been listening to him. Sugar held Mrs. Sawyer's arm as they walked out of the church. As they started down the steps, I saw Sugar lean forward and say something, and over and over I could hear Mrs. Sawyer asking in a faraway voice, "Huh? What? What?"

By that afternoon everybody knew that J. D. had been killed in action. J. D. was Hazel's older brother, but they were as different as night and day. Only the good die young, people said, thinking of Hazel.

I was standing on the sidewalk in front of the Sawyers' house watching the people come and go when I saw Hazel come out on the porch holding the baby. Walking closer to the porch, I called to her softly, "I'm real sorry about J. D., Hazel."

She stopped patting the baby's back and looked down at me.

142

"How would you know anything about it? You never had a brother. Never will. You think you're so smart, why don't you think about that sometime? Just think about it, Anna Lee." For one fleeting instant there was a moment of painful recognition, and then it was gone. Hazel was a thief and a liar.

Perhaps it had arrived later for us than for others, but the war was becoming a real thing, more real all of a sudden than the Civil War. Air raid drills had been nothing more than a game to see who could leave a light on without getting caught, but now even in the light of day we were afraid inside our own living rooms. J. D. wouldn't come marching home again. I tried to imagine him dead and couldn't. I talked to Uncle Johnn about it, trying to understand why it had happened. Miss Red said God punished the wicked, but J. D. had been so nice.

"And so very young," Uncle Johnn replied sadly. "So very young. But there are worse things than death, honey. Death can be merciful. Death isn't punishment. It's the price we pay for living."

"You're thinking about Miss Amy's husband, aren't you?"

"They weren't married when he died, Anna Lee, but yes, I suppose I was."

I sighed. No matter what Uncle Johnn and I talked about anymore, it seemed we always got around to Miss Amy.

We hadn't adjusted to the shock of J. D.'s death when Uncle Johnn brought home the news about Bubba Whitehead. "Lost at sea," he told us. The doctor had called in some medicine to quiet his mother. "Bay Harbor is fortunate to have been spared so long," he said quietly.

We'd all liked Bubba. He'd driven the ice truck before he was drafted, always smiling and waving to people, a regular Pied Piper with a crowd of children chasing the creaking, dripping truck as it eased in and out of alleyways and streets.

Old people died, not young boys like J. D. and Bubba. The war wasn't dying. It was being quiet so Mama could hear the news and doing without bubble gum and candy. It was buying war bonds and paying money to ride in a jeep. Ration stamps and pictures hanging in the dining room. Blackout shades and air drills. But all of a sudden World War II was having people you knew get killed. If only Chester's punctured eardrum hadn't made him 4F!

As I walked through the woods to the sand cave, I thought about my conversation with Uncle Johnn. He was right. There were things worse than death. I put the food down and sat on a concrete slab, waiting. Finally I looked inside the cave and saw that it was empty. My heart tightened with fear that he'd gone. Wouldn't he say good-bye? Bent over, I was backing out of the cave when I heard him clear his throat. I jumped, but he stood perfectly still where I'd left the food. I'd given him some of Uncle Johnn's old clothes, and a breeze whipped the loose folds, giving him the hollowed-out look of a scarecrow.

"I thought you'd left, and I didn't even know your name."

"What's in a name?"

"You know mine."

"Yes, I know yours, but 'that which we call a rose by any other name would smell as sweet.'"

"Did you just make that up?"

"No, I didn't just make that up."

"It sounds like something you'd say."

He gave me a funny look and began eating.

"Two people I know were killed in the war. Do you suppose your family thinks you're dead?"

"Probably."

"Don't you want them to know you aren't?"

"Not really."

"But why—"

He squeezed his eyes shut. "Anna Lee, *please*."

"Then will you tell me your name?"

He shook his head.

"You know I can keep a secret."

"Some secrets get the best of people."

"I need to call you something."

"What's your favorite name?"

"Ashley."

"What?"

"You know, Ashley from *Gone With the Wind*."

"That book?"

"Didn't you see the show?"

"No."

"I thought everybody but Daddy had seen it. Did you read the book?"

"I may have. I don't remember."

"I didn't think anybody could forget *Gone With the Wind*."

"You learn something new every day, don't you?"

"I didn't mean to make you mad."

"Dogs are mad. People are angry."

"See, you are ma — uh, angry."

"I wish I had a cigarette."

"I didn't know you smoked. My Uncle Johnn smokes."

"Uncle Johnn?"

"I told you. He lives with us. Is Ashley okay, then?"

"Ashley?"

What was wrong with him? "To call you."

"Oh, sure."

"I wish you could remember if you read the book."

"Sometimes it's better not to remember."

"When the war's over, it'll be okay. You'll see."

"Sure," his voice broke, "when the war's over."

"I have worries, too."

"You?" He smiled for the first time, and it was as out of place as thunder on a sunny day.

"Sure. Things bother me. Bad things. And then there are other things. I don't know how to describe it, but I have a problem. I know it's a terrible problem, I feel it hurting me sometimes, but I can't remember what it is. Isn't that crazy?"

His eyes grew black and hard. "What are you getting at?"

"I'm just telling you my problems." Tears welled up in my eyes.

"They sound so like my own," he said numbly and stared hard at the bay.

Later that night as I lay awake worrying because I knew Chester was due back the next day, I heard Daddy go into Uncle

Johnn's room. I tensed, knowing what was coming. Daddy was always lecturing Uncle Johnn about something, most often about his drinking. Uncle Johnn didn't like the moonshine Uncle Henry drank, and Daddy about had a heart attack every time he saw Uncle Johnn come in with a brown paper sack twisted tight around the neck of a wine bottle.

The lectures were always late at night after Daddy got off work and I was supposed to be asleep. Trying not to hear Daddy in the next room, I'd cover my ears with my hands, but it was no use. I could always hear him.

"Johnn, I'm a-warnin' you." That's how Daddy always started out. "You just go on a-buyin' your likker and draggin' it home for the whole town to see. Next thing you know, people'll say your hands shake, and then they won't buy the medicine you make up for them. Mark my words, you'll ruin your business. Our business," he corrected. Over Mama's protest, Daddy had put up some of the money for the drugstore when Uncle Johnn came to Bay Harbor.

"If you're goin' to make your home with us, I think I should have some say so in the goin's-on. I'm not a-tellin' you a thing you don't already know when I tell you that you can't afford to ruin your name a second time. Me and Estelle have never brought up the past, and I never wanted to. It ain't pretty. You know how close me and Earl was, but you're my brother, too. I always took your part, Johnn. I always stood by you no matter what anybody said, but I won't let you ruin yourself a second time, not and take me with you."

"Oh, God," Uncle Johnn groaned, "not that again. All those evil-minded people. I don't care what people think about me, but how could anybody who knew her believe those stories? If she had any fault, I suppose it was loving Earl too much. And you never forgave her for that, did you, Robert? Admit it for once in your life, goddammit. Admit she wouldn't have you!"

"That's enough, Johnn," Daddy said threateningly. "If you want to be livin' here tomorrow morning, you shut your mouth right now."

"You're good at keeping your mouth shut, aren't you, Robert, taking my part all these years. Do you really want me to leave so you can go back to living on a deputy sheriff's salary? You can sell your new guns and the outboard motor and all the things you're able to buy from the money you get off the drugstore and my rent. Don't tell me you don't find that money sweet."

"You're drunk," Daddy said, "and you don't know what you're sayin', but I'm cold sober, son, and I ain't about to forget it. I could tell you plenty. I could sober you up real fast, but I got me a wife and youngun to think about. I carry heavy responsibilities. You ever wondered what it'd be like to go to work every mornin' and not know if you're going to be alive by evening? I never know who's gone be behind the next door or where the next bullet is headed, but I don't take to drinkin' so I can live with it. Start actin' like a man!"

Uncle Johnn said something I couldn't make out, and Daddy's voice softened. They reached an agreement, deciding Daddy would buy the wine for Uncle Johnn at some out-of-the-way place. Mama wasn't to throw the bottles in the garbage, either. Daddy would carry them off in the car. But he needn't have worried about Uncle Johnn's hands shaking. Any one of the men at O'Kelly's knew Uncle Johnn had the steadiest hands in town.

I stayed inside all the following day, seeing Chester's car drive by the house three or four times. My nerves were pretty well shot by the time Daddy appeared at the front door that night around nine-thirty. Mama and Uncle Johnn and I were sitting in the living room listening to the radio when, out of the dark, Daddy raced up the front steps to the screen door and yelled, *"Don't drink any water!"* That's all in the world he said before he disappeared again, "Don't drink any water." We looked at each other, and Uncle Johnn shrugged his shoulders and smiled. Mama was crocheting and never dropped a stitch, but she was immediately thirsty. I wasn't thirsty; I was sick to my stomach with worry that it might have something to do with Ashley. When Daddy came back to the house a little later, Mama was in the kitchen breaking up saltine crackers in a glass of cold milk.

"It's okay," Daddy told her, "you can drink the water. I guess we're all kinda edgy with all the talk about spies and submarines. Everybody thinks they're a-bein' spied on, always a-thinkin' somebody's watchin' 'em. Otis Favor saw somebody on the water tank, and until we knew better, we had to figure it was a spy tryin' to poison the water. Turned out it was just a drunk sailor. He thought he was climbin' on board his ship," Daddy said, drawing himself a glass of tap water.

"I don't know how we'll win this war with everybody drunk," Mama complained.

"It's the American way, Estelle," Uncle Johnn said gently from the kitchen door.

Daddy drained the glass and wiped his mouth on his sleeve. He hitched his holster up a bit and started back out. "All I got to say is, we better hope the other side's drunk, too."

Mama lifted a soggy cracker out with a spoon. "Your daddy always did look on the bright side of things."

Uncle Johnn came back to the door of the kitchen, stretched, and yawned. "I think I'll go for a walk. I'm about to fall asleep just sitting here."

I started up from my chair, but Mama pushed me back down. "You're staying here with me, Anna Lee. All this talk about spies. I'm not wild to be left alone here in the house by myself. Not that that would ever occur to any of you." I knew she was hoping Uncle Johnn heard her, but he made no answer and came out a few minutes later and left by the front door.

"A regular Paul Revere," Mama said.

"Ma'am?"

"Mark my words, Amy Walker won't go thirsty tonight."

"Maybe he's just walking."

"Maybe," she answered, but she didn't sound convinced.

When Mama went into the bathroom, I headed back to the living room and was turning on the porch light when a sudden chilling fear racked my body. Just because Ashley hadn't been on the water tank didn't prove he wasn't a spy. What was a deserter but the back side of a spy? Sick with misgiving, I turned toward the front window and saw a face staring in at me. Unreasoning fear sent me screaming into the bathroom with Mama. I scared her so bad she dropped the hose to her enema bag, and water sprayed out all over the bathroom. I saw her hands shaking without any crochet thread to calm them.

"What is it?" she kept shouting at me. "What is it?"

"A face," I gasped. "A face in the living room window."

Even afraid, Mama was practical. "What kind of face?"

I hadn't known myself until I answered her. "A dog's face!" I hollered. Had fear not clouded my reasoning, I would have lied to her, but until that moment I hadn't realized myself that it was only a stray dog that had wandered onto the porch and looked in at the window.

"A dog's face!" she yelled. "You nearly give me a heart attack over a dog's face?"

"It was the face of a red dog," I said, not yet released from my fright.

"A red dog! What the hell do I care what color it was?" Her breath came in short gasps as she struggled to gain control of the ribbed hose. When she looked up and saw me still standing there, her face was nearly the color of the enema bag. "Get out!" she yelled. "Get out of my sight!"

My legs were still shaking as I returned to the living room. I looked out the front window to the porch, but the dog was gone, obviously scared by my screams and Mama's yelling. I knew then that if a German soldier came to the front door, I wouldn't tell Mama, and if I told her about Ashley, she wouldn't believe me.

Too worried to sleep, I was the first one up the next morning. I waited impatiently for Mama to fix breakfast and was ready to leave before Daddy started his second cup of coffee. My stomach growled and knotted with thoughts of Chester and the fear that Ashley might be a clever spy after all. Out of sheer habit I grabbed a piece of hoecake and an apple. As I walked down the side of the house Miss Red hollered, "Remember the Sabbath day, Anna Lee, to keep it holy."

"Yes, ma'am," I answered, wondering what her problem was. It was only Thursday.

I was weak with worry as I made my way toward the woods, as concerned for Ashley's well-being as for the safety of Bay Harbor. We'd heard stories about German spies in Florida. Dear God, I prayed, please don't let him be a spy. Please, please don't let him be a spy. Clearing the woods, I paused and searched the bay. There was always the chance I'd spot a submarine. Staring so hard at times, I'd think I really had seen one, had become unable to tell the imagined from the real thing. Maybe there was one out there now, waiting for a spy on the beach. Still watching the bay, I started forward, and my heart stopped. He grabbed me from behind, one hand over my mouth, the other over my stomach, pressing me tight against his body. Oh, God, no, not again, I pleaded wordlessly. We fell as he leaped sideways into a grassy clearing. The breath was knocked out of me by the fall, and when I tried to rise, he held me tighter, dragging me with him along the ground. I opened my mouth to scream when I saw the snake. It was as big as a man's arm, a diamondback rattler coiled to strike. Less than a foot away, the apple glistened like blood in its path. Ashley held his finger against my lips, and we lay motionless until the snake uncoiled and slithered away.

"Th-th-thank you, Ashley," I stuttered as I began to whimper and shake.

"I didn't mean to hurt you."

"I—I . . . I'm just scared."

"You should be. You've no business coming here. It's dangerous. That snake could have killed you."

"He could have killed you, too."

"I suppose so. But I don't have many friends. I'd like to keep the ones I have." He stood up and started toward the beach.

I grabbed the apple and followed. "Are you a spy?"

"Do you think I'd risk my life for you if I was a spy?" he asked without even turning around.

The memory of the snake made me suddenly weak, and, unable to stand any longer, I knelt in the sand. "I don't know. I've never known a spy before."

"You don't know one now, either."

"Last night there was somebody on the water tank. It could have been a spy poisoning the water. I was afraid it was you."

"Well, it wasn't me."

"I know that. It was a drunk sailor, but are you a spy?" I fished the flattened hoecake out of my pocket and handed it to him.

"I told you already. I deserted."

"I kept praying that's all you were. Mama says we're sitting ducks with those oil tanks over there. She says if one of those tanks goes, it'll blow Bay Harbor sky-high. A spy could blow them up easy. I have nightmares about it."

"Your mother has no business saying things like that in front of a child."

"Do you think a real mother would say something like that?"

He looked at me funny. "What do you mean, a *real* mother?"

"I mean your own mother. If you're not adopted."

"Are you adopted?"

"No, sir. Oh, no." Unbidden tears filled my eyes. "I couldn't bear it if I was adopted."

"There's nothing wrong with it."

"Sure there is. You're an outsider. It's like hiding your light."

"Hiding your light?"

"You know, under a bushel. Not knowing who you are is like hiding your light. I know who I am all right, but how can I help hiding my light if I don't know what it is?"

"Beats me."

"I worry about it 'cause I know it's wrong. Sometimes I think I don't have one, that God overlooked me."

"How old are you?"

"Nine."

"Only nine?"

"I'm tall for my age, but I'll be ten in a few weeks."

"Maybe when you're older, your light'll be brighter, and then you can see it."

"What's your light?"

"Mine?" He picked up a shell and threw it. "Mine burned out a long time ago."

"I never heard of that. That'd be worse almost than being adopted."

"Some people have all the luck, I guess. I'm adopted, too."

"How do you know?"

"Why, my parents told me, of course."

"They just told you? They didn't try to make you think you were their own child?"

He shook his head and stared at the bay.

"Don't you ever wonder who your real parents are?"

"Yes." He made a harsh sound deep in his throat. "I've thought about that a lot."

"When the war's over, maybe you should ask your adopted mother about them."

"I don't have any family."

"But you said you did. You told me you did."

"You made a mistake. I don't have any family."

"No, sir, I remember, you said—"

"*Stop it!*" he yelled and stood up with his fists clenched at his sides.

Suddenly afraid, I backed away from him. "I have to go now," I said quietly and began running.

"Don't do that," he called, but I kept on running until he tackled me in the soft sand. He was so mad he was shaking.

"Don't you know that snake could still be there? Are you determined to get yourself killed? Go the beach route."

"I can't."

"What the hell do you mean? Of course you can. Don't go near those woods again."

"I can't."

He shook me by the shoulders. "Are you stupid? Don't you know what a close call you had?" He spoke slowly, distinctly. "There are snakes in those woods."

"I can't go down the beach. Somebody bad waits for me."

"Somebody bad?"

I nodded. "He does—" I hesitated. "He does bad things."

"Tell your daddy. Hell, he'll shoot him."

"That's why I can't tell."

"Good God. You make no sense at all. Come on." He picked up a piece of driftwood and a chunk of concrete. Beating the bushes with the stick, he led me to the road. "Don't come back," he called softly.

Mama didn't even notice my dirty clothes when I walked in the house. She was on the phone to Than Carter. "Come by after work," she said. "I've got a dilly for you."

Not even noticing that I'd changed my dress, she told me what she was saving for Than. "You'll never believe what Miss Red's done, and in this heat. She's baked her fruitcake! In August! God, I'd hate to know what she put in it. Verna better quit gallivanting around Chicago and get back here to see about her mother once in a while."

But Miss Red's fruitcake took a back seat to Uncle Johnn's news. Passing the fried chicken at dinner, he announced that he was buying a car. Mama nearly dropped the platter, and she and Daddy both raised their eyes to the ceiling as though seeking divine help.

"A car?" Daddy asked in disbelief. "But you don't even know how to drive!"

"I'll learn. There can't be much to it."

"There's more to it than lighting a stove," Mama said, but nobody was paying any attention to her.

Daddy went on. "You'd be foolish to buy one now even if you did. Why, man, don't you know you can't buy gas or tires or anythin' anymore? Did you forget there's a war on? There's a world war ragin' practically at our doorstep." Daddy narrowed his eyes. "Where you gettin' this car?"

"I won it." His voice sounded hard, almost cynical, not at all like Uncle Johnn, and the strangeness of it was disturbing.

Mama gasped, and Uncle Johnn smiled. "I didn't win it. It's just an old car I'm buying from a friend."

"No. No, you're not." Daddy stopped. "What friend?"

"What difference does it make? I've already bought it."

"But, Johnn," Mama interrupted, "you know you get such good exercise walking to work. Being shut up like you are all day, you need to be out some. And anyway, with two cars in the front yard, we'd never get the grass to grow."

"I'm surprised at you, Estelle. I thought you'd be glad to have me out of all that hot sun you're always worrying about. I can still walk if I feel like it, but I surely can't walk if I decide to take a trip."

"You drive a car out of town?" Daddy was about beside himself. "My God!" He didn't say another word. He just got up and left the table.

After he'd gone, Mama asked, "What color is your car, Johnn?"

"Black."

"Oh," she said quietly. "I always liked a blue car myself."

"Well, if you don't mind driving a black one, I'll leave it for you some of the time and get some fresh air. How'd that be?"

That put the starch back in her, and she sat up straighter in her chair. "That would be a help, Johnn. Yes, it would be a help."

We didn't see it arrive, but Uncle Johnn's car was parked in our front yard later that same afternoon. Despite his offer to let her use it, it was about as welcome with Mama as an invasion of tanks.

Uncle Johnn spent every spare minute learning to drive, but he could never do it to suit Mama and Daddy. He always raced the motor before turning off the ignition. That really set Mama's nerves on edge. She closed her eyes and shook her head every time he did it.

While Uncle Johnn sat out front in his car, Mama and Daddy kept watching him from the window. Daddy warned me never to stand behind the car when Uncle Johnn was in it. "Matter of fact," he said, "I wouldn't stand in front of it, either. I consider myself lucky he ain't parked it in that cottonwood yet. Furthermore, Anna Lee, don't ride with him, neither. You'd be safer in the front line of battle."

"But, Daddy," I protested, "once he gets his license and all—"

"Now just wait," Daddy interrupted. "Let's wait and see. Now listen to what I'm tellin' you. If Johnn learns to drive that car to my satisfaction, then we'll see. In the meantime, stay clear of him and that car. I don't want you gettin' crippled up or killed 'cause Johnn Owens decides to learn how to drive."

Mama picked up her crocheting and slipped the straight pin further down the page of her pattern book. "I think he's got bigger fish to fry than Anna Lee, anyway," she added.

14

With so many soldiers and sailors in town, Daddy said there was a good chance Bay Harbor might regain its reputation of earlier times. No longer were the fights restricted to the Quarters. Daddy never knew where the next one would break out. It was almost more than he and the chief of police could handle. More and more often the sheriff had to get involved, too. "Maybe it's a good thing," Daddy told Mama. "Let him see more'n votes out there."

The biggest fights were still in the Quarters, though, and Fly had warned Daddy of a bootleg operation that threatened to make things worse than ever. When Daddy came home for dinner at noon on Friday, he told us he thought he had things in hand.

"I took out a search warrant," he said. "Don't never go nowhere, not nowhere, without a search warrant," he warned us. "Well, I knocked on this here nigger's door and asked him if Jake Brown was there. 'Naw, sir,' he says to me, 'I don't know no Jake Brown. There ain't no Jake Brown here, Sheriff.'

"'That's too bad,' I says to him. 'Somebody come into the police station and left a mess of sweet potatoes and possum for Jake Brown. Guess I'll have to give 'em to somebody else.'

"'Jake Brown!' he says to me and starts laughing. 'Why, that there's me, Sheriff. I plumb forgot,'" Daddy mocked. "'Everybody around here calls me Shuffle. I jes forgot.'"

Daddy narrowed his eyes. "That's when I moved in on Mister Jake Brown. I didn't have far to go to find what I was lookin' for, neither. It was right there in the bathtub waitin' to be bottled."

"Tsk, tsk," Mama said, shaking her head. "They have to be animals to drink such filth."

Daddy started laughing. "Shuffle, Mr. Brown, starts unbuttoning his shirt. 'I was jes about to git a bath, Sheriff. You come up jes when I was ready to get in this here tub.'

"'I interrupted you all right,' I told him. 'Now, you pull the plug on that thing and get out here with me.'

"'Don't make me do that, Mr. Owens, sir,' he begged. I thought to my soul he was gone cry when I made him drain that shine."

Uncle Johnn wiped his mouth with his napkin. "You ought to be in Hollywood, Robert. You're the best mimic I've ever heard."

"Hollywood, hell," Daddy said and left the table.

None of us thought anything unusual about Daddy's run-in with Jake Brown. We'd heard the same story in other forms before. But this time it was different. Daddy was seldom home before midnight, but around ten o'clock that night he stood in the living room door. He just stood there, white-faced, and didn't move.

Mama was intent on her crocheting while she and Uncle Johnn and I listened to the radio. I don't know how long Daddy had been there before any of us noticed him. Nobody moved. We all sat frozen. Only Mama's hands continued moving, workin in and out of the crochet thread as though they didn't belong to her. It seemed an eternity before she dropped the crocheting, stood up, and walked toward Daddy. He stood still as a picture framed in the screen door. Mama pushed the door slightly and asked uncertainly, "Are you all right, Robert?"

"Can we drink the water, Daddy?" I asked.

He still didn't move. "Fly's dead," he said dully from the other side of the screen. "Fly's dead."

Mama let out a sigh of relief and regained control of herself. "Is that all? Why, you about scared me half to death. Come on in the house." She opened the door and pulled at Daddy's arm. When he came inside, there were tears running down his cheeks. Daddy, who could kill somebody, stood there crying.

Uncle Johnn went over and gripped his shoulder. "What happened, Robert?"

"Some son-of-a-bitchin' Yankee nigger from the army base posted bail for Jake Brown. Nobody's ever posted bail for one of our niggers before, so Jake thought he was Mister Big Shot. He started drinkin' shine the minute they turned him loose. By eight o'clock, he was naturally tearin' things up in the Quarters. Fly come and got me and the chief, and we went right over there. When we walked in the juke, Jake and this yellow nigger had their knives out and were startin' their fancy footwork. I grabbed my nightstick and started swinging. The yellow nigger dived under the table, but Jake come for me. When I looked up and saw that knife bearin' down on me, I thought for sure I was about to meet my Maker. But Fly was there between us, faster'n I'd ever seen him move. The knife caught him in the neck. He was dead before he hit the floor." Daddy turned to me. "Didn't I tell you Fly was a hero? If it wasn't for Fly, you wouldn't have a daddy tonight." Daddy moaned and broke into sobs.

"Come on in the kitchen, Robert, and I'll make you some coffee. There's no use making yourself sick over this," Mama advised.

"No use making myself sick? Woman, do you realize a man, a nigger, saved my life tonight? Didn't just save my life but gave his? Oh, Fly," Daddy moaned.

I'd never even liked Fly, but I felt tears welling in my eyes.

"Poor little nigger," Daddy cried. "All he ever wanted was to be a deputy sheriff."

I couldn't stand seeing him cry like that and looked away.

Uncle Johnn stood in the kitchen door. "What'd you do with Jake?"

"What'd I do with him? I beat him half to death, that's what. When I seen what he'd done to Fly, I went crazy and naturally let into him with my nightstick. He's a big son of a bitch. Must be near as tall as Earl, but I beat him to the ground. I beat his son-of-a-bitchin' head in before the chief pulled me off him. If he lives long enough to go to the electric chair, he won't know no more'n if he was goin' for a haircut. The bastard bled all over the back seat of the car. For all I know, he bled to death. I didn't even get out of the car when they took him in the hospital. I let Sheriff and the chief handle it. I don't never want to see that son of a bitch again as long as I live."

Daddy didn't go to work the next morning. He was still grieving over Fly, but Mama had had about all she could take. "Now, Robert, I know you thought a lot of Fly. He was a good darkie, and he was a good friend to you, but he's dead and gone. All this carrying on's not going to bring him back. I'm really surprised at you."

Daddy's voice was hard with anger and grief. "I'm surprised you ain't realized I'm lucky to be a settin' here! If it wasn't for that good darkie, you'd be out buyin' yourself a black dress about now. Fly saved my life, and I won't never forget that to my dyin' day." Daddy poured his coffee in a saucer and blew gently so that tiny waves rippled across its surface. He sipped noisily from the side of the saucer and then announced, "You'd best go buy that black dress anyhow, Estelle. Get one for Anna Lee, too. We're goin' to Fly's funeral."

"Oh no we're not," Mama retorted. "You may be going to Fly's funeral, but you can leave me and Anna Lee out of it."

Daddy poured more coffee in his saucer and proceeded to roll a cigarette. He tipped the can of Prince Albert and tapped tobacco into the trough his fingers shaped with the cigarette paper. He did it carefully, as though he was giving it great thought, which he wasn't, because he'd rolled a million of them. He could roll a cigarette and steer the car at the same time. He licked the seam and twisted the ends of the paper, carefully brushing shreds of tobacco from the top of the kitchen table before he said another word. "I'm not aimin' to have trouble, Estelle. You just better get them black dresses I was a-tellin' you about. I figure the funeral won't be before Monday, and we're going to be there as a family. I owe a debt over there, and I aim to pay it."

Mama pushed her chair back from the table. "You've gone crazy, Robert Owens, so I'll humor you, but Anna Lee isn't getting any black dress. Any idiot knows they don't make black dresses for children."

"Then sew her one. We're all wearing black."

Out of respect to Fly, Daddy didn't want me to go to the show that afternoon, either, but Mama talked him out of that. "She's just a child, Robert. There's no use making her sit around the house and be in the way all afternoon. It's not as though Fly was a relative or anything."

"He's damn near it," Daddy insisted. "You can't get much closer than to give up your life for somebody."

"I never thought I'd see this day," Mama sighed.

"Neither did I," Daddy said with amazement, shaking his head from side to side. His eyes filled with tears again. "Neither did I."

Broken up as Daddy was, it didn't hurt his appetite any. He wasn't accustomed to a leisurely noon meal, and while he didn't do much talking, he ate enough for two people. When he finished eating, Daddy went to the bedroom, and I heard the whining of the cork as he struggled with the bottle of moonshine. He still hadn't come out when I left the house.

As I ran down the front steps, I looked back over my shoulder and saw that I needn't have hurried. Miss Red hadn't even waited for me. To avoid the chance of running into Chester, I didn't follow the sidewalk but cut through people's backyards instead. Finally emerging on the edge of town, I joined the waiting line in front of the show, giving special attention to the line of Nigras facing us from the other side of the ticket booth. I couldn't see that any of them had stayed home out of respect to Fly, either. The Nigras filed into the show through a narrow door on the back side of the ticket booth. It led upstairs to the balcony. I suppose they were lucky there was any place for them at all, but I always felt bad that they weren't allowed to buy anything to eat or drink.

There were a lot of soldiers in the lobby as I waited for fresh popcorn to boil out of the popper. Hazel leaned over the counter toward me and said, softly as a secret, "Bonnie."

"You got that from—"

"I thought of it myself," she snapped.

Sure she did. She had to be mighty slow to have taken so long to copy her baby's name from everybody's favorite show. All of Bay Harbor would know she got it from *Gone With the Wind*. She prissed away, and a couple of soldiers leaned over the counter and started talking to her. She began telling them about her awful sunburn, neglecting to mention why her skin had grown so unaccustomed to the sun. She acted like she was any other young girl, not at all like she had a baby with its ear grown to its head waiting for her at home.

One of the soldiers raised his eyebrows and looked at his buddy. "You gotta be kidding. I don't see any sunburn, do you, Bert?"

They leaned further over the counter. Bert said he didn't see a sign of a sunburn. Hazel smiled, exposing the straight edge of her doll-like teeth. She took a few steps back and hiked her dress up. I turned my head the other way, but not before I'd seen her white underpants and shapely legs. She was right, though. She sure did have a sunburn. Her legs were fiery red. The boys laughed and whistled so she dropped her dress.

Quick as a snake, she turned to me. "Well, smarty, when you get your eyes full, open your mouth."

My face felt as red as her legs, and I rushed inside and dropped into the first empty seat I could find, wishing Uncle Johnn had kept his word. He was always saying he was going to rent a seat for me at the show, and I'd be like the people in New York City who had their own church pews. He always said that, but he never did it.

I'd seen the newsreel and a short subject before the screen went blank. At first I thought it was just a delay, but when nothing appeared on the screen for about five minutes, I began to worry — for once, not about Jesus. What if Daddy had something to do with it? Would he arrest the man at the projector and close the show down out of respect to Fly? I'd about decided that's what had happened when a voice announced from the darkness above me that the projector had broken and our money would be refunded. Daddy had his way after all, but he didn't know it yet.

I hadn't seen Ashley since Thursday, but I couldn't risk running into Chester. Taking the long way home once more, I hurried through people's yards, hidden from passing cars. When I crossed the street to our house, I saw that the shades were still pulled in the front bedroom, so I went around back and let myself in through the porch door in case Daddy was sleeping. He wasn't asleep, though. He and Mama were still arguing. Daddy sounded surly, and Mama's voice was high and unnatural.

"I'll tell you something, Robert Owens. I've never brought this up, but you force me to it. Yes, I was jealous of Fly. What's more, I've always been jealous of Grace. And why shouldn't I be? Have you ever acted like I was anything more than a servant and a mother for Anna Lee? Sometimes I wonder why you married me. Was it because Grace turned you down? Did you propose to her and she turned you down? That's something I'd like to know."

Daddy's words were slow and slurred. "I married you 'cause you had the biggest bosoms I'd ever seen," he said and started laughing.

"It's funny to me you never showed that much interest in them until after Grace and Earl were married. I was just as big before that wedding as I was after. I was built far better than Grace even if I was older than her. And that's the truth if I say it myself."

"It's the truth," Daddy said jovially. "I just didn't get to know you that well till after they was married. Why, I never thought a good-lookin' woman like you would give a fella like me a second glance."

"Maybe I shouldn't have. You act like you don't care a thing about me half the time."

"I know what's really important to you, Stelle. I know how you've felt all these years about your mama runnin' off with another man. I don't run around on you none, and I don't beat you. That ought to show you I care."

"Well, I can't help but wonder. I couldn't believe it when you wanted to bring Johnn in here to live under the same roof with us. There was only one thing we were sure he knew how to do, and you put him under the same roof with your wife."

Daddy's voice was low, serious. "Has he ever laid a hand on you?"

"No. Of course not. You know he hasn't. I admit he's been a perfect gentleman. A perfect gentleman. But I had no way of knowing that beforehand, and neither did you."

"I didn't take no chances in bringin' Johnn in here. I know Johnn, and I knew what I was a-doing. We got no way of knowin' there was one scrap of truth to any of that."

"We've got Anna Lee. What further proof do you want?"

"If I thought for one minute you believed that, I never would of let him come here to live. Do you think if that was true I'd of let him live here with us, here in the same house with her? I want you to settle that in your mind once and for all. Earl's death was an accident. It had nothin' to do with Johnn and Grace. And Anna Lee is Earl's. His spittin' image. You've only got to look at her to know that."

"I know, but at times I can't help but worry. She worships Johnn so, and then I remember it was mighty funny Grace never said a word about being in a family way until after Earl died. And even funnier that she carried the baby over nine months" — Mama hesitated — "if it was Earl's."

"There's nothin' funny about it," Daddy said. "Grace was sick. She died, for God's sake! You must love misery to torture yourself like this. Can't you just love Anna Lee and let it go at that?"

Quietly, I began walking backwards with leaden feet. Back across the kitchen and across the porch to the door. Weak, I slumped to the floor and stayed there. I had difficulty comprehending what I'd heard, and yet it was familiar. Uncle Daddy, Aunt Mama, I thought crazily. Aunt Mama. I sat there remembering all the bits and pieces, the sudden silences, Aunt Wilda's funeral, fitting them together like a jigsaw puzzle. I didn't see through a glass darkly anymore. I was face-to-face with it. "I'm adopted," I acknowledged to myself in a whisper, surprised that, after all this time, the pain was so great. Beyond that, I trembled to think that Uncle Johnn was more than an uncle, that he might be my daddy. With that realization, I waited for the joy that didn't come. I wanted to die instead. I'd never seen my own mother. I knew nothing about her, really. But worst of all, I couldn't feel anything. I should hurt for her or care, but my mother was a graveyard figure, a story, no more real than the fever victims. My head hurt and my eyeballs ached, but I couldn't move until I heard Mama come out of the bedroom. I leaped to my feet and slammed the screen door hard. I felt removed from myself, outside my own body looking in. From a hollow distance I heard my voice calling, "I'm home everybody. I'm home."

Mama walked to the dining room door. "Well, what of it? You've been here before."

Daddy walked out of the bedroom in his undershirt and pants.

"The projector broke. We got out early. They gave us our money back and sent everybody home."

"Well, I'm sure glad," Daddy said. "If President Roosevelt was to die, don't you think they'd close the show down? Sure they would. And Fly's a hero. I'm glad the show's closed."

"Maybe it's God's way," Mama said, and I stared hard at the face I couldn't claim as my own.

But it was Daddy's way for the rest of the weekend. Mama spent most of her time getting ready for Fly's funeral. She aired the dress she'd worn to Aunt Wilda's funeral and pedaled the sewing machine furiously all Saturday afternoon to make the ugliest black dress I'd ever seen, but I was too numb to put up any fuss about wearing it. When she finished my dress and took out the fingernail polish, I knew she was getting back at Daddy. With a steady and deliberate motion, she drew the tiny brush across her nails, leaving them bright crimson except for their rounded tips and the white half moons around her cuticles. She held her hand at a distance to inspect it. Seeming pleased with the result, she asked, "You see Hazel at the show?"

"Yes, ma'am," I answered without revealing just how much I had seen of Hazel.

"I'll bet her mother'll never know the show's closed down. I knew all along Hazel's working didn't have anything to do with money. Edna Sawyer's not dumb. Working is what keeps Hazel out of trouble, and Edna knows it."

I didn't tell her any different. Mama never went to the show except to see *Gone With the Wind,* and I wondered what she'd say if she knew about the soldiers or how the sailors crowded the lobby around the candy counter every time a boat came to town. All Mama knew was that one of the soldiers from the base had been arrested for giving Peggy Andrews some candy so she'd sit on his lap during the show. He said she'd reminded him of his own little girl, that he didn't do a thing to her, but they arrested him anyway.

Mama looked at me for the first time. "You're white as a sheet. Nobody bothered you in the show, did they, Anna Lee?" she asked, not for the first time.

"No, ma'am. Would Daddy shoot them if they did?"

"Just don't ever put yourself in a position to find out, you hear?"

"Yes, ma'am, I hear. Mama?" I asked, thinking I might strangle on the word.

She blew on her nails. "Uh huh?"

"Mama?" I began.

"What is it?"

I threw my arms around her, burying my face against her damp neck, smelling the sour odor of her hair.

"Anna Lee, what's got into you?" She held her hands high in the air. "You're going to smear my nail polish if you're not careful. Whew. It's too hot for you to be standing so close. Mama loves you. Now go on and play."

Play? But for my throbbing head, I felt paralyzed. I went to my room and stayed there, my silence taken for grief, mistakenly, for Fly. Like Daddy, I knew I owed Fly a debt, too. No way would Daddy let us go to the boarding house that night.

Daddy knew no one would dare ask him, so he volunteered to be a pallbearer and had Mama order a flower arrangement in the shape of a huge white cross. Mama did it, but she wasn't happy about it. Daddy volunteered to pay for the funeral as well, and Mama thought that was cross enough for Fly or anybody else.

When we arrived at the Nigra church on Monday, it was the first time I'd actually set foot in the Quarters since I'd been to

Edith's house. As we approached the door of the church, Daddy took his hat off and guided us to a seat in the back, but one of the ushers came over and whispered, "Sheriff, Miz Owens, please sit in the front. Fly don't have no family." We left the chief and the sheriff, the only other white people at the service, standing in the back of the church and made our way down the aisle. It was a terribly long, hot service, and the smell of Royal Crown hair dressing threatened to make me sick. They not only sang and preached, they read all the sympathy messages out loud. When it seemed we'd heard a hundred times how broken up everyone was at Fly's passing, they read the cards off the flowers. There were only two, ours and one signed "Law Enforcement." Beyond that there were any number of home grown zinnias and petunias, all cardless.

Mama kept her veil pulled tight over her face and didn't move or turn her head the entire time. Staring straight ahead, I was past seeing or thinking when Mama jerked my arm and motioned me to get up. I turned to go back up the aisle toward the door, but facing me was a long line of people walking toward the front of the church. I turned and shuffled slowly ahead to the casket for the viewing. When Daddy looked down at Fly, he stopped dead in his tracks, and the line grew still. I seemed to wake up then and watched, fascinated, as Daddy reached in his pocket and drew out his badge. He leaned over and pinned it on Fly's coat.

"There you go, Fly," he said out loud. "You're goin' to heaven a deputy sheriff!"

Within seconds everybody in the church knew what he'd done, and up and down the line, the swell of whispers stirred like rustling leaves as they chanted, "Praise Jesus, Praise Jesus, Praise Jesus."

Leaving the church, I saw Uncle Johnn standing in the back. So fair and tall, he was like an angel come to guide Fly to heaven. Out of respect and gratitude to Fly, he had closed the drugstore for the entire afternoon.

When we were back home that night, Mama told Daddy she didn't think it was legal for him to give away a badge of office like that. "It's not as though it was yours to give, Robert."

"I'll tell you one thing. I'll kill the first son of a bitch that tries to dig it up."

"That was a beautiful gesture, Robert," Uncle Johnn said. "It really was."

"It just seemed like the thing to do at the time," Daddy answered sadly. "I may never do anythin' right again, but I think that was right. I'd of given him a medal if I could."

"That's what you did, Robert," Mama added, "that's what you did."

15

More varied than anything Mama could crochet, my mind fashioned nightmares that threaded through the still night on the raw edge of dreams. I was choked by green mists from exploding oil tanks, my clothes were torn by unseen hands, and a faceless woman waited for me with outstretched arms. Mama always caught me before I ran out the front door. "Shh, shh." She laughed. "There's no Ashley here. You're just dreaming a picture show. Come on back to bed now."

At once curious and afraid of Uncle Johnn's involvement, I couldn't go to him. But Ashley was adopted; he'd know what I should do. And with the first rays of light I finally slept.

Fully aware now of the danger, I cut through the woods, picking my way more carefully than if I were avoiding quicksand. Coming over the rise, I forgot to scan the bay. Like some kind of signal, I saw that the concrete slabs in front of the cave were gone. Losing my footing, I slid down the incline, my heart racing as I hurried to an empty cave on a deserted stretch of beach. One piece of concrete lay conspicuously in the cave's entrance. In uneven letters, he'd scratched on the rough surface, "Watch out for snakes. Love, A."

How could I bear so much pain and disappointment? There was nowhere to turn. "Oh, Ashley," I cried, at last giving voice to my grief, "I'm adopted. I'm adopted." I said it over and over, let it be carried on a warm salt breeze that blew it back against my face. I'd known all along. Deep down, I'd known. I was part of some unspeakable crime, some hurt Mama couldn't face, and without anyone Daddy could kill to settle the score. I didn't have any choice. I never had, really. I'd have to go on protecting them with my ignorance, hiding my light under a bushel.

Tears blurred my eyes as I ran down the beach, trying to escape events that would never release me. I'd rounded the bend, bringing the pier into view, when I heard him calling my name. I'd forgotten to cut through the woods! Chester was leaning against one of the tree roots, cleaning his nails with a pocket-knife. He was wearing a hat with a black bill like he was some ship's captain and not a common laborer on a dirty old dredge. How could I have missed seeing him? My legs were stiff and unnatural, not at all a part of me, as I tried to run. He tossed the knife like it was a piece of trash and grabbed me by the arm. He pulled me to his side, wrapping his arm around my shoulders.

"I ain't seen you in a coon's age. How you been doin', little Anna Lee? You miss old Chester, huh?"

I shook my head from side to side, and he laughed. "I bet you did. I bet you think about me lots of times. Lots of times, huh? I think of you all right. Out there on the *Blackwater,* I'm thinkin' of you jes like I bet you're thinkin' of me. You're jes modest, little Anna Lee." I could feel my whole body going rigid as his hand came around my shoulder and worked its way down inside my dress.

"My goodness, but your heart is beating fast. I knew you'd be glad to see me again." He ran his hand back and forth over my chest. "You're so glad to see me you got goose bumps. Whew! I'm sure tired. I guess we better go inside here out of the sun and sit down a bit." He withdrew his hand and was turning to go in the cave under the tree roots when two people started up the beach in our direction.

"Sure am glad I ran into you, Anna Lee," he said loudly. "Me and Helen love you just the same as if you was our own youngun." He swatted my rear end and said, "Run along home now, sugar, so your mama won't be worryin' about you none."

I felt a chill pass over me as I walked down the beach away from him. How like a spider's web he was, visible only when it held the morning dew but always there, waiting.

Mama wasn't worried about me. She didn't know she had any reason to be. When I walked in, she was standing at the kitchen table sprinkling clothes. I watched her restless hands dipping in and out of a pan of water. She rolled one of my dresses expertly and placed it in the clothes basket before she looked up. "What's wrong? What are you crying about now?" she asked and resumed sprinkling the clothes.

I stared at her head bent over the laundry, the only mother I knew, and had to clear my throat several times before I could talk. "I . . . I couldn't find the cat. I looked everywhere."

"Good riddance, I say. I never liked you carrying food off in all kinds of weather. I'd have soon put a stop to it anyway. She probably followed some tom off."

"I guess," I sighed and went into the bathroom. I soaped a cloth and scrubbed my chest until it burned.

The very next day, Helen found the lovebirds. They were both dead on the floor of their cage when she uncovered them. She said it looked like someone had put cigarette ashes in their water. The boarders wouldn't have harmed those birds. It was the very kind of thing Chester would do. He probably killed them and dumped ashes in their water after the fact. I didn't even feel bad. I was glad they were dead, free of Chester, but I was left with the uneasy feeling that he was giving me a warning.

There were times when I felt that the war and the summer heat were traveling down the same road, side by side, and I could see no end in sight for either of them. Even the rain didn't cool things off, steam rising from the ground the minute it began to slack. People tried frying eggs on the sidewalk and made bets on how long it'd take a block of ice to melt in front of the post office.

When school started I had a gold stretch bracelet, a birthday present from Uncle Johnn. Mama wouldn't let me wear it to school, but there was nothing she could do about the heart-shaped heat rash on my arm. Unknowing teachers invited dog flies when they propped the doors open in hopes of catching a breeze. More vicious and daring than mosquitoes, they nested in the seaweed and wouldn't leave until we had a cold snap. Ashley would have been eaten alive, but I'd never quit hoping he'd come back. When Chester wasn't around, I still checked the cave from time to time. I'd turned the concrete slab over and written, "I love you, A. L.," but there was never any sign that he'd been there to read it.

Uncle Johnn seemed very much at home in his familiar Pontiac now, but he never could drive to suit Daddy and Mama. Daddy insisted people weren't safe on the streets anymore. I knew, too, that Uncle Johnn's car was parked at Miss Amy's far more than I cared to think about. He said it was only because Miss Amy was so jumpy any more that he went to her house as often as he did. She kept feeling like somebody was watching her. Even with the shades down, she felt like she was being watched.

"That's her guilty conscience," Mama said. "Until now I wasn't sure she had one."

"We'd better hope that's all it is," Daddy offered one night after Uncle Johnn excused himself from the table early and left the house. "God only knows, a guilty conscience is about the only thing Johnn could rassle with." He paused. "Course, he could prove to be a real help if she's got some Peeping Tom over there. I wouldn't be a bit surprised to hear Johnn's run over him some night. How in the world he ever talked Purvis into givin' him a driver's license, I don't know," he said and slapped the table with the palm of his hand. "I guess he could sweet-talk the devil. He damn sure couldn't drive him noplace."

Like a war coming to an end, summer was finally over, skidding into the welcome change of an early fall. The leaves on the cottonwood trees turned to light yellow and here and there drifted to the ground like butterflies in summer. People sitting in their cars on Saturday night would soon roll up their windows against the chill night air, and there would be an odor of mothballs about the country people who clung to the sidewalks. We hadn't begun to light fires, but wood had been ordered and dumped in backyards, where it lay in clean, sweet-smelling hills. Fall was my favorite time of the year. Like a preview of things to come, it was filled with the promise of Halloween and Thanksgiving and Christmas. Apples and nuts would arrive from places we might never see, and there would be eggnog and cold nights and warm fires against the winter rains.

Sitting on Helen's front porch, we talked of these things and enjoyed those nights most of all, knowing we'd soon have to shut the door that led to the porch and sit around the wood stove in the living room, hating the cold air that came up from the open stairs.

It was then in the early fall that Joel arrived. I still hated myself for having believed Mr. Rollins, and I viewed all the boarders with a wary eye, but of all the men we'd seen at the boarding house, Joel was special. We saw that right from the start. He stood out from all the others, so handsome and tall in his uniform. He was handsome enough to have been a movie star.

Mama had made chocolate fudge the night he arrived, and we were sitting on Helen's porch passing the platter back and forth down the line of rockers, pushing up fudge with a flat-blade knife. Chester was on the *Blackwater,* and we were feeling especially happy when we heard whistling from the sidewalk below and leaned forward in our rockers. We couldn't see who it was because the sound came from directly under the porch. Quietly chewing the fudge, we listened to the footsteps go to the end of the sidewalk and stop.

"Must be a stranger," Helen said. "He's out of luck if he wants a room. I don't have a one left."

A few minutes later, the whistling cut through the crisp air once again, and the footsteps continued. Up the stairs and through the swinging doors, the tune grew louder. I hummed along with the stranger to "This Is the Army, Mr. Jones."

He stopped at the porch door and dropped his canvas bag onto the linoleum floor.

"Looks like I'm just in time," he said and drew a deep breath. "If sugar wasn't rationed, I'd swear that was homemade fudge."

I kept on pushing up fudge. I wasn't taking up with any more strangers. Mama snatched the platter from my hands and shoved it into Helen's stomach. Extending the platter before her, Helen walked toward him. "Won't you have some? My friend here, Miz Owens, takes the credit for making it."

"That's very kind of you," Joel answered, "very kind indeed." He helped himself and then waved his hands in a downward motion like a bandleader. "But just sit down, sit down. Don't let me interrupt. If you have a room where I can stay, I'll just make myself at home."

"You're welcome to join us," Helen replied, "but I don't have a room in the house. I don't know when I will have one."

He took off his narrow hat, slapping it against his hand and revealing an abundance of short-cropped hair. He was so handsome it almost took your breath away to look at him, but unlike Uncle Johnn he didn't look like a gentleman.

"I have to go back to the base hospital soon for more tests, but I'd planned to spend some time here just roaming the beach and relaxing. What's the next closest town?"

I started to answer when Helen interrupted me. "If you don't mind something makeshift, I could put a cot out here for you, there at the end of the porch. It won't be the first time I've done it. I'll just hang a curtain there." She pointed to the ceiling where a wire was strung the width of the porch. "It won't be too comfortable or private, though, and the nights are getting cool. I could tack something against the screen, but it'd still be cool."

He held up his hand to stop her from talking.

"I'll take it! It'll be more private than the hospital bed I just vacated, believe me."

"But if you've been ill—" Helen began, and he interrupted her again.

"Oh, no, nothing to worry about. They needed my bed and kicked me out to recuperate on my own for a while. And don't worry about the cool nights. Where I come from, our hottest summers are colder than it is here right now."

That was our first meeting with Joel. He never was a stranger, and he ate nearly all our fudge without even apologizing.

Mama said it wasn't enough that Joel was good-looking. He was happy with life. Maybe I saw that more clearly than any of them because I'd known the stark sadness of Ashley. Joel did enjoy himself, always whistling or talking to someone. From time to time I'd see him in the drugstore talking to Uncle Johnn.

They were both so handsome but in such different ways. Though Joel was probably older than Uncle Johnn, he seemed younger because he was always searching for ways to have a good time. He could make almost anything fun. One night he sent me to the drugstore for some wooden spoons, the kind that came with ice cream.

"But, Joel," I protested, "it's too cold for ice cream now."

"Who said anything about ice cream? Get those spoons and I'll show you something you've never seen before."

He did, too. I came back with the spoons, and he passed out K rations just like the soldiers ate overseas. We didn't know how he came by them and were polite enough not to ask.

Mama told Daddy later, "Now, wasn't that something? Who would ever have thought of doing something like that but Joel? Why, Robert, I wish you could have tasted that stuff."

"Well, I don't. Why in the name of God would I want to eat that garbage when I have fresh vegetables on the table?"

"I mean for the experience, to say you've eaten K rations."

"That's one experience I'll do without, thank you. You sit up there with Helen night after night talkin' to them soldiers and listenin' to the line they spin until you don't have your wits about you. One day you're a-tellin' me how glad you are that I'm too old for the draft, and the next you're a-wantin' me to eat K rations. First thing I know, you'll be wantin' me to enlist just for the experience."

Mama didn't have so much to say about Joel after that. We were spending more and more time at the boarding house, and there were some things Daddy just couldn't understand.

As we came to know Joel, we took a renewed interest in the war effort. Mama rolled Red Cross bandages and gave me some old pot lids to throw over the side of the chicken-wire pen with the other scrap metal. I was about to leave when I noticed something glinting gold like a ring against the dull scrap. Poking a stick through the wire, I saw that it wasn't a ring after all. Never having had an original thought in her life, Hazel had gone and donated my knife to the cause. Taking something from the scrap pile was worse than taking change from the offering plate at church, but I took my knife without a second thought. Maybe now my luck would change. If it could only make me forget about Chester and being adopted.

Instead of roaming the beaches the way he'd said he would, Joel spent most of his time talking to Helen. I spent as much time as I could with them, making a beeline for the boarding house every day after school. I was never scared of Joel. He wasn't anything like Chester. I loved hearing him tell about snow and ice skating and sled riding. He made snow sound like the most beautiful thing in all the world.

"Oh, Joel, I'd love to see snow," Helen said. "It's wet, but it's not like rain. That's hard to imagine, isn't it?" She laughed. "I wish you could box it up and mail it like fruit."

"That would spoil it," he said, "even if you could. You have to walk in snow with it falling all around you to really experience the joy of it."

"Maybe," she said thoughtfully, "Chester and I could drive north some winter, just drive until we come to snow. That would be something to do, going to meet snow."

Joel acted like he hadn't even heard her. "I wish I could take you to Vermont," he said. "I'd like to be with you the first time you see snow. It would be a wonderful thing to share, wouldn't it?"

Helen's hands worked rapidly in her lap, struggling with the folds of her dress. "Why, that's kind of you, Joel. That's an awfully kind thing to say." She took her glasses off for a moment and pressed the bridge of her nose with her fingers, closing her eyes as she did so.

Joel looked at her and frowned. His voice was little more than a whisper when he spoke. "I wasn't being kind." He stared at Helen, and neither of them spoke.

I felt uncomfortable and wished we'd never started talking about snow. I put my hand over my mouth, and Helen turned and looked at me, seeming to see me there for the first time.

"Why, look, Joel," she said, breaking the silence. "Look at those long fingers. They could span an octave easy as anything."

She took both my hands in hers. "These hands were meant to play the piano."

She'd said that so often I had begun to believe it myself. I expected great things from my hands because she believed in them. Whenever she started talking about them that way, I couldn't keep them still, and I sat there cracking my knuckles.

"Oh yes, Anna Lee, your hands were meant for the piano. See how limber they are, Joel?" She watched me bend my thumb back until it touched my arm. "How I'd love to hear you play!"

I was embarrassed because I could see Joel wasn't interested in my hands. For once he made me feel like an intruder.

"If you don't quit cracking your knuckles and doing all those contortions, Anna Lee, you won't be able to play the piano or find a wedding ring big enough to go over your finger," he said and shoved his own hands into his pockets. He went behind the curtained-off space where he slept and returned a few minutes later with his shaving things and walked off down the hall. When I left I could hear him whistling, "In my arms, in my arms, ain't I never gonna get a girl in my arms."

It worried me that Helen continued to talk about my hands when I never came any closer to being able to play the piano for her. I didn't even bother to remind her that we didn't own a piano, for when she talked that way, my hands trembled for the touch of ivory keys, and I could believe that they were destined to play the piano for her. But that was all a dream that was part of the boarding house. She talked about the piano the way she did hats. How she did love hats! Box upon box was stacked in her bedroom, and in each there was a hat she had never worn. Mama and I had seen them all once, the ones under the bed and lining the walls and even those in yellowed boxes high on top of her wardrobe.

Reaching into the depths of a box, she'd fuss gently with the crisp paper covering the hat and then hold it out in her hand at arm's length for us to see.

"Now, isn't this a pretty one? I think this is the nicest one yet," she'd say.

Her newest one was always the nicest.

"Are you going to wear this one, Helen, or do you plan to leave it in the box like all the rest?" Mama would ask. She'd laugh as she said it, already knowing the answer.

"Why, of course I'll wear it—when the time comes. When the time comes, I'll wear it."

She'd been saying that for years, but the time she waited for had never arrived. Buried in their boxes so many years, the hats seemed almost alive, a part of Helen that remained unchanged and passed through life unseen.

Joel said he'd take her someplace where she could wear a hat. Not laughing the way she had with Mr. Rollins, Helen answered, "No. No, Joel, that would never do."

Joel even bought her a hat. He gave it to her in front of all of us. Mama said that was the only way a single man could decently make a gift to a married woman.

Helen took a long time removing the hat from the box, and she touched it gently with her fingertips, the way a blind person would to learn its shape.

"You're so thoughtful, Joel, but I can't accept it."

"Oh, Helen, go on," Mama urged.

Helen looked up and faced Joel. "It is truly lovely, but I just can't."

Right then Joel took it out back and jammed it down into the garbage can. It wasn't even fit for the cooks to wear when they lifted it out the next morning.

"It wouldn't have done any harm to take that hat, Helen," Mama told her later. "You wouldn't have worn it anyway."

"A person has to do what he has to do, Miz Owens. It wasn't that I wanted to hurt him."

Apparently trying to make it up to Joel, Helen let him go grocery shopping with her a few days later. He carried the things she bought, and people teasingly asked if she was making him earn his keep.

Mama always said that's where all the trouble started. "If she'd have taken the hat, that would have been the end of it, but buying groceries is such a domestic thing. Somebody probably shot his mouth off to Chester, knowing full well he doesn't have any use for soldiers anyway."

But the boarding house soon had one less soldier. As abruptly as he'd arrived, the time came for Joel to return for the tests he'd told us about. On a Sunday afternoon he shook our hands, even mine, and told us all good-bye. When he came to Helen, though, he cupped her hand gently in both of his, the way you would to keep a bird from flying. "I'll be back," he promised. "It may not be until this damn war's over, but I'll be back."

16

My urges were always a mystery. Like drop-in visitors, they came unbidden and demanded attention. What was little more than an inkling, a teasing darting in and out of my thoughts on Friday morning was by afternoon full-blown and possessive. Nothing would do but that I go to the cemetery after school. I didn't know why; I just had to. Mark didn't question my change of plans when I told him I wouldn't be walking with him and cut off in the opposite direction, away from school and home.

It was a long walk. I was tired by the time I saw the pines and oaks climbing upward on the only hill in Bay Harbor other than Miss Amy's, and this one was higher. I looked up trying to identify the topmost tree, where the ship's captain had lashed himself during the storm. The tidal wave never reached the cemetery, but even if it had, we were sure the towering tree would have saved him.

Searching skyward, I hadn't noticed Uncle Johnn's car parked there at the foot of the hill. But seeing it, I understood my urge. Uncle Johnn had been thinking of me. I'd picked up those thoughts, and we could meet and talk alone at last. I could tell him what I'd learned about Grace, and maybe he'd claim me, tell me that he was really my daddy. I started up the path through the trees when I heard voices. We wouldn't be alone after all. I fought the hatred and bitter taste that filled my mouth. Hidden by trees, I worked my way closer to the top. Uncle Johnn and Miss Amy stood by the little white picket fence surrounding her baby's grave. Uncle Johnn had his arm around her, and I could hear them talking.

"It isn't that I don't love you, Johnn," she was saying. "Oh, I do love you. Truly I do." There was a huskiness to her voice, and I willed the roaring in my ears to stop so that I could hear better. Uncle Johnn said something I couldn't make out, and she pulled away from him. "I'm afraid," she said. Well, we all knew that. She surely didn't have to meet him in the cemetery to tell him why he'd been going to her house so often at night. "My life," she continued, "seems like a series of tragedies. Something terrible has happened to everyone I've loved. I can't let something happen to you, too, Johnn."

At last there was something she and I could agree on. But Uncle Johnn was talking about shadows. He sounded resigned, beaten. "Sometimes it seems as though my whole life has been clouded by the shadows of men who came before me. That just shouldn't be," he said as he tapped the top of the picket fence lightly with his hand. "That just shouldn't be. I can't allow shadows to go on interfering with my life."

And then he did a terrible thing. As though exploring familiar territory, he pulled her close, letting his steady, pool-wise hand glide downward from her waist, caressing, so that the hem of her skirt rose and fell with the motion. She didn't protest or pull away, and a vision of Chester fogged my brain. I closed my eyes tight, trying to squeeze the memory beyond recognition, when I became aware of a rustling in the thicket on my left. I turned away and hurried past Uncle Johnn's car toward the road. If they left soon, I didn't want them suspicious at finding me this far from home.

I had nearly reached the school when I heard a car behind me. I looked the other way so I wouldn't see them, hoping they wouldn't notice me. But it wasn't Uncle Johnn's car. Chester slowed to a snail's pace, driving right along beside me. "Get in, Anna Lee, and I'll give you a lift home."

"No, thanks, I'm nearly there now."

He laughed. "Don't you think I know where you live? Get in!" His voice was harsh, no longer wheedling. Forcing me over with the car, he eased off the road and leaned over, opening the door on the passenger side.

I shook my head and backed away.

"You're asking for trouble, sugar. You best git in this car if you know what's good for your Uncle Johnn. Now!"

Uncle Johnn was alone up there in the woods with Miss Amy. I got in the car, sitting as close to the door as possible. He let it stall, and I heard a thumping sound coming from a Maxwell House coffee can on the seat between us. "Before I start this car, sugar, you better move over a little closer so it don't look like you're scared of me. Fact is, I want you to prove to Chester you ain't scared. Put that sweet little hand of yours right here." He pointed to the inside of his right leg, and I reached for the door handle, but not before he'd grabbed my wrist.

"Maybe you'd rather put it in here," he said, removing the lid from the can. I shuddered as he pushed my hand toward a big hairy spider trying to crawl up the side of the can.

"No, no, please," I begged.

"It's your choice, sugar." He released my hand, and fingers that could reach an octave lay where he'd pointed.

"That's better. That's a lot better. Now Chester can take you home."

And he did. He drove me straight home. My relief was short-lived however,. As I was opening the door he said, "You be to the beach in a hour, you hear? You be there if you know what's good for you."

Mama came to the screen door and waved to Chester. "Estelle," he said and nodded his head before driving off.

"I wondered where in the world you were," Mama said. "Did you thank Chester for giving you a ride home?"

"Yes, ma'am."

"Are you sure? I didn't see you saying anything to him."

I nodded my head.

"Don't get smart with me now. You answer me when I talk to you, you hear me?"

"Yes, ma'am, I thanked Chester for the ride."

"Well, all right then. Just 'cause you're in the fifth grade doesn't mean you're too old for manners. You're never too old for manners."

I didn't leave the house the rest of the afternoon. I could always tell Chester Mama wouldn't let me leave because I came home so late. I saw his car drive slowly by the house a few times, but I never showed my face.

When we sat down to supper and Uncle Johnn still wasn't home, I began to worry. If Chester had done something to him because I hadn't gone to the beach, I'd never forgive myself. Mama wasn't worried—she was mad. It was bad enough that Uncle Johnn wasn't around enough to do any serious betting with her, but to let food get cold was unforgivable.

"Nobody likes being taken for granted," she was saying to Daddy, "and any more Johnn just seems to take living here with us for granted. I, for one, am tired of it. You'd think, with a car and all, he could be on time for meals, but it's the other way around."

About that time we heard Uncle Johnn's car drive up in the front yard. He raced the motor, and Daddy muttered a low "God."

I started up to meet him, but Mama stopped me. "Just sit still, Anna Lee. He doesn't need any welcoming committee."

"Hi, Uncle Johnn," I called from my chair as he came in the door.

"Hi, baby. Sorry I'm late, Estelle. I had a bit of an accident today."

The word *accident* had a warming effect on the frost Mama reserved for people who let their food get cold. "Accident, Johnn?"

"Well, in a way. It was the strangest thing. Somebody must have let all the air out of my tires. Amy wanted to go up to the cemetery to her baby's grave, and I drove her up there. The car was fine when we left it, I'm sure, but all four tires were flat when we went to leave. I could hardly believe it."

Neither could I. The tires hadn't been flat when I left. I was sure of that.

Daddy looked Uncle Johnn up and down. "You look mighty clean for a man's been workin' on his car."

Uncle Johnn chuckled. "I walked to the nearest house and called the filling station, Robert. They took care of the situation for me. Amy and I sat in the car and waited for them. It was really quite comfortable, this season of year. But then by the time I got back to the store, I was backlogged with work."

Daddy squinted his eyes. "You called the fillin' station," he asked incredulously, "and just sat there and let somebody work on your own car for you?" As though he didn't expect an answer, he added, "I'm not a bit surprised. I wouldn't of expected any different, I don't suppose."

I could tell by the hurt look on Daddy's face that Uncle Johnn had embarrassed him again.

Uncle Johnn smiled at Daddy knowingly. "He was well paid, Robert. That's his job, not mine."

"That's the God's truth," Daddy muttered. "God's truth." That settled, Daddy finished his meal in silence.

Mama was washing the dishes and I was drying when we heard the tapping at the back door. My heart missed a beat, and my hands began to tremble as I wondered what Chester could be up to now. I didn't even realize Mama was talking to me until, without ever taking her hands out of the dishpan, she jabbed me in the ribs with her elbow. "Help Miss Red in the door, Anna Lee. What in the world's the matter with you, anyway?"

"Yes, ma'am." Weak with relief, I draped the towel over the dishes and opened the door. I could feel a tremor in Miss Red's arm as I guided her to the kitchen table. There had been a time when she came to the house quite often in the evenings, but that hadn't been recently. There may have been a time when age was as kind to Miss Red as it was to Helen, but as I looked at her, I knew that time was long gone. Her health was failing fast. She hadn't rented rooms out to teachers in the fall, and she stayed in bed more and more often. When she did get up, she was careless about her appearance. She was careless about a lot of things. I didn't like the way she talked about Mark at all. She was doing her best to turn Mama against him, even now as she sat at the table and talked to us while we finished the dishes.

"Yes," she said to Mama as she played with a strand of loose hair, "as soon as Anna Lee graduates from high school, she'll up and marry some shirt-tail boy. I bet I know who it'll be, too. It'll be Anna Lee and Mark before you know it, Mrs. Owens."

It made me sick to my stomach to hear her say that. "Mark and I are just good friends, Miss Red."

She laughed. "That's what they all say until they decide they want to get married. Oh, it'll happen before you know it."

"Anna Lee is much too young to be thinking seriously about boys," Mama said, but she looked at me with eyes hard as marbles.

"I'm not going to get married the minute I graduate from high school, and if I did, it wouldn't be to Mark."

Miss Red laughed again. "What's the matter, Anna Lee? He done something we don't know about?"

I looked at Mama. "You know Mark likes pretty girls."

"There's nothing wrong with the way you look," Mama snapped.

"Oh, Mama, you know I'm not pretty, not like Nancy or Virginia. How many times have we seen Mark going to those parties at Nancy's house? And everybody knows how pretty Nancy is."

Being reminded of the parties set Miss Red to thinking. The next thing I knew, I heard her saying to Mama, "Well, to tell you the truth, Mrs. Owens, I wouldn't let a daughter of mine date Mark Thomas if she had tin pants on. I just wouldn't do it."

If Miss Red's suspicions required tin pants, Mama didn't want me hearing about it and sent me out of the room.

I could hardly wait for recess at school the next morning. When I told Mark what Miss Red had said about him, he broke into a big grin and acted as though she'd paid him a compliment. Maybe she had, at that. After it was told around town enough, people quit calling him a bookworm. He even wrote his daddy overseas about it.

The leaves of the chinaberry tree were burnished to a golden hue when we realized there was something wrong with Miss

Red, but it wasn't until she began walking around the yard in her nightgown that Mama wrote to Verna.

More and more often we'd find Miss Red outside the house with her hair hanging loose around her shoulders and her gown trailing in the dust. The gowns were always heavy and long sleeved, but Mama said it was the principle of the thing. She said she should have realized something was wrong back in August when Miss Red baked her fruitcake.

Until Verna arrived, the whole town took it upon itself to look after Miss Red. Old Dr. Hardy went by the house every night and gave her a powder to make her sleep. About all he could do was make her comfortable. "The moving parts are running down," he said and walked slowly to his car, as though foretelling his own future. Different ladies from the Baptist church took turns spending the night, and Mama and I would go over and sit with them from time to time. I'd carry the little fan and put it in the living room so Mama could crochet while she talked. Summer had long since melted into fall, but Mama insisted that her fingers perspired so in the old house that she could hardly hold her thread. The house was old, and very little breeze squeezed through the straight panels of lace curtains covering the tall, narrow windows.

Miss Red had grown up in the house, and she wanted everything just the way it had been when she was a girl. She kept the flower beds bordered with little wooden planks the way her mother had done before her. The flowers never varied, but each year she tore the tops off seed packages and propped them up on little sticks as though she might be surprised at what came up. For as long as anyone could remember, there had been a vegetable garden on the east end of her property, and when Daddy spaded up land for a victory garden, he lined it up with Miss Red's.

Even when her bifocals started making her dizzy as she made her crab-like way down the back steps and Daddy had offered to put up a handrail for her, Miss Red's first concern had been for the house. She hated to add or change anything. Daddy had really done her a favor to put the thing up, but all the while he worked at it—and Daddy wasn't handy with tools—she sat under her chinaberry tree calling out a word of advice here and there the same as if she'd hired him to do the job. Miss Red had never been able to accept a compliment or gift without some sort of protest or justification, and by the time Daddy had the railing up and she emerged from the umbrella shade of her chinaberry tree, she acted as though she had done Daddy a favor by allowing him to put it up at all. His shirt was soaking wet, and he kept wiping his forehead with his arm as he gathered up his tools. Miss Red, on the other hand, looked as cool and powdered as when she'd eased herself into the chair to supervise his work.

"It doesn't look too bad, does it, Mr. Owens?"

Daddy just blinked sweat from his eyes and didn't answer her.

"I don't think it takes anything away from the house, do you?"

She didn't wait for him to answer but continued talking to herself, trying to justify the thing. "Yes, it looks like it might have been there all the while. As soon as you get it painted, it should do very nicely."

Startled, Daddy asked, "Painted?"

"That ought to do it. Just a little paint, and no one would ever guess it'd just been put up."

That was as much of a thank-you as Daddy ever got, but he went ahead and painted it anyway. That had been some time ago, and now, with the paint all chipped and falling off, the railing did look as though it had always been there.

Miss Red kept the inside of her house the same as she did the outside—like a shrine. Her father's mustache cup sat on a corner shelf in the living room, and over the fireplace hung a portrait of her mother standing with one hand resting on the back of a chair and the other holding a closed fan against the folds of her long skirt. The family Bible lay beneath an oil lamp that filled the room with the sound of bells each time the fan blew the glass prisms against one another. The only changes we'd ever known Miss Red to make were the handrail and the blackout shades. She hadn't wanted the blackout shades, but Brother Palmer had pleaded with her, for her own safety and that of the town, to put them up. He finally won, but everything else in the house was to remind her of her youth.

Sitting at the big round table in the dining room, I tried to study by the dim overhead light, but it was hard to concentrate. It was always hardest to get my mind on my homework when it was Than's turn to spend the night because she always had so much news from the telegraph office. It was more like a party when Than was there. She and Mama took turns bringing things to eat, each one trying to outdo the other by turning up with something they'd been hoarding since the war started.

It had been years since I'd heard anybody talk about Miss Red's marriage. I'd nearly forgotten about it, but her sickness brought it to everyone's mind again, and people began to recount things they'd been told. We'd all heard stories, but we didn't know anything definite or firsthand. As long as Mama or Than or anybody else who'd talk about it could remember, Miss Red had been old and faded. It was as though she'd sprung into the world that way, but there had to be some accounting for Verna, and none of us had ever known a man to live in Miss Red's house.

Mama and Than compared notes and pieced the story together pretty well. Years before, Miss Red had been married to an Irishman named Lon. He'd come to town from nowhere that anybody ever knew and swept Miss Red right off her feet. Her folks hadn't gone for the idea of their only child marrying a stranger, but he treated them nice enough, and Miss Red was to an age where she had few gentlemen callers. After they were married, Lon moved in with Miss Red and her parents. There was just no getting her away from that house. Mama and Than thought that had to have been part of the trouble all along.

It was told that Lon was big and loud and laughed a lot. Noises came out of the house such as the town had never heard before. And in what hardly seemed a decent length of time, it was obvious that Miss Red was going to have a baby. She'd been a slip of a girl, and it showed right off. Lon was more attentive than ever, but instead of sewing and making things for the baby, Miss Red had spent her time taking care of her hair, forever washing, brushing, and arranging it. It was her hair, people said, that had attracted him to her in the first place, but it was beautiful in its own right and hadn't needed all the attention she lavished on it.

Every evening when it cooled off, Lon was seen taking his bride for a stroll, holding her hand against his arm as they walked along. He even went so far as to place a cushion under her feet when she sat in the rocker on her front porch. It was generally felt that that was going a little too far. No other woman in Bay Harbor had a man at her feet, much less a cushion.

When it had looked as though Miss Red would be an old maid, people felt sorry for her and put her on every kind of church committee, sort of marrying her off to the church. Those same people objected to her marriage, and as things grew strained, she resigned from most of the committees and specialized in being a bride. Her husband, though, was somehow too much — too loud, too attentive, too big for Bay Harbor. But he kept on fussing over her and being gallant right up until the day he left her.

He'd been a fireman, and it suited him. People expected no less of him. A man with all that intensity was suited to emergencies. He was always on the move, at the center of all excitement, and he was able to bring dash and glamour to an ordinary brush fire. To see him hanging from the fire wagon, yelling and waving his arms about, was like watching a show at which Miss Red had the best seat. Any time there was a fire, she dashed to the front porch as excited as a school girl to watch for a glimpse of him as he passed the house. She was seated on her front porch the day the Staffords' house burned, her feet propped up on a satin cushion. Lon was hanging onto the side of the fire wagon when it passed the house. He waved to her and yelled something. At the time everybody thought he said, "Hi, darlin'," but later on they figured he must have said "Bye" instead. That was the last time she ever saw him. She was left with the echo of his voice and the memory of his big hand waving to her. Not even the firemen saw him leave. One minute he was there, and the next he wasn't. Her daddy tried to trace him, but nothing ever came of it. She never mentioned his name again or showed any sign of being hurt, except that she had practically all her hair cut off. She took back her maiden name and went on with her church work after Verna was born.

I was glad Miss Red had been given the sleeping powder so there was no chance of her overhearing Than and Mama talking about her. Sick and alone, those memories would be doubly painful, but then maybe that was why she was sick after all. That and Verna. She and Verna had never hit it off. Maybe Verna reminded her of the Irishman. But Verna was vain, too, and pushed her mother as far as she could and still remain on speaking terms. She'd "almost" do things so that Miss Red could never say too much. She wouldn't curse in front of her mother, but she'd come close to it. Verna thought she was so cute. She used expressions like *bass ackwards* and *mell of a hess*. And Miss Red would get upset over *gee whiz* if I said it.

"It's the same as saying 'God whiz,' Anna Lee," she'd said to me many a time. "Just remember that, you hear?"

Before Verna married and moved away, she was always coming over to our house to smoke. She'd never lit a cigarette inside her mother's house. I always thought Mama enjoyed sharing Verna's secret, but she never let on to Verna. None of us quite trusted her.

She and Mama would sit in the living room, Verna taking a chair in the corner so she could put her cigarette out if she saw her mother coming. She made smoking look so delicious. With her legs crossed and her dress hiked up, she'd stretch both arms out to the sides of the chair, the cigarette hanging downward from her tapered fingers. Just when I'd think the long ash would fall on the floor, she'd lay the cigarette on the edge of the metal ashtray and tap it with her forefinger. I could almost feel the taut white paper under my own fingers as I watched her. Putting the cigarette to her lips, she'd lean her head so that the thick dark hair seemed to pull her backwards. She'd draw deeper and deeper on the cigarette and then sling both arms out again, driving the smoke downward through slightly parted lips.

I thought Mama enjoyed watching her, too. "If your mother could see you now, Verna," Mama would say and laugh. "She's such a good woman, a regular pillar of the church."

"A *fluted* pillar," Verna corrected before going on with her delicious cigarette.

Verna's cigarettes always smelled like perfume, as though they'd been hidden with some sachet in her underwear drawer. When nobody was looking, I'd take the lid off the smoking stand and press my face to the round metal bowl, smelling the odor of Verna's cigarettes. It was a forbidden odor, the same as the one that crept through the screen door of O'Kelly's Bar. Verna told us once that next to cigarettes, she liked beer best of anything in the world. "Never puts an ounce on me, either," she said, slapping her flat abdomen with the palm of her hand.

Afterward I asked her what beer tasted like. She laughed and threw her head back the way she did when she smoked.

"Cow pee, Anna Lee. It tastes just like cow pee!"

I knew then what I'd always suspected. Verna didn't like me. She just put up with me so she could come over to our house and smoke.

None of us knew how old Verna was, but she was no spring chicken when she'd married a Protestant soldier she hardly knew. Of course, we'd heard the same thing about Miss Red. Daddy said you could hear the sigh of relief all over town when Verna finally caught a man of her own. Somebody was even spiteful enough to start talk about not letting her wear a white wedding dress. I guess that was the only time I ever heard Verna talk back to her mother.

"You know, don't you, Mama," she'd shouted, "that if you'd let Neil and me alone, nobody would have had anything to say about me wearing white for my wedding. It's your fault. Neil and I were in love, Mama. In love! I knew it was because of you that his folks sent him away. His being Jewish made it real easy for you, but that wasn't the real reason, was it? You couldn't hold on to the man you loved, so I shouldn't be happy either. Wasn't that it?"

Miss Red never uttered a word that I could hear. There was only the sound of my own indrawn breath and Verna's crying. "Oh, Mama, I didn't mean it. I'm sorry, Mama. Won't you please forgive me?" Apologizing was so unlike Verna, I was embarrassed to listen any more.

Verna wore white for her wedding, but the absence of color in her dress couldn't really change anything. That church wedding was probably the only thing Verna and Miss Red had ever agreed on. There was a steady stream of Baptists calling at their house with gifts that were displayed on long tables set up in the living room. Silver and crystal and china gleamed with a worldliness I'd never seen at Miss Red's before. Verna had about the biggest wedding the town had ever seen, but I'd heard her crying upstairs in her room the night before she was married.

As soon as Verna was a wife, she was worse than ever about exposing her legs. Mama said Verna knew that her legs were her best feature and that was why she was always sashaying around and hiking her dress up. I'd noticed lots of women who didn't have pretty legs, though, and as soon as they were married, up came their dresses the minute they got a little warm. They'd be so prim and proper one month, and the next they'd sit around fanning themselves with their skirts.

Mama was making biscuits when the wire came. We hadn't expected it, and Mama caught her breath when she saw Clarence standing at the door with the yellow envelope in his hand. Bits of biscuit dough still clung to her hands, small pieces falling to the floor as she tore open the envelope with trembling fingers. She sank into a chair with a sigh of relief.

"It's just Verna," she said. "She's coming home. She must of collected plenty of insurance off that soldier to be sending telegrams."

Two days later, we met Verna at the bus station. She came home bag and baggage as though to stay, but she didn't appear too upset over her mother. When she walked into the house, Miss Red sat propped up against pillows on the living room sofa.

"Verna," she said softly, nothing more, and made no move to get up.

"How are tricks, Mama?" Verna said, banging her suitcase on the floor. She kissed Miss Red on the cheek. "The old place looks the same as ever," she said, glancing around.

I don't suppose truer words were ever spoken, but coming from Verna they were cruel.

After the first night or two she was home, Verna started going out in the evening after she got Miss Red to sleep. There were no ladies from the Baptist church there any more, and it fell to Mama to keep an eye on things. Mama had never made a mistake in her life, but I knew she was hard put not to question her judgment in having written to Verna in the first place. Instead, she fumed and accused Verna of putting on airs. "Why, she talks just like a Yankee. She hasn't been in Chicago long enough to be talking like that. It's put on, that's what!"

Verna was quick to tell Mama she'd learned to play bridge. She was probably the only Baptist in Bay Harbor acquainted with a deck of cards, much less bridge, but she didn't dare risk playing for fear of giving Miss Red a setback should she find out about it. Nevertheless, she continued to worry that her game might suffer. She worried right up until the night she found herself a boyfriend. After that, bridge was a lost art as far as Verna was concerned. She'd captured a real prize, a captain off a tanker that docked in Bay Harbor. I could see her through the kitchen window with a little white apron on, peeking into the oven and clicking around in high heels as she cooked for him.

Mama didn't like the looks of things at all. "Mark my words," she said at the supper table one night, "Verna is out to get a man. First thing you know, she'll have her poor old mother up in Chattahoochee to get her out of the way. Miss Red won't live long after that, either. Verna'll put her away, and I'll give her three months to live. Mark my words!"

Miss Red got into the habit of wandering. That was about the worst of it, that and the pair of pink underpants that always hung from her pocketbook. As she walked along, children gathered behind her asking her where she was going. Miss Red always gave them the same answer. She was looking for her mother's house. She always found it, too. She'd walk all over town and then come back home. There were times when she'd seem okay and be her old self again, but it was when Verna's captain was in town that things really came to a head.

It was early one Saturday morning when Miss Red started walking down the street, but in place of her pocketbook, she'd slung a slop jar over her arm. She was wearing her nightgown too, and Verna about had a fit. She went running down the street in a bright colored Japanese kimono trying to catch up with Miss Red.

"Well, well, well," Mama commented, "I'd sure like to know where she got that."

Verna had all sorts of things. She had a blouse made out of a parachute, and you could see through it. And when she came over to smoke one day, she gave me a compact. There were little flowers on it, and it was all scratched up, but she claimed it had come from Germany. I was so proud of it, but I'd accidentally dropped it in the toilet at the show one day and hadn't enjoyed it as much since.

I stood on the front porch and watched as Verna finally caught up with Miss Red and tried to lead her home. Verna's long hair kept falling over her face, and she pushed it away with her free hand until Miss Red insisted she hold the slop jar. With her hair in her face, Miss Red holding onto one arm, and the slop jar in the other, Verna still managed to carry things off pretty well until somebody drove by and yelled, "Hey, Verna, couldn't you wait?" Without even looking back, Verna hurled the slop jar at the passing car and continued on home.

Later that morning I heard Verna calling to Mama from the back door. She didn't bring any presents this time, only her cigarettes. Pale and strangely quiet, she asked if it was okay for her to smoke. Mama eyed her warily but nodded and followed her into the living room. Verna went to her usual place, the chair in the corner, and sat with her legs crossed, one foot swinging back and forth, but I saw her hands tremble when she lit her cigarette. She shook the match out, blew smoke through her nose, and said, "My nerves are shot to hell and back." It wasn't long, five minutes maybe, before she tapped the cigarette out in the ashtray, gently at first and then with a grinding force that reduced it to a small heap of tobacco shreds.

"Mind if I use your phone to make a long-distance call, Mrs. Owens? I'll get the charges from the operator."

Speechless, Mama inclined her head, having known all along this was coming.

The phone was in Uncle Johnn's room, but we could hear every word Verna said. We were the only people on our block with a phone, but we didn't use it often. It was Uncle Johnn's, placed by his bed for emergencies. My mouth went dry as a traitor's at the thought that Verna would come to our house to make all the arrangements. As deputy sheriff, Daddy would be the one to take Miss Red up for Verna. He always did in cases like this. I looked at Mama, and she had that I-told-you-so expression written all over her face. I wondered why she didn't just throw in with Carlotta and start reading palms.

When Verna finished making her calls, Mama invited her into the kitchen for coffee. Mama filled Verna's cup and apologized for the coffee. "I couldn't find any without chicory, Verna. I'm sorry."

"I'm used to it now. In fact, I rather like it."

"I'll never like it. It takes all the pleasure out of drinking coffee as far as I'm concerned. Just give me plain old Maxwell House any day," Mama said, pushing the cup away in distaste. "That stuff's strong enough to walk."

Verna sat with both elbows on the table, cradling the cup in her palms. "Maybe that's why I like it so much," she answered listlessly.

"Do you think you're doing the right thing, Verna?" Mama asked. "She is your mother. Don't do something you'll regret later on."

Verna put her cup down and sat up straight. "Of course I'm doing the right thing," she assured us, but the nervous tapping of her nails on the metal table top implied otherwise. "I'm not a nursemaid. She'll get better care there than I can give her. It'll be better all the way around. God only knows what she'll do next." Verna stared at the ceiling and blew a lock of hair that fell over her face.

When Verna left a short time later, Mama turned to me. "She'll live to regret it. Don't ever put anything on the shelf, Anna Lee, that you wouldn't want to take down for yourself."

Perhaps it was only because Mama was sad, but that was just the sort of thing Miss Red would have said. It was the strangest feeling, knowing Miss Red was really going to Chattahoochee. I hadn't thought it would ever come to that. There were so many things I could have done for her, so many things I wouldn't have said about her had I known this would be the end of it.

I woke up early the day Daddy was to take her away. I kept thinking of what Mama had said. Maybe she'd be dead soon. She'd held herself and that old house together all these years. She loved the house so, and now she was being taken away from it. I didn't think I could bear to see her go. More than any of us, she belonged.

No one else was awake as I tiptoed quietly through the house. The floor felt cold to my bare feet as I slipped out the back door. I stood on the steps a minute hugging myself against the chill autumn air. I remained motionless for a time, memorizing the moment when I first noticed Miss Red sitting beneath her chinaberry tree. There was a grayness about everything, an unreal quality of seeing an old and faded photograph. But for the morning dew that clung to them, the tree limbs were bare, their wildly spreading branches a picture of my own grief. A slight breeze sent the last of the yellowed cottonwood leaves tumbling over the grass to Miss Red's feet, but she didn't notice. She was slumped forward as though she'd fallen asleep. I was relieved to see that she had on a dress, and her hair was neatly done up with tortoiseshell combs holding it in place. In place of a purse, there was a box on her lap.

I walked over to her, my toes curling against the cold, damp grass. "Miss Red?" I was hesitant to wake her, but this might be our last chance to talk. I touched her arm, and the box slipped to the ground, spilling some of the auburn hair. I shook her. "Miss Red?" I called louder. When she didn't wake up, I ran inside the house yelling for Verna. She came running down the stairs pulling the the kimono around her.

"What in the world do you mean, Anna Lee, coming in here yelling like that?" Then she seemed to notice I was crying. She held tight to the banister railing, and I could see the veins in her hands stand out.

"It's Mama! Where's Mama, Anna Lee?"

She didn't wait for me to answer but ran down the stairs and out into the backyard. When she saw Miss Red, she screamed. I could feel the gooseflesh creeping down my arms. Verna kept on screaming until Mama came and slapped her across the mouth.

Uncle Johnn carried Miss Red inside the house. Daddy was probably rushing around trying to find something to put on, but Uncle Johnn wore his brown robe with the initials *JO* embroidered on the pocket, where Miss Red drooled and caused a dark spot to form over his heart. I knew Carlotta would say it was a sign that something bad was going to happen to him, and for an instant I hated Miss Red. While everybody was running around fussing over Miss Red and trying to reach the doctor, I went outside and picked up the box of hair. I took it to Verna.

"What do you want me to do with this?" I asked her.

"With what?"

"This box of hair. Miss Red was holding it."

"Throw it in the garbage. Do anything with it! Just don't bother me. Of all the stupid things to ask at a time like this!"

I wanted more than anything to throw the hair away, to be rid of it, but I just couldn't. It was the last thing in the world I wanted, but I took it home. Standing in the middle of my room, I looked around, searching for a place, finally hiding it under a box of paper dolls in the back of my closet. Miss Red's youth in the back of my closet. That was even worse than an old trunk, but then, where could one find a hiding place worthy of remembered youth?

Miss Red lapsed into a coma. She lay still as if she were in a coffin, face up in her own bed. Dr. Hardy said it was just a matter of time. Miss Red had had several small strokes already.

Verna cried and carried on like she was the most devoted daughter in the world. I carried plates of hot food over for her to eat. Steam clouded the waxed paper covering the food, and the palms of my hands burned, but Verna never touched a thing. I carried the plates home cold in the evening. Verna sat and stroked Miss Red's hair and talked to her. She told her intimate things and whispered into the darkness of the powdery white ears. She begged and pleaded with Miss Red to hear her, but Verna was too late.

The second day, it rained. It wasn't a hard rain, just cold and piercing. I willed Miss Red to think it was summer and that we were sitting in her kitchen waiting for the teachers to come downstairs. Surely from her darkened bedroom it might sound like the summer rain she'd loved so well. But I wouldn't know how it sounded to her or if she even heard it, because she never woke again. On the third day she died, passing away as her eyes stared sightlessly at the ceiling above her bed.

When the funeral was over and the people who had flocked to the house with food and sympathy were gone, Verna locked the doors and refused to come out.

Mama thought she'd commit suicide. "Mark my words, they'll carry her out of there feet first!" But Mama was wrong. Verna lived to open the house and face the world again. She was pale and thinner but very much alive when she came over and asked Mama if she could smoke. It was the closest I'd ever seen her come to being embarrassed. She shook her head and tried to smile. "I can't do it. I think I'd choke to death if I lit a cigarette over there." She inhaled deeply, as though drawing courage into her lungs. "I'm closing up the house, Mrs. Owens. I'm going back to Chicago." She laid her cigarette on the ashtray and tapped it gently with her forefinger. "I'll be back, though. I just need some time away from here, away from that damned house. For Mama it was a way of life. I always thought it was nothing but a house, just an old house, but now, you see, it's my only living relative. How's that for retribution?"

I looked at Mama, but she didn't answer, appearing intent on her crocheting.

I was in school when Mama drove Verna to the bus station. "She's hard," Mama told us that evening, "harder than I'd ever care to be no matter what kind of hand I'd been dealt. But," she sighed, "you can't live somebody else's life for them."

I couldn't quit looking at Miss Red's house. It was as stark and lonely as her chinaberry tree. It might have been the only house left standing in Bay Harbor. I tried to tell myself it didn't look any different than it had any other time, but it did, and I looked at it again and again, worrying it like a loose tooth. One night I was out back lying on the woodpile staring at it when I thought I saw a light inside, like a candle flickering. I skinned my legs getting off the woodpile to run in the house and tell Mama, but she wouldn't believe me.

"Anna Lee, you just saw car lights reflecting off the glass, that's all. If you weren't so mean, you wouldn't be scared and thinking of ghosts."

"I didn't say it was a ghost."

Mama laughed and turned the page of her pattern book. "You didn't have to. It's written all over your face."

The next morning before school, I went over and looked through the window at the back door. I ran home to tell Mama. "There's dishes on the table, Mama, just like somebody had breakfast at Miss Red's. I know somebody's in there. I just know it."

"Anna Lee, I'm absolutely certain there's dishes on that table. I don't even have to look. Did you ever know Verna to clean up after herself one little bit? If she thinks I'm going over there and clean for her, though, she's got another thought coming. That house'll rot and fall in before I do her dirty work for her."

I asked Mark if he'd noticed any lights at Miss Red's. He said he hadn't, but then he hadn't been looking, either. After school one afternoon, together at Miss Red's once more, we walked all around the house, looking in the windows and listening at the walls. There was a loud creaking noise, and we both jumped, but Mark said it was only the wind. We tiptoed up the front porch steps the same as if Miss Red had been asleep inside the house. Despite saying she wouldn't help Verna, I noticed Mama was watering the ferns. She'd moved them back against the wall to protect them from the wind, and they looked as healthy as if

Miss Red had been around to care. The lace curtains at the windows cast uneven shadows on the living room walls, and spiders were spinning webs across the doors. "There's a funny odor," I said, rubbing my nose. "Don't you smell it, Mark?"

He took a deep breath. "I don't think so," he said uncertainly. "What's it smell like?"

"Oh, I don't know. Just funny." I was ashamed to tell him. I knew, though. It smelled like Miss Red. Miss Red was seeping out around the windows and doors. I walked back down the steps. My eyes stung. "I don't want to come here again."

Just then Mama saw us. "Anna Lee, you younguns get away from that house. You've got no business over there, you hear me?"

Mark shrugged his shoulders. "She's right, you know. We shouldn't be here. Not anymore."

"I know, we'd already let go, long before she died, but now there's no way, no hope of . . . " I hesitated.

"There wasn't any hope then, other than our own." His eyes looked bright, as though he might cry, so I turned away and started toward home.

I told Mama I'd go to town and check the mail, but first I intended to go by the drugstore and see if Uncle Johnn was too busy to talk to me. We had so little time together now that he seemed more like a stranger than a member of our family. Avoiding Chester still, I cut through people's yards and back alleys, letting myself in the little side door where I could slip behind the counter without being noticed. Uncle Johnn was pouring a red liquid into a bottle, holding it high in front of his face. It was pretty, the color of a melted Santa Claus.

"Uncle Johnn?"

"Huh?" he asked absently. He stopped pouring and looked at me. "Just a minute, honey, until I'm finished here, okay? Get yourself some ice cream and something to drink."

"Thanks. No, sir. I'll just wait."

He put the bottle down, closed it with a black cap, and then held it up to the light again. "That's a pretty color, don't you think?"

I smiled and nodded. Maybe it'd be like old times.

"Bet you'd look pretty in a dress that color. You find one that looks like this bottle of vile-tasting stuff and I'll buy it for you. Okay?" He stared at me a moment and then asked, "Is something the matter?"

"I'm not sure, Uncle Johnn. Do you believe in ghosts?"

"Yes and no."

"Both?"

He nodded. "I don't believe ghosts exist except as we create them, and, God knows, there are enough of that kind. Too many! But if you believe in something enough, it can be as real as you and me. Amy's struggling with the same problem."

"Oh, her again!" I hadn't meant to sound so ugly. I never wanted to sound hateful to Uncle Johnn.

"Anna Lee?"

"Sir?"

"Anna Lee . . . "

I waited for him to continue.

"You're getting old enough to understand things now, and, still, I don't know quite how to put it." He stopped again.

But now I knew what he was trying to say. He was uncovering something I had tried to keep hidden. He was going to tell me he was really my daddy. I held my breath, willing him to go on. Tell me, I pleaded silently. Tell me!

"You see, honey, Amy and I —"

"*No!*"

He looked stunned and frowned.

I started to cry, but gently as the soft purring of a cat. Crying and not quite crying. "Please don't say it, Uncle Johnn. Please."

"Okay. I won't. Not now, anyway. But it has to be said sooner or later, and I wanted you to know before anyone else. Not saying it won't change things, Anna Lee. This isn't the place, though. You and I need to go off someplace and have a good, long talk. I know how you love the beach. Why don't we meet down there and talk, just the two of us?"

I shook my head rapidly. "I have to go now," I said and left without anyone seeing I'd been there, left before he could settle on a place to discuss something I never wanted to hear.

That night at supper Mama told us she'd talked to Helen. "I guess Chester made quite a mess at the boarding house last night," she said and waited until we all stopped eating and looked at her. "He'd been out to some juke joint with a bunch of drunks discussing the war, and when he came in, she said he was mad as a hornet. He broke just about everything they had that was made in Japan. You know what a path that would cut through those souvenirs, and here with Christmas less than two months away, he broke half her Christmas ornaments before she could stop him. Course, Helen never did have a tree pretty as ours, I didn't think. God only knows what she'll have this year. I wouldn't put up with that kind of nonsense five minutes."

"See how lucky you are, Stelle," Daddy put in, "that you have two fellas as sweet as me and Johnn. Not many women are as lucky as you are," Daddy said and gave her a big smile.

"Just because my Christmas ornaments aren't broken doesn't mean I've got a bed of roses, Robert Owens, and don't ever forget it. You'll be getting fried eggs and rice for supper if you aren't careful."

Daddy knew which side his bread was buttered on. "If you cooked it, sugar, it'd taste like nectar and ambrosia."

"You underestimate me, Robert. That's the kind of food you'd be cooking, not me." But she smiled when she said it, so I relaxed while she and Daddy bantered back and forth at each other for a while. Uncle Johnn told me once that Mama and Daddy reminded him of a couple of cats playing with each other. "Only trouble is," he said, "sometimes they draw blood."

17

It was the last week in November, and I sat at my desk making out my Christmas list and eating dry oatmeal from a saucer. I'd just printed BICYCLE in big block letters when Mama walked up and looked over my shoulder.

"Put your list away, Anna Lee. You'll have plenty of time for that later. I want you to get your things together and go to the boarding house. Helen wants you to sleep there tonight."

"Sleep at the boarding house?"

"It won't be the first time you've slept there."

That was true. Once when Chester was away, some years before, I'd stayed there with Helen and pretended I was a roomer passing through town. I even took a shower before I went to bed. Helen was the only person I knew who had a shower, and I loved the novelty of bathing standing up. I stirred the oatmeal with my finger and didn't look up.

"Anna Lee!" Mama spoke sharply, and I jumped. "Helen asked for you. Now get your things together. If you don't shake a leg, it'll be dark. Hurry up now."

"Mama, I can't. Please don't make me go. Please?"

"You ought to be ashamed of yourself, Anna Lee Owens. Helen thinks a lot of you. She and Chester both do. You're just like their own youngun. Now Chester's away and she wants you to stay with her tonight."

"But I can't, Mama. I can't. You know Chester sometimes comes back when she's not expecting him."

"That's all the more reason for you to be there. I can't believe you could be so selfish and ungrateful. I'd die if Helen knew you were acting like this. She has a little surprise I think you'll like. Now I don't want to hear another word out of you."

"Please, Mama. I can't. I don't want the surprise. Not even a donkey."

"Okay, Anna Lee, I've taken all of this I'm going to. You're not too big to spank, you know. There's not one reason for you not to stay there, and you know it. Tomorrow's Saturday so there's no school, and there's not a thing to keep you here at home tonight. Get your things."

"You can't make me."

"Oh yes I can, young lady! Don't give me any sass!" She grabbed my arm to pull me up from the desk, and I blurted out, "No! You're not my mother . . . " As the color drained from her face and her hand fell from my arm, I continued, " . . . and Daddy both. I'll ask Daddy." Her hand shook, and I thought she would hit me, but she didn't.

"I've been good to you, Anna Lee. Don't push me. Get your things together."

I'd come so close, too close to the edge of something Mama wasn't prepared to face. I put some clothes in a paper sack and hurried to leave before it was dark.

"You ought to be ashamed," Mama called as I walked out the door, and then, louder, "And it's not a donkey!"

In the front yard I hesitated and drew a deep breath. A gray mist lay over Bay Harbor, and the air was clammy and cold. I looked toward Miss Red's, but the darkened house was grim and lonely, no longer a source of comfort. As I walked across the street, the wind picked up, and leaves and sand blew across my shoes. Ahead of me the sidewalk stretched unevenly, and on either side houses hugged themselves behind closed doors. Their lighted windows, promising more than they could deliver, looked dim and far away. I shivered and thought, Somebody's walking across my grave. Half a block away, I could hear the creak of the swinging sign at the boarding house, but as I started up the steps, the creaking gave way to whistling. Joel was back! Joel was back! I rushed up the stairs, and, sure enough, Joel and Helen sat in the living room. There was a fire in the stove, and Helen rocked back and forth slowly, smiling when she saw me at the landing.

"How's this for a surprise, Anna Lee? Look who's feeling stronger than ever and back to visit us again."

Joel stood up and grabbed me by the waist and swung me around. Then he pushed me away from him and said, "I swear to goodness, but I do believe she's growing again. I wonder . . . By the time I get back . . . " He stopped and Helen continued, "Let's don't talk about that, Joel. Let's just enjoy your being here for a time. Joel has a pass, Anna Lee, and he thinks he's being shipped overseas. We're going to give him special treatment, you hear?"

Despite watching the door for Chester, we did have a good evening. We ate downstairs in the dining room and then sat around the stove visiting. But as the evening wore on, even Joel couldn't lessen my dread of sleeping beside Helen in Chester's bed. There wasn't a room for me, though. Even Joel had taken up his old quarters on the porch outside Helen and Chester's bedroom.

Later that evening one of the boarders came in drunk and started singing and making so much racket Helen had to keep going to his room to ask him to be quiet. She told him she'd have to call the sheriff if he didn't quiet down.

"Aw," he slurred, "you wouldn't do me thata way would you, honey?"

Helen laughed and assured him that she would. Finally she did put in a call to Daddy, but he was out, and the police chief came. The chief and Joel carried the man out to the car. He'd have to sleep it off in the jail, where he wouldn't be disturbing any paying guests. I thought Helen would give his room to Joel, but she didn't. She said I could have it.

Joel was staring out the window of the porch door when I started down the hall to bed. I hadn't gone far when I heard him snap his fingers and say excitedly, "I know! Let's go for a walk on the beach."

"Oh, Joel," Helen replied sadly, "I don't think so. It's late and awfully raw out."

"Let's go anyway! I need to do something totally impractical, unplanned. There's a full moon. It'll be beautiful."

"It wouldn't look right, Joel. A married woman—"

"A married woman and a child! Anna Lee can go with us. You know I'd never do anything to hurt your reputation."

"Well," Helen began hesitantly and then replied firmly, "I don't mean to be difficult, but you don't understand how things are here in Bay Harbor. I'm sorry."

"Don't mention it," he snapped and, grabbing his jacket off a chair, started downstairs.

I looked at Helen and her eyes were full and shiny. "Get your coat, honey. We'll just take a short walk."

She was rushing me so, I didn't have time to be frightened. By the time we reached the sidewalk, Joel was nearly to the corner. I ran ahead and told him to wait for Helen. He did, never taking his eyes off her.

Helen was right. It was cold, and we walked at a brisk pace until we reached the soft, sandy beach. I'd never been there late at night before, and I was surprised that it was so beautiful. Helen and Joel didn't seem to notice when I dropped behind to stare at the shimmering luster that lay like a film of oil over the surface of the bay. Seeking shelter from the wind, I knelt in the sand beside a palm and watched the moon lapping at the shore. I could have stayed that way indefinitely had I not seen a movement from the corner of my eye. I searched the pier's dark shadows and decided I'd only imagined it. Uneasy now, I saw that Helen and Joel were far down the beach, too far, but before I could stand up to call to them, they turned and started back. Helen was nearly as tall as Joel, and they were like a golden-haired god and goddess striding along the shore together. Helen stumbled, and for a moment their shadows blended into one as Joel bent to help her. Erect again, they faced each other, and neither moved until Helen, seeming suddenly frantic, began running down the beach in my direction. I figured she'd missed me and started once more to call her when I saw that I hadn't imagined the shadow on the pier. Crouched, Chester was stealing silently down the walkway toward them. I moved deeper into the shadows of the tree.

Searching for me, I suppose, and because they were moving away from the water now, they apparently didn't notice him. Joel was ahead of Helen, who passed the pier just as Chester's feet hit the sand. Quickly closing the distance between them, Chester grabbed Helen roughly by the arm. I heard her exclaim, "Chester! It's not —" The rest was swallowed by the sound of his hand striking her. She fell to the sand crying, and Joel was by her side in an instant. And then I saw how impartial moonlight can be. It glinted off the water, off Helen's hair, and off the blade of Chester's knife. He yanked Joel away from Helen, and they began to struggle. Like sunlight reflecting off a fish in shallow water, I saw the knife glide through the air and hit the sand. So did Helen. She lunged for it. Pulling herself to her feet, she ran a few steps in the direction of the water and then stopped and drew her arm backward to throw the knife into the bay. In that same moment, Chester gave Joel a vicious kick, and he cried out in pain. Still in the act of flinging the knife away, Helen spun around. There was a startled yelp when the knife struck home. Chester remained standing for long seconds before he dropped to the ground beside Joel.

Terror-struck, I ran, leaving Helen and Joel on the beach with Chester. Mama always said fear could give you untold strength, and she was right. I made it back to the boarding house in what seemed like a single bound. I ran to the empty room and locking the door, jumped into bed with my clothes on. I hugged my knees to my chest, but they still knocked together. It wasn't long before I heard the familiar sound of tires squealing and knew a car was leaving the police station. I hadn't quit shaking when Daddy started banging on the door, yelling for me to wake up.

"Have we been attacked by the Germans?" I called from the bed.

"Dammit, Anna Lee, open this here door and hurry up about it. No, we haven't been attacked by the Germans, but you get out here right now."

"Is there a fire?" I truly did not think I would ever be able to get up and leave that room.

"You're not too big to whip, youngun. The only fire is going to be in the seat of your pants if you don't get out here. Now Chester's hurt, and Helen's been worried sick wondering where you were."

Stalling for time, I called, "Let me get dressed, Daddy." The last thing I wanted was to have the boarders see me get a spanking. I lingered a few more minutes and then opened the door and followed him down the hall.

Helen was sitting in the living room, still and white as a perfect statue, except that her face was beginning to swell where Chester had hit her. I saw blood on Joel's pants, and when Daddy and I approached, he touched Helen's arm and asked if she was able to walk.

Daddy had no intention of carrying Helen, so he brushed Joel aside and said, "Of course she can walk. Come on, Helen. You're not doin' Chester one bit of good a-settin' here. Come home with me and Anna Lee." She started crying softly as we started down the stairs. I thought how much like a queen she was to be so gentle and quiet no matter what was happening to her. She was still crying when Daddy guided her by the elbow to our kitchen, where Mama poured her a cup of coffee. I felt light-headed and weak, but nobody paid any attention to me until Uncle Johnn put his arm around my shoulders and held me against his side the same as if I'd been Miss Amy. Mama remembered I was home then and told me to go to bed, but going to sleep was out of the question. I stretched out on the couch in the living room and listened to them talking. After a bit Uncle Johnn said, "Robert, she needs something stronger than coffee to steady her nerves." A few minutes later I heard Daddy rummaging around in the bedroom closet for the moonshine. That must have been what she needed because she finally stopped crying and was able to tell them what had happened.

"Joel wanted to go for a walk on the beach. I said no at first, but then I thought about the war and all, never knowing who'd be taken next, and it seemed so innocent with Anna Lee along. She started out with us anyway. I suppose she was cold and went back to the boarding house to bed. We were looking for her when

Chester jumped out at us. I wasn't expecting him for a couple of days yet, but I guess he'd been in town all night drinking. Lord knows, it wasn't the first time he'd spent the evening at the pier with a bottle. I tried to explain, but he wouldn't listen." She touched her face where he'd hit her. "He was," she hesitated, "the way he gets when he drinks." I thought he might kill us all. I swear, though, I didn't mean to. I only meant to throw the knife into the bay, but then Joel screamed, and I turned toward the sound. I turned before the knife left my hand, and it hit Chester instead. I feel so awful to have involved Joel in something so sordid. He's been so good to me, and now to involve him in all this mess." Helen started crying again, and Mama and Daddy both talked at once. She was still crying when I finally fell asleep.

By the time Daddy got to the hospital to see Chester the next day, the sheriff and police chief had already been there. Chester told them it was Joel who'd stabbed him. He denied that Helen went near the knife.

At the dinner table that noon Daddy told us all about it. "Helen wouldn't hurt me," Chester had said to Daddy. "That pretty boy's mighty slick with a knife or he wouldn't have got the best of me. Maybe he got the best of Helen, too, Robert. You know what I mean, don't you? The very best of her?"

"A knifing ain't changed Chester none," Daddy said. "Spite of his pain, he had a good laugh at his own joke. But Helen, now, she's another matter. I thought she was a-goin' to fall over when she found out what Chester was sayin'." Daddy poured coffee in his saucer and blew on it, making pale ripples on its khaki surface. He took a sip and continued. "Over and over, over and over, she kept repeatin', 'I've got to make him tell the truth. I've just got to make him tell the truth.'"

"Poor Joel," Uncle Johnn said. "This could ruin him."

"They're trainin' him to kill, ain't they?" Daddy asked. "Bad as we need men to win this war, though, it might not be as tough on him as you think."

"Helen's in no shape to be left alone," Mama said. "If I can't be with her, you can stay, Anna Lee. A child's better than nobody. Anyway, until Joel leaves, it's best they not be alone together.

You'll have to stay there when I can't, and I don't want any more arguments, you hear?"

"Yes, ma'am." And then I ventured the question I'd been holding in since the night before. "Is Chester going to die?"

"Pshaw," Daddy said. "It'd take more'n a knife wound to kill that scoundrel. You don't need to worry about Chester none. He's tough as nails."

Mama shook her head. "So much happening. It seems like it was only yesterday Joel came here. It wasn't too much more than that, really. People live faster when there's a war on."

Much as I admired Helen's gentle ways, I didn't think any less of her for having stabbed Chester. I just wished she'd killed him. That would have solved so many things, and it would have made it easier for me to tell Daddy what I knew. I cleared my throat, but my voice was hoarse. "Daddy?"

"Yeah, baby?"

"Helen did stab Chester."

"That's what she's a-claimin', Anna Lee."

"No, sir. I mean she really did. I saw her."

Daddy narrowed his eyes. "You *saw* her?"

"Yes, sir."

"No you didn't, Anna Lee, and don't you go lyin', now, tryin' to get mixed up in something that don't concern you, you hear?"

"But I did see her. Honest. I was there on the beach all the time."

"*You were what?*" Mama exclaimed. "A child of mine spying on friends. I've never been so humiliated in my entire life. Why . . ."

"Hush, Estelle," Daddy interrupted. "Anna Lee ain't seen nothin'. She was locked in her room when I got there, and I like to never talked her out of it. She can't tell me she'd been down there through all of that. The moon was bright. They'd of seen her if she'd been there." Daddy took a noisy sip of coffee and leveled a gaze at me. "I didn't raise no liars. You know what I'm a-talkin' about, don't you, Anna Lee?"

"Yes, sir, but . . ."

"Now, don't but me!"

"Robert . . . " Uncle Johnn put in, but Daddy stopped him, too.

"Stay out of this, Johnn. This ain't no concern of yours. We're going to act like you never said what you did, Anna Lee. It'll never leave this house. I'm not goin' to have you mixin' our name up in no scandal, and I don't never want you lyin' to me again, you hear?"

I pressed my lips together and gave a half nod.

"I don't know what's got into her lately," Mama said. "Her imagination seems to be running away with her. She even thinks she sees lights over at Miss Red's."

"Maybe you're seeing too many picture shows," Daddy said. "I think you better cut out some of your show goin'."

"That'll work out just fine," Mama said. "She needs to stay with Helen anyway."

Uncle Johnn excused himself from the table, but he paused at my chair and put his hand on my shoulder for just one moment. He believed me. I knew he did.

True to her word, Mama sent me to the boarding house that same afternoon. If Helen noticed my reluctance to talk to her, she didn't say anything about it. She didn't talk much herself. She just sat on the side of her bed and stared at nothing, not even seeming to notice me until she started to change clothes. Then she asked me to leave the room for a few minutes. Reluctantly, I left the soft-padded rocker and walked to the door, where I paused and looked back at the spacious room with its frilly white curtains and pillow shams. I was frightened when she closed the door, but I didn't know what else to do but wait. It seemed a long time before the door opened again, and she stood there wearing one of her hats. The dark veil fit close, helping to conceal her bruised and swollen face. She was pulling on a pair of navy blue gloves, just the color of the hat. I'd never seen her look so nice, and yet the hat looked out of place, as though it still belonged inside its box.

I heard the give of springs in Joel's cot, and he walked to the porch door, which Helen had propped open with the green frog to catch the warmth of the afternoon sun.

"Helen?"

I don't think I'd ever heard him say her name before, not quite that way, and it didn't sound right, seeming to belong to someone else.

Helen didn't even look at him. She stared straight ahead at the stairs. "I'm going to the hospital to see Chester."

"No! Please. Don't do that."

"It's the only way, Joel. I won't let you go to jail over this. It's only my word against his that has you out of jail now, and how long can we count on that?"

Joel just stood there, and I followed Helen as she walked down into the darkness of the stairs and out into the bright light of day. Watching her walk along wearing her hat so proudly was sadder than I could have imagined. People stepped outside of stores to speak to her, and looking back, I saw them standing in groups still watching as she walked past them and on down the street. I saw, too, that Joel stood on the front porch staring down at her. I waved to him, but he didn't move. Some of the people on the sidewalk waved to me, though.

We got into the back seat of a taxi parked in front of the picture show. It felt strange to ride in a taxi, stranger still to have Josh Lincoln's mother doing the driving, but with so many men drafted, women had begun to take over their jobs. The war made all kinds of changes in people. I sat as still and quiet as Helen, wondering if she even knew I was there. At the hospital I followed her to the door of Chester's room. Being careful that he didn't see me, I stood outside and listened to them talking.

"Chester?"

"Well, well, well," he answered hoarsely, as though he'd been asleep. "And what have we got here? If she ain't wearin' one of her fancy hats. Surely you ain't wearin' that for me. You must be on your way home from buyin' groceries."

"That's no occasion for a hat, Chester."

"Oh, no, surely it ain't. But when your lover tries to kill your husband, now that's an occasion, ain't it?"

"You can't ruin that boy, Chester."

"Boy? Boys don't go around fuckin' other men's wives."

"That's not true. You know it isn't. He's never done a thing to me or you, and you know it."

"Now, Helen, don't go tellin' me that, not me of all people. They found his fingerprints on the knife, didn't they?"

"Chester, he tried to help you. I never intended to hurt you, and I was in a state of shock. He pulled the knife from your body. My prints are on there, too, and yours."

"Well, who wouldn't expect them to be? When I go to bed at night, that knife sets right there aside a the bed. You've probably touched it a dozen times. Don't lie and tell me that bastard tried to help me down there at the beach. I'm in his way. He's after you like a dog in heat."

"Chester, that isn't true. I swear to you, he tried to help. He took the knife from your side and tried to stop the bleeding."

"Yeah, you tell me that, Helen. Am I supposed to think my wife was down on the beach playing patty cake with that son of a bitch? What do you take me for?"

"We were just walking, Chester. Anna Lee was with us."

"Anna Lee?"

"Yes. We didn't want to start any rumors so we took Anna Lee along, but she left and went back to the boarding house."

"I never knew a woman to lie like you, Helen, and now you'll try to involve an innocent child to cover your guilt. I bet that bastard's used more'n my knife. You standing there with your dress blowing up over your head almost, and me on the ground bleeding to death. It's a sorry business."

"Chester!" Her voice rose and she sounded frightened, but she didn't say anything more because a nurse came in and told her she'd have to leave.

I couldn't get over Mama's surprise when I told her I'd gone to the hospital with Helen in a taxi. After all, I was only doing what she'd told me to do, just as I was when I repeated for her everything I'd heard them say. The next day Mama borrowed Uncle Johnn's car and drove Helen to the hospital herself.

"I was so silly not to learn to drive," Helen said. "I never bothered to learn because I always wanted to look at things. It never occurred to me that I'd need to know how some day."

"Don't let it worry you," Mama replied. "I'll drive you to the hospital any time you want to go. Johnn'll let me use his car to help you out. That's what friends are for."

Mama had taken her crocheting along, and as we sat in the lobby waiting for Helen, several of the nurses came over and exclaimed over how fast she could crochet. It seemed to me that the only thing safe from rationing was Mama's crochet thread. Her hands were frantic, always shaping the thread to her will. At home every table was topped with a doily, spidery shapes protected the backs and arms of all the furniture, and our coat hangers wore crocheted covers to protect our clothes from rust marks. Now Mama was beginning to crochet lamp shades. I worried where it would all end.

For a while we were driving Helen to the hospital every day after school, and every day she wore a different hat. She seemed almost of two minds, going there to plead with Chester on the one hand and driving him wild with her hats on the other. After sleeping in the same room with those hats for years, Chester acted like a crazy man every time she came in wearing another one. We couldn't figure out if Helen enjoyed his discomfort or if she was trying to force him to agree to her side of the story.

"I never saw a grown man scared of a hat before," one of the nurses said to Mama.

"Oh, it's just an obsession, I guess, and he's sick, too." Mama laughed. "Why, I once knew a girl who was scared of chicken necks."

I didn't understand any of it, much less what happened next. Helen never did get anywhere with Chester, and he continued to raise cain over the shooting. "I'm gonna cut him," we heard him hollering one day. "When I get out of here, I'm gonna have me a slice of pretty boy's face."

"That's one opportunity you'll be denied," Helen told him. "Joel left already."

I ran back to the lobby and asked Mama, but she said, "No, he's not gone. Not yet, anyway. Helen's just baiting Chester, that's all."

As we drove back to the boarding house, Helen told us that Joel really would be leaving the next day. "The sheriff says they've got no

legal reason to hold him, especially not when we need every able-
bodied man we can get to win this war. They can't prove it wasn't
self-defense. He's free. Almost." She sighed. "I have to tell somebody, Miz Owens. Joel's proposed."

Not totally at ease with Uncle Johnn's car, Mama accidentally hit
the brake and nearly sent Helen through the windshield. The car
choked down, and she was so nervous she flooded it. There was
nothing to do but just sit there awhile. Helen was so calm. She
might have been sitting in one of the porch rockers telling us about
it.

"Why, I never dreamed of such a thing," she emphasized to
Mama. "Last night he asked me if I'd come sit on the porch with
him."

"Where were you, Anna Lee?" Mama asked accusingly, just as
though I could have stopped him. Helen looked back at me and
smiled. "She fell asleep listening to the radio. Anyway, he said there
was something we needed to discuss in private. Naturally, I thought
he meant the stabbing. I got my sweater and met him on the porch.
Why, nobody could have been more surprised than me. 'When
you're free,' he says to me, 'When you're free, Helen, I want you to
marry me.' I still can't believe it. It all seems so unreal."

It seemed unreal to me, too. It just didn't seem possible that Joel
would want to marry Helen, that he could feel that way about her. I
loved her, but that was different. He could have had the prettiest girl
in town, Miss Amy even, so why would he want to marry Helen?
She belonged to the boarding house. Joel didn't.

When Mama finally started the car again, she speeded all the way
to the boarding house. She sent me to the post office for the mail,
and she and Helen were still in the car talking when I got back. I
waited outside the car for Helen.

"She won't be needing you tonight," Mama said. "Get in and
let's take the car back to your Uncle Johnn. He can drop us off at
the house."

At the supper table that night Mama told Daddy and Uncle
Johnn what Helen had said. "I cautioned her not to tell anyone else
about it. Joel's free now, but something like this could start everything up again. First people saw him out shopping with her, and

then them out on the beach together late at night. Why, every word they ever exchanged has taken on special meaning since the stabbling. I said all along that Helen should never have let him go shopping with her. Didn't I say that? And God knows, she should never have gone down there on the beach with him, even if she did think Anna Lee was along. I think the world of Helen, but she surely doesn't have a drop of common sense. You know how some people are, always looking for trouble. You can't be too careful. Why, she's my best friend, and it even seems kinda funny to me how she hit Chester with that knife. She said he broke her glasses when he hit her, and if he turned sideways, you couldn't see him."

"You believe Helen, don't you, Mama?"

"Yes, I guess I believe her, Anna Lee. She's told me quite a bit about her feelings for Joel, too," Mama continued. She'd like to marry him all right. What woman wouldn't? If I had a man that looked like Joel, I'd lock him in a room and slip food under the door."

"No you wouldn't," Daddy said. "You got as good-lookin' a fella as you'd ever want right here, and I ain't never caught you a-tryin' to lock me up."

"The trouble with you, Robert Owens, is that you believe that. Joel's not the least bit stuck up about his looks."

"Huh! I'd just like to buy that bastard for what he's worth and sell him for what he thinks he's worth. And I'm not so sure he'd marry Helen if she was free today. She don't know but what he's got a wife and younguns up north some place. You can't put any stock in what these soldiers say."

"Robert, you just don't understand."

"I understand a lot more'n you think I do, Estelle. But you stay out of it. This thing ain't finished yet. Chester's still in the hospital. There could be more trouble when he gets out of there."

"Well, let's hope not," Uncle Johnn said. "I like Joel and Helen, and I'd like to see them happy. If a man and woman are in love, they're not complete without each other." Uncle Johnn winked at me, but this time he was telling me a secret I didn't want to hear.

"Well, we all better be rememberin' one thing," Daddy said. "Right now Helen's still complete with Chester. They ain't got no divorce yet. I don't care who it is, a married woman's got no business fooling around with a soldier." He pushed his chair up to the table and hitched up his pants. "Nasty's nasty."

After Mama and I cleared the table, Uncle Johnn motioned me to follow him to his room. He closed the door and picked up the twin hair brushes from the dresser and began smoothing the sides of his hair.

"I've missed you, Uncle Johnn."

"Why, I haven't been anywhere, honey."

"You might as well have been. It seems like we never get to talk anymore."

"No, I guess we don't. As a matter of fact, I've had the distinct impression you've been avoiding me." He picked up a pack of Chesterfields and sat on the bed beside me.

I lowered my eyes and shook my head from side to side.

He looked toward the hateful catalpa tree that grew outside his window. In the summer Uncle Johnn's room was filled with the dry, scratching sound of crawling worms. The catalpa tree was alive with them. Like Mama's hands, they were never still.

I looked toward the window, too, but I couldn't see the catalpa tree, only our reflections in the glass. "Uncle Johnn, why don't you ask Daddy to cut that catalpa tree down? Don't those worms give you the creeps?"

He smiled. "I don't have a fondness for them. Oh, but I could never ask Robert to cut it down. He likes to fish too much. They're good bait. And now, without Fly, it'd be hard for him to buy worms from anyone else."

"They'd keep me awake at night."

"Lots of things keep me awake, honey." He tilted his chin back slightly and blew smoke rings. After a few minutes he turned to me. "How are you doing in school these days? Got those multiplication tables down yet?"

I thought he was only teasing. "Oh, Uncle Johnn, you know that was last year."

"Last year? Was it?" He smiled and, sounding more like Daddy than I'd ever thought he could, said "Yes, I guess it was." He turned away from me. "Time is passing me by."

"Anna Lee, I've always wished there were some way I could tell you how much you've meant to me, mean to me now. How you'll always remind . . . "

"Remind, Uncle Johnn?"

"No. I don't know what I was going to say. I guess I'm ill at ease about what I have to tell you."

Now he was going to tell me he was my real daddy. That's why he closed the door, so Mama and Daddy wouldn't know.

"You've probably suspected for a long time now."

I nodded my head.

"I'd always been a happy man, you see. No, not happy, not really. I was content, content to share your life and your parents'. Content to share your home. All I had of happiness came from you, and I was content to live on the fringe of your life. Until I fell in love."

"Sir? What?" What was he trying to say? I felt I'd missed something, had been asleep and missed the point of what he was telling me.

"Christmas wedding," I heard him say. "You're the only one who knows. We wanted you to be the first to know."

"Wedding?" I asked, my mouth suddenly dry.

"That's the way it's usually done," he laughed.

"Do you want me to come live with you?"

"Live with us, Anna Lee? Why, darling, you'll stay here with your parents. I love you. I'll always love you, but you must live with your parents."

"My parents?" Wasn't he ever going to be my daddy?

"I thought you understood, hon. I'm afraid I've been clumsy. This isn't turning out the way I thought it would at all. I thought, I'd hoped, you'd be happy for us."

"You thought I'd be happy to lose you?" I got out jerkily, my tongue sticking to my mouth.

"You won't be losing me. You'll always be my special love. Always."

"Is Miss Amy your first love?" I prodded in a choked voice.

"No, she isn't my first love. Not even you, my sweet, are my first love."

"Who was?" I pushed for the answer I wanted to hear.

"My first love," he sighed. "It wasn't a romantic love, Anna Lee. Under different circumstances it might have been, but I was in school. She was older, and later she loved someone else."

"Do you ever see her anymore?"

"Only when I look at you." He coughed and looked trapped. "I mean, your youth is like my first love, like the joy and tenderness of new leaves in spring."

"And Miss Amy's like a rousing game of pool, isn't she?" I never meant to say it, but there it was between us.

Uncle Johnn was stunned, absolutely speechless, but I didn't care. If he didn't want to be my daddy, I didn't care what he thought. I jumped off the bed and ran from the room. I locked myself in the bathroom, and later I could hear him and Mama talking about a Marine invasion in the Pacific. Still later, I heard his car drive off into the night.

"Anna Lee, what are you doing in there?" Mama asked from outside the door. "Do you need some castor oil?"

I came out then. I'd had enough bad news without castor oil. The dishes were stacked on the drain board, so I went in and began drying them.

"You were in there with Johnn so long, they almost dried themselves."

"Yes'm."

"Did you hear what I said?" Mama snapped, and I realized I hadn't been listening to her.

"No, ma'am."

"I swear to goodness, you're hard of hearing sometimes. When I want you to hear something, you don't, but if I whisper in the front room, you know every word I've said. I asked if you knew Chester was out of the hospital. They finally got that infection cleared up and let him out a couple of days ago. He and Helen are separated, though. She's filing for divorce like she should of done years ago."

"Where's he living?"

"He's rented a cabin down near the river. Be close to his work. Helen's never told him she intends marrying Joel, and don't you go saying anything to anybody, either, especially not Chester. Helen's smart to keep it to herself. Course, Chester's trying to put a good face on things" — she hesitated a moment, whispering, "three, four, five," as the crochet hook kept time with her, and continued in midsentence — "saying he wouldn't go back if she begged him. He told your daddy he wasn't taking a chance on any more of Helen's boyfriends stabbing him again. He still won't admit she's the one that did it. Guess it hurts his pride too much."

I slept in fits and starts all night, and when I woke up, I knew it was beginning all over again. When Uncle Johnn raised his shade that morning, he had a ragged view of the catalpa tree. His window screen was torn to pieces.

"Looks like a mad dog got hold of it," Daddy said.

I knew that was exactly what had happened.

"You got any ideas who would of done somethin' like that, Johnn?"

Uncle Johnn shook his head, puzzled. "No, Robert. It doesn't make sense. I mean, if somebody wanted to break in here, they'd do it so it wouldn't be noticed. This way, I don't know."

"You're sure then there's nothin' going' on you need to tell me about?"

"For God's sake, Robert. I'm certain not everybody in this town likes me, but no, I don't know who my son-of-a-bitching enemies are." He turned to Mama and me. "Excuse me, Anna Lee, Estelle. All I'm trying to do is plan a wedding."

"Wedding?" Mama asked, sounding stunned and hurt at the same time. "Did you say 'wedding'?"

"I can't seem to do this right no matter how I try. I didn't mean to blurt it out that way, Estelle. Amy planned to have you over, and we'd tell you then. We're getting married at Christmas."

"Christmas? Why, that's just around the corner," Mama commented, sounding more hurt by the minute.

"I know, but I don't want to give her time to change her mind. I had enough trouble convincing her to marry me as it was."

"Maybe then, son, you'd best not go through with it."

"It's nothing like that, Robert. She just felt, after what's happened and all, that she wasn't meant to be married, to be happy."

"But you convinced her otherwise," Mama said.

"That's right. We have to put our pasts behind us."

"That's where they've always been," Mama countered, beginning to sound disgusted now.

"No, Estelle. Sometimes we carry them around with us. That's what we have to guard against."

"Well, I have to admit, that makes sense," she conceded. "Still and all, this is so sudden. It'll take some getting used to."

When I left for school, Mama was outside measuring Uncle Johnn's window. I wondered if Chester was trying to scare me or if he'd really hurt Uncle Johnn. I knew one thing for sure. I had to talk to somebody. If only Ashley hadn't left. If he could have stayed on and become part of Bay Harbor. By the time I reached school, my mind was made up. I'd talk to Helen. At least I wouldn't have to worry about Chester being there anymore.

After school I dropped my books off at home and walked to town. I'd dressed with special care that morning. I wore the new coat dress Mama had made me. It was blue with a big lacy collar and white pearl buttons down the front. I thought it made me look older. Even so, I was scared. I stopped at the steps of the boarding house and drew a deep breath. Maybe I'd walk around to the dining room first to see if it was open. The door was locked, so I went back around front, this time continuing up the stairs. There was an eerie quiet, and the door to Helen's empty room stood open. The porch door was stuck, but I jarred it open and looked around. No one was there, either. The rockers had been turned so they faced the house, and were tipped forward, propped against the wall. I faced the end of the porch outside Helen's room. Joel had been different from all the others, but he had been, after all, only a boarder. When his time came, he left too. Helen had taken the curtain down and shoved his cot down the hall to one of the rooms. Still, it wasn't as though he'd never been there. Only the wind and dust were in Joel's space now, but none of us would ever forget he'd been there.

I closed the door quietly, as on a funeral. Helen had to be around someplace or the door to her room would have been closed. I walked to the end of the hall, thinking she might be in one of the bathrooms, but they were empty, too. I turned to leave when I heard voices downstairs. Slipping quietly into the bigger bathroom, I closed the door and knelt on the floor beside the tub. I'd discovered a long time before that by moving a piece of loose linoleum surrounding the bathtub pipes, I could look through a hole into the kitchen below. Very carefully, I slipped the linoleum aside. There, directly under me stood Chester and Helen. Hardly daring to breathe, I eased myself to the floor and lay flat to get a closer look. Helen wore a flowered dress and stood so close to Chester they were almost touching. Without ever taking her eyes off his face, she reached down inside her brassiere and took out the little black change purse. She removed several folded bills and handed them to Chester. He tucked them inside his shirt pocket and laid his calloused hand on her breast. She made a low sound I'd never heard before and yet was instantly familiar. Tiny nerves flicked down either side of my tongue the way they would if I held a cat too close to my face. Hastily I shoved the linoleum back into place and rushed on tiptoe out of the bathroom and down the hall to the front stairs. Everything was coming to me at once. Bits of conversations and memories of the boarding house rushed through my head. "Yoohoo?" I kept hearing her say, "Yoohoo?"

One minute I was at the boarding house, and the next I was standing in Miss Red's front yard. I remembered nothing in between. I didn't even know why I was there. I didn't want to be anyplace, not anyplace at all. How could a queen be that way? Nothing made any sense any more. I willed myself to concentrate on Miss Red's house. The steps and porch were filthy. Leaves and trash had blown into the corners, and the ferns were wind-shredded. I started up the steps and stopped. Spiderwebs were everywhere. I pulled a sticky strand from my hand and shivered. Turning, I walked around the bedroom wing to the big side yard. It stretched all the way to the next street. Once, when I was little, I'd run away from home and gone there to hide in the cottonwood trees. Now it was overgrown and tangled with weeds and dried sandspurs. Miss Red's room was at the very back of the house, nearest the kitchen. I tried to look in at the windows, but Verna had left the blackout shades down, and I couldn't see anything. I continued on around back, picking my way carefully over some rusting cans and pieces of broken brick. I started back up the steps to peek in at the kitchen window when Mama saw me. I heard her hit our kitchen window with the edge of her hand to unstick it. Pushing it up, she yelled, "Anna Lee Owens, if I catch you at that house one more time I'm going to tell your daddy, now, you hear? That's Verna's house now, and she hasn't sent any messages telling me to have you over there. Come on home. If you've got so much time on your hands, you can help me get supper started in a little while."

All Mama could talk about that night was Uncle Johnn's wedding. She was split right down the middle. On the one hand, it was like a contest she'd lost, and on the other, it was quite a plum to have Miss Amy for a relative.

"You didn't mean Christmas Day did you, Johnn?" Mama asked at supper.

"I don't know yet, Estelle. Sometime over the holidays. Amy doesn't want to be married in her home. You can understand that. But then the courthouse seems too impersonal. I don't know how we'll wind up doing it."

"Well, you sure better decide pretty soon. You're talking about something less than three weeks."

"Three weeks?" Uncle Johnn repeated in a faraway, dreamy voice.

"You sure you can wait that long?" Daddy asked. "You sound like a lovesick cow."

"Robert!" Mama scolded, already beginning to pull away and treat Uncle Johnn like company.

When Uncle Johnn excused himself and left for Miss Amy's, I stared at his empty chair and wondered if it would have been better had he never come to live with us in the first place. If Miss Amy could take him away so easily, maybe he'd never really belonged to us after all.

I was miserable all evening, sure sleep would never come, and when it did, it arrived on a crocheted nightmare. Dreaming, I woke up in a dim room and noticed how the sun cast tight little shadows on all the walls. I couldn't see out any of the windows or doors because spiderwebs, giant crocheted spiderwebs, covered everything. I pulled and pushed, but Clark's white O.N.T. ball thread held firm, and all the while Mama sat there crocheting faster and faster, never seeming to notice what was happening.

"Mama, do you know what crochet means? Ashley says it's a French word meaning crook . . . " I woke with a strangling noise, sitting bolt upright in bed. I was wringing wet. Because I slept curled into a tight ball, Mama was always thinking I was cold and putting extra covers on me. I kicked the heavy quilts to the bottom of the bed and recalled something very important. But it would have to wait. Mama was already up and rushing me off to school.

At noon I hurried home for dinner, but Uncle Johnn was already in the front yard waiting for me, and we walked inside the house together.

"It looks like it might rain, Anna Lee," Mama said. "I'm surprised they didn't declare a rainy day session and let you all out for the rest of the day. You better hurry up and eat and get on back before it lets loose with a downpour."

I knew there'd be no getting around her. I'd just have to wait now until school let out. It didn't rain, but the day was gloomy and cold. It was so dark in our classroom we could hardly see our books, and there was a heavy smell of damp chalk dust and paste. The hours dragged until the bell rang. "I'll blind you with heel dust," I called to Mark as I ran across the school yard. He was talking to Nancy and didn't even try to follow me. At the corner I cut across the street into Miss Red's side yard. I'd run all the way so Mama wouldn't be expecting to see me yet, especially not the back way. I looked at Miss Red's kitchen steps and door.

I was right. It just hadn't registered until I woke from the nightmare. Practically the whole house was wrapped in spiderwebs, all but the back door. It was as free and clear as if somebody was coming and going regularly. I slipped quietly up the steps and turned the knob. The door opened, and I stepped inside. I bet they'd believe me now. There in the sink were the remains of a gutted candle. There were dishes on the table. Clean ones. Everything looked pretty clean. No spiderwebs inside. It didn't even look dusty. Empty food cans had been stacked on one corner of the kitchen counter. They'd all been rinsed clean and stacked so neat. Everything was so neat!

Ashley! Of course, Ashley, always cleaning his hands, so neat and tidy with his little concrete fence. Ashley was staying here! I knew it!

I ran through the house softly calling his name. It was dark as night inside, and I bumped into the lamp with the glass prisms and started its bell-like ringing. I stilled it with my hands, and again there was only silence. Of course! He'd be at the beach now. He just came here at night when he wouldn't be seen. But I couldn't wait that long to see him again. Running bent over so there'd be no chance of Mama seeing me in the windows, I ran out the back door, down the steps, and across the side yard to the corner.

As I cut across the street toward the beach road, I realized that if Ashley was truly back, then God did answer prayers after all. I ran to the end of the block and then cut around the corner at Larkin's and ran toward the pier. The wind whipped sand into a swirling white mist that stung my legs as I rushed through the stormy darkness. I lowered my head against the sand and kept running even when my sides began to ache. I stopped just short of the seawall. There was no fence that I could make out. I crawled out of the wind into the sand cave. Feeling around, trying to find the piece of concrete where I'd left my message, I called, "Ashley? Ashley?" He was probably up in the woods, and it was so dark out already. Maybe the storm would come in the night, I thought excitedly, and I could sneak over to Miss Red's and visit with him. He knew how good I was at keeping secrets. I started backing out of the cave, uneasy now because of the growing darkness. My hand felt something, and I dug down, able to see just enough to make out the empty citronella bottle.

"What you got there, sugar?"

God. No. Please, no!

"Well now. Ain't this cozy? You pick this out just for Chester? I knew you was thinkin' about me all the time. All the time I been sick, I knew you was thinkin' about me, waitin' for me. I've been waitin' for you a long time, Anna Lee. I think I been waitin' too long." He left the mouth of the cave and began crawling toward me.

"You've been drinking."

He laughed. "That's a fact, sugar. I have. Don't you think I got reason enough to drink after all's happened to me? You gone make it all better now, ain't you? He grabbed my arm and pulled me backward with him further up into the cave. "You been playing *Gone With the Wind* down here? Are you Scarlett looking for

Ashley? I hate to disappoint you, sugar, but you just found Rhett Butler." He loosened his belt, and I began crying.

"I'm gonna tell. Don't you touch me!"

"I ain't gone touch you. I just want to show you my battle scar. I want you to put your hand into my wound." He laughed again and grunted as he struggled with his pants. Even above the wind I could hear the zipper. He grabbed my hand and said, "Here!" My fingers recoiled from the warm, sticky flesh beneath my hand. I screamed, and he rolled over me on all fours like a dog. Yanking my raincoat open, he tore my dress and pulled at my underpants. I kept screaming until he pressed sand in my mouth. He forced one of his bony legs between mine, and I felt a pressure, the beginning of pain, and then there was a thud, and Chester moaned. Someone was in there with us. Ashley! Ashley had hit Chester in the back with a piece of concrete.

Like a mad dog, Chester rolled sideways and charged. Spitting sand, I screamed, *"Ashley, run, Ashley. Run quick!"* But Chester tackled him, and I heard Ashley's head hit one of the jagged pieces of concrete that had once been part of his fence. "Ashley!" I cried. "Ashley!" He didn't move, and my hand felt wet when I touched his head. I struggled to find a rock, anything. I grabbed fistfuls of sand and began pelting Chester as he tried to zip his pants and fasten his belt. "Just hold on a minute now, sister, and I'll tend to you," he said, but as he turned toward me, we both heard voices. People were running up the beach, flashlights bobbing up and down like buoys in a heavy sea.

"You'll be sorry now," I cried. "You'll be sorry. I'll see you dead, Chester. I'll see you dead."

"What's all the commotion?"

I recognized Mr. Meyers's voice.

"What's going on here?" he asked as they drew closer. "First Eula thought it was just the wind, but I was sure I heard somebody screaming."

I was struggling to turn Ashley on his back when I heard Chester saying, "We're mighty glad to see you, Mr. Meyers. I heard screams, too, from out there on the pier. That tramp there" — he pointed to Ashley — "was trying to rape this child. We struggled, and he fell on a piece of cement or something. I think the child's in shock. She ain't made no sense atall. Not atall."

"That's not true, and you know it!" I shouted. "Mrs. Meyers, he's lying. Honest. It was him, not Ashley."

"Ashley?" Mr. Meyers questioned, shining the light toward us.

"He's my friend, Mr. Meyers. Get a doctor, please. He's hurt bad. Please get a doctor."

"She's in a bad way, Mr. Meyers. I best take her on home to her mama. I'm gettin' worried, her thinkin' she knows that bearded tramp."

"No, Mr. Meyers, don't let him take me. Please don't let him take me. *Please!*"

"It's all right, Anna Lee, honey," Mrs. Meyers said. "Mr. Armstrong's a friend of your family. Now go with him like a good girl."

I screamed then, and I couldn't stop. My throat hurt, and there was sand in my mouth, but I couldn't stop. Chester tried to pick me up, and I kicked him. I grabbed hold of Ashley's leg and held tight, but they pried my fingers away.

Mrs. Meyers bent down to me. "Come on now, honey, hold my hand. Mr. Armstrong and I will take you home. Just hush now, you hear?"

Sand crunched in my teeth. "You'll go with us?"

"I'll go with you, Mr. Armstrong. I think she needs a woman with her after what she's been through."

"Sure thing, Miz Meyers. Sure thing."

"But Ashley—" I began.

"That man has to go to the hospital," Mrs. Meyers said. "There's nothing we can do for him." She turned to her husband. "I'll stop at the house and call the doctor and send for help. You better stay here."

When Chester drove into our front yard, Mama was standing on the front porch. She ran out to the car. "Have you seen Anna Lee, Chester? Oh, my God! My baby! What's happened to my baby?"

As Mama took in my torn dress and all the blood, she made a whimpering noise, and Mrs. Meyers took command again. "Now, Mrs. Owens, we have to keep calm for the child's sake. Let's get her inside, and we'll explain what's happened. You can thank Mr. Armstrong here that things aren't any worse than they are."

We walked in the front door, and Chester started in. "She's just like my own youngun. Me and Helen—" His voice broke into a sob. "Well, anyway, I just wish I could of kept somethin' like this from ever happenin' to Anna Lee."

I spit on him then and shoved my bloody hands against his stomach. "You lie. Ashley's never hurt anybody. It's you. It's you, and you know it. *Liar!*" I screamed. "*Liar!*"

"Anna Lee!" Mama said sharply. "Stop that this instant. I—I'm all confused about what's been going on, but don't you ever talk to anyone that way, especially not someone who apparently just saved your life."

Chester shook his head back and forth and put his finger to his lips. "Don't, Estelle. She's had a terrible shock. She's out of her head. Don't know a word she's saying."

"Oh yes I do know what I'm saying. You know I do. You know I do. You know I do. You know I do. You know I—" Mama hit me then, right across the mouth. "Oh, my baby, I'm so sorry. Mama didn't mean to do that." She was crying and grabbed me around the waist, hugging me to her. "Please forgive Mama, please." I just looked at her. I wouldn't forgive her. You're not my mother, my brain shouted, but I couldn't. My throat closed, and nothing would come out, not one word.

Mama walked out on the porch with Chester and Mrs. Meyers. I could hear them talking, but I didn't care any more. Let them talk. When Mama came back inside, she brought a cloth and a basin of water and started sponging me off. I pulled away from her and went to the kitchen. I drew a glass of water and filled my mouth again and again, spitting right into the sink.

Daddy and Uncle Johnn came home then. "What happened, Estelle?" Uncle Johnn asked, stopping when he saw me coming out of the kitchen. Daddy stared at me, all the while taking a can of Prince Albert out of his pocket and beginning to roll a cigarette.

"There was some tramp got hold of her down on the beach. Chester heard her screaming and went running down there to help her. I guess he hurt the man pretty bad. They've taken him to the hospital." Mama started talking low then, as though that would keep me from hearing her and me sitting right there in the room with them. "Trouble is, Anna Lee is in shock and all confused. She thinks it was Chester messing with her. And him rescuing her and always thinking so much of her. He broke down and cried trying to tell me about it."

"Well, that son of a bitch better be in the hospital, 'cause if he ain't, I'm gonna kill the bastard. Maybe I'll kill him anyway."

"Robert, shut up!" I'd never heard Uncle Johnn speak that way to Daddy before. "The child's right here. Your responsibility is to her now. I think we'd better take her to the hospital and have her looked at. Don't you think that'd be a good idea, Estelle?"

"Oh," Mama said. "Of course it is. I hadn't thought. I guess I didn't want to think about . . . about . . . " She left the room without finishing the sentence.

Daddy was still staring at me as Uncle Johnn knelt down. "Anna Lee? Baby? Anna Lee, we're going to have you checked over by a doctor, okay? He'll give you something to help you sleep and forget all about this. Can you hold Uncle Johnn's hand and come out to the car?" He was talking to me like I was two years old. That was all right. I wasn't feeling any older than that, really.

The exam at the hospital was the most embarrassing of my entire life. My main concern, though, was not with the exam but how to sneak away and find Ashley. It wasn't going to be easy. The nurse helped me dress and stayed in the room until Mama came to get me.

"She hasn't spoken a word," the nurse whispered. The doctor came in then and motioned Mama to the door. I listened numbly, able to make out only snatches of what he was saying. "Lucky. Didn't finish job."

When Mama came back for me her eyes were glazed and staring. They brought in a wheelchair, and she rolled me off toward the lobby where Daddy and Uncle Johnn were sitting. We arrived there the same time as Miss Amy. She came running in the door whiter than any ghost could have been. I hadn't realized she cared so much about me. Uncle Johnn stood up and called her name, but she rushed past him like he wasn't even there. I don't believe she even noticed me. We just stood there and stared after her as she ran off down the hall. None of us moved until we heard her scream. Uncle Johnn was after her in an instant.

"What in the world—" Mama began, but Daddy touched her arm. "Have a seat, Estelle. I better see what's a-goin' on here."

It seemed a long time before Daddy came back, alone. He pressed his bottom lip in and sucked air through his teeth. He sat down beside Mama and spoke in the hushed voice usually reserved for funerals. "I swear to God," he said. "I wouldn't have believed it possible. You know who that was down on the beach with Anna Lee?" Mama shook her head slowly as though she wasn't sure she wanted to find out.

"W. T. Walker!"

"What?"

"I swear to God. He must of escaped in that fire, and it was the other poor sucker that was burned to death. God knows, that bastard must have nine lives. And he's gone need 'em if he ever wakes up."

"Robert! He's not responsible. He's, well, you know."

"Hell, you think I care! Look what he's done. She can't even talk about it."

Not Ashley? W. T.? He couldn't be Miss Amy's W. T. Ashley wasn't crazy. I loved him. It wouldn't be fair. She couldn't have Ashley and Uncle Johnn both.

In a little while I saw Uncle Johnn coming back down the hall. He didn't have much more color than Miss Amy, and he looked stiff and uncomfortable.

"Let's go," he said. "She won't leave him. I don't suppose I'd love her as much if she felt otherwise, but it still hurts."

18

In the beginning Daddy thought he could trick me into talking, and when that didn't work, he and Mama treated me as though my hearing had been affected too. Right in front of me, they talked, said things about me, as though I wasn't there.

Uncle Johnn was home every night now. Ashley had never regained consciousness. Uncle Johnn tried going to the hospital to be with Miss Amy, but she didn't want him there. "I've lost him twice already," she told Uncle Johnn. "If there is to be a third time, he must know I'm here with him. He must know someone believes in him."

"What'd she mean by that?" Daddy asked Uncle Johnn suspiciously. "Believes in him?"

Uncle Johnn cleared his throat. "She doesn't think he would have harmed a child. Amy believes Anna Lee was telling the truth about Chester."

Yes, yes, my mind screamed, she's right, but my throat closed achingly tight and dry. I opened my mouth and struggled for words that wouldn't come.

Daddy propped his elbow on the supper table and pinched the bridge of his nose between his thumb and forefinger. "She believes a crazy man and a child that's so mixed up she can't even talk?" He shook his head. "You marry that woman and you don't have the brains I thought you had."

"I may not be marrying her," Uncle Johnn said dully. "She feels now, after all that's happened, that it was never meant to be. Her first loyalty, she says, must be to W. T."

No wedding? Ashley had saved me twice.

Daddy wanted me to go with him to cut down the Christmas tree, but I shook my head. All I wanted to do was sleep, welcome dreamless sleep, blank as the screen at the picture show with a broken projector. Mama forced me to get out of bed in the morning, but I'd fall asleep on the couch listening to the radio. Mark came by and sat with me. He talked but never expected anything of me. Best friends are that way. We stared at Mama as she hung ornaments on the tree. Normally it would have given me so much pleasure, the smell and sight of it all, but I let go of the best holiday of the year, refusing to be the little girl in the warm lighted house.

On Christmas Eve Daddy came home with a paper sack in his hand and sat down beside me on the couch. "Now, baby, somebody's sent you a present. I want you to think now and remember things like they're supposed to be." He reached in the sack and pulled out a cluster of mistletoe. "Chester found this growin' on an oak tree and sent it to you. Wasn't that nice?"

I knocked it to the floor and ran from the room. Couldn't they put two and two together? Didn't they know mistletoe was poison?

Christmas morning came, and they had to wake me up. Near the tree was a secondhand bicycle. "Bicycles have gone to war, baby," Daddy said. "Guess old Santy Claus talked somebody out of this one."

Well, he could have saved his breath. Everybody was still looking at me, waiting for my reaction, and I realized I hadn't said it after all. Maybe I smiled. The wooden roller skates weren't secondhand. Painted green, I was absolutely certain no one else had used them.

"This is some Christmas," Mama kept sniffing. "Some Christmas."

But old habits die hard. After dinner Mama went to the boarding house to take Helen her gift. I lay down on the floor in front of the tree and fell asleep among the presents. I don't know how long I'd been there when I was roused by voices. It sounded as though Daddy was in Uncle John's room lecturing him again.

"No way! We're not takin' her away from here."

"Be sensible, Robert. You and Estelle don't seem to realize how serious this could be. She hasn't spoken a word since that night, not a word. Surely even you will admit that's not normal."

"Let me tell you one thing. Anna Lee's not crazy. I ain't takin' her off to some fancy doctor and have 'em lockin' her up with a bunch of crazies like W. T. Walker. You got a lot of nerve even suggestin' it."

"Nobody's suggesting she's crazy, Robert, but there is a problem. I don't think you realize how serious this could be. People have had nervous breakdowns over less than she's been through."

"Children ain't got nerves."

"Well, we can't just let her sit here like this. All she wants to do is sleep! If you won't get help for her, then I'll take her myself."

"Oh no. You ain't takin' Anna Lee noplace. Not noplace! She's my youngun."

"Are you ready to prove that?" Uncle Johnn asked wearily.

"You wait just a damn minute, son. What in hell are you trying to pull now? Don't think you're going to start something with me. I stood up for you all these years and never said a word against you when everybody else was saying Earl's accident was really suicide 'cause you was foolin' around with Grace. You want to go through hell twice? I can put you through it."

I'd never heard Daddy so mad. Angry. I'd never heard Daddy so angry.

"I've had just about all I'm going to take out of you. Me and Estelle took you in our home when nobody else would ever speak to you. We let you live with us, and this is how you show your gratitude. Don't push me, Johnn. Everybody knew you was in love with Grace. You stayed there at the house with them every chance you got so you could moon around her like some lovesick schoolboy."

"You're disgusting! Yes, I admit it. I loved Grace. Was in love with her, but it transcended anything physical, if you can understand that. She was the most beautiful person I'd ever known, but she was my brother's wife, and I never forgot it, not once. You just couldn't stand it because she didn't have any use for you. Her husband's twin, and she couldn't bear the sight of you."

"Earl may have been a lot taller'n me, but I was more of a man than he ever thought of being."

"That's all you ever thought about, wasn't it? Being a man. That wasn't important to Grace."

"Like hell! I made it important to her. She was plenty glad to see me after Earl died."

"She was in shock. Half the time she thought you were Earl!"

"Yes, she did," Daddy said quietly, "and that's why you're not goin' to stir up any trouble and try to take Anna Lee anywhere. I know she ain't yours 'cause she's mine. I ain't never said a word to nobody 'cause it would break Stelle's heart. I ain't never let on, but that's my baby in there, not yours, and I aim to see to it that she goes on thinkin' me and Stelle are her real mama and daddy and that Stelle goes on thinkin' we ain't. I never meant to be unfaithful to Stelle. Her mama bein' what she was, I knew that was the one thing that was important to her, and I never intended to do it. You know how Grace took to her bed after Earl died. She was always so frail and delicate-like. I think she might have died then and there if we hadn't hired that nurse to go stay with her. Well, I was sittin' up with her one night, waitin' for the nurse to come, when she woke up and called me Earl. She reached her hand up and touched my face. 'Come to bed, Earl,' she said to me. I tried, I swear to God I did. I said, 'Grace, this is Robert, not Earl,' but she didn't seem to hear me. She stood up out of the bed in that thin nightgown and put her arms around my neck and started kissing me. For a long time I told myself I was tryin' to help her, to give Earl back to her for a few minutes, but it wasn't Earl I was thinkin' about. I couldn't help myself."

"I know that," Uncle Johnn said.

"What do you mean, you know?" Daddy asked hoarsely.

"Grace told me, after Anna Lee was born, when she knew she was dying. At first she believed you were Earl, and then when she realized you weren't, well, it was too late. For the child's sake, she wanted someone to know, to look after her."

When Daddy answered, his voice was tight with something, anger maybe, or disbelief. "Being noble again, huh?"

"No, Robert, not noble. Just because I'm not Earl, not your twin, doesn't mean I don't care about you. You're still my brother. I was young and single. I didn't have a wife to worry about. It didn't matter if people talked and said things about me. Anyway, I envied you. I wished it had been me."

The floor swayed back and forth beneath me. I wasn't Uncle Johnn's after all. I'd belonged to Daddy all the time.

"Lingering." That's what Uncle Johnn said each day. Lingering, and we all knew he meant Ashley. They were afraid to move him, and Miss Amy had been unable to get a doctor to come down and see about him. They'd gone to war, too.

It was a cold December day, and I sat at the kitchen table watching Mama cook dinner. In the middle of the table were a pepper shaker, a box of Morton Iodized Salt, and a can of Pet milk left there from breakfast. Like eyes stuck with sleepy, the ice pick holes in the top of the can were crusted over with dried milk. I shifted my gaze to the box of salt, where the paper was firm and shiny. It was my favorite of all wrappers. "When it rains it pours." I loved the slogan, but I was most fascinated by the picture of the little girl repeated on the box tucked under her arm. On that box was another picture, it being repeated over and over again forever. I stared hard at the shiny blue paper, imagining smaller and smaller pictures on smaller and smaller boxes of salt, smaller and smaller little girls with stepmothers, a word I'd never say out loud if I could. Stepmother. Poor Mama. If she ever found out, not even her crocheting would calm her, but she'd never find out from me. Never.

"Anna Lee! Are you deaf? Here," Mama said, and thrust a bag of oleomargarine at me. "Make yourself useful, youngun." She smiled, but I knew she was tired of being patient and understanding. She'd give more time to a simple chain stitch. I pinched the orange bead and watched how, if I didn't leave it alone, if I kneaded it enough, it spread out and covered everything until the white glob looked like real butter, which it wasn't.

It was all fake. I tried to form the word *fake,* but I couldn't. It was trapped, caught with all the other unspoken words.

When Daddy and Uncle Johnn came home for dinner, I knew Mama was at the end of her rope. "Robert," she began, "maybe Johnn's right after all. Maybe we should have somebody take a look at Anna Lee. School'll be starting in less than a week now."

Daddy stopped right in the middle of cutting his meat. He didn't even put his fork down when he answered her. "Anna Lee's goin' back to school," he said. "I don't see her wantin' to be held back a year and let all her friends go ahead of her. She'll talk. Just hold your horses and your big ideas. She'll talk."

Would I? I didn't even much care anymore. If they'd just leave me alone so I could sleep.

"I think she needs to get out more," Uncle Johnn suggested. "She needs to be out of this house. Get her around people and things that are happening."

"That's fine," Daddy said. "I got no objections to that."

After we cleaned up the kitchen, Mama said we'd go see Helen. She handed me my coat, and we walked to town. When we reached the boarding house, I tugged at her hand and pointed to the drugstore.

"You want to go there? Well, that's all right. It was his idea." She walked over with me and told Uncle Johnn she had some company for him. He smiled, and I went behind the counter and sat on a low box where nobody would see me. All the while he worked, he kept talking to me, telling me all kinds of things. I was beginning to feel real comfortable when the phone rang.

"What! Got away? How? Right away. Oh yes, wait. Call the boarding house and ask for Mrs. Owens. Tell her what you've told me. Anna Lee will be with her."

He didn't even take off his white coat. "Come on, Anna Lee, run." We went out the side door to his car. He backed it around and skidded on the brakes at the corner. He turned right and then made a U-turn in the middle of the street. U-turns were forbidden in Bay Harbor. He pulled up in front of the boarding house steps. "Anna Lee, if you love Uncle Johnn at all, do what I say. Get up those steps quick and stay with your mama. I have to find Amy."

It was Ashley. I knew it was. I got out of the car and walked up the steps. I stopped just inside the swinging doors and waited. When I heard his car pull away, I went back outside and started toward home. I didn't run the way I wanted to for fear someone would take notice and try to stop me. Everybody in town knew what had happened at the beach. At least they thought they knew what happened. Chester was a hero.

When I reached home, I walked in the front door and out the back. I ran to Miss Red's. Inside the house I called, "Ashley? Ashley?" Thinking I heard something, I went into Miss Red's bedroom. The shades were down, and it was dark and musty. A candle burned on the bedside table, and Ashley lay on top of the bedspread. There was a white bandage all around his head, and his beard had been shaved.

"Oh, Ashley." I knelt by the bed and took his hand.

"Amy?"

"It's Anna Lee."

He whispered carefully, "Anna Lee?"

"You know, Ashley, from the beach."

He sighed. "You're okay?"

"I'm okay. Do you want me to turn the light on?" For the first time in a long while, I wasn't sleepy. I didn't want to be in the darkness anymore.

"No! They'd see. No light." He tried to lick his lips, and I could see they were parched and swollen. I touched his face. He was burning up with fever. I went into the bathroom and held a towel under running water. I wrung it out and returned to his bedside. I kept touching it to his face and hands. "It's okay, Ashley. It'll be okay."

"My head!" He grabbed his head with both hands and threw up. He strangled, and I shoved and pushed until he turned on his side. Grabbing the shawl off Miss Red's trunk at the foot of the bed, I covered the brackish foam and wiped his mouth with the towel. "Ashley, I have to get a doctor."

"Aspirin. Get me aspirin." He moaned, "My head."

"Okay. I'll get some and be right back. Then I'm getting a doctor."

At home I searched the medicine cabinet. I looked in Uncle Johnn's dresser. When I finally found them in the kitchen cabinet with the glasses, I wondered why I'd left. I should have looked at Miss Red's and not left him. Just as I went out the back door, I heard Uncle Johnn's car drive up. Ducking, I ran to Miss Red's. The minute I opened the door, I smelled it, and I heard it. Running to the bedroom, I saw that Ashley had knocked the candle over. The curtains, everything was catching on fire.

"Ashley!" I screamed. I was choking on smoke, but I couldn't move him. His mouth hung open, and I couldn't wake him up. "Ashley, please," I pleaded. A piece of curtain fell on the bed, and it was in flames. I pulled him to the floor and jerked his arm. I could hear Uncle Johnn calling me. *"Anna Lee! Anna Lee!"* He crawled to us on all fours. *"Get out! Get out!* I'll bring him. *Hurry!"*

The house was filling with smoke, and Miss Red's room was a mass of flames as we crawled to the back door, Uncle Johnn dragging Ashley with him. When we were outside, he picked Ashley up, and I noticed how limp he was in Uncle Johnn's arms, hanging there like a rag doll. The fire truck came, and in all the confusion I lost sight of them.

There wasn't much that could be done about Miss Red's house. They kept wetting ours down and hosing the trees to keep them from going. Later Mama cooked fried eggs and rice for supper. Daddy clearly wasn't happy about it, so she said, "Be glad you've got supper at all after what I've been through today."

Daddy ignored her and poured milk in his coffee. Slowly stirring it, he spoke to Uncle Johnn. "That was a close one, son. You messed up, leavin' my youngun like that. You know how close she come to bein' killed?"

"I watched her go up the stairs. I thought she was with Estelle. I'd asked the hospital to notify her of what had happened. I thought she was with her mother, and I didn't know what might be happening to Amy. She'd left the hospital to go home, and in that space of time he woke up. No one was with him, and he just walked out of the place. Just walked out. He knew his way around. Just slipped out the delivery door, they figure."

I cleared my throat. "Did they give him something for his headache?"

They all turned and looked at me. Daddy was saucering his coffee and burned his mouth.

"Praise Jesus," Mama said and started to cry.

"Did they help Ashley's headache?"

"God, her mind's still bad," Daddy said, shaking his head.

I looked at Daddy. "W. T. A rose by any other —" I began. Uncle Johnn got up from the table and walked around to my chair.

"W. T. — Ashley — " Uncle Johnn corrected, "won't have headaches anymore, honey."

My eyes brimmed, and my throat swelled. "He's — he's . . . " I stood up, holding to the table, but I couldn't say it. Neither could Uncle Johnn. He merely nodded and sat in my chair, pulling me to his lap. "There's something else that needs settling," he said. "A child doesn't risk her life to save someone who's harmed her. I think we should all look at that." He cradled me like a baby, his baby.

"Ashley was my friend." I spoke to Uncle Johnn's shirt. "He said he was a deserter, and I believed him."

"Mother of Jesus," Daddy said, and Mama kicked him under the table.

"He went away. At least he said he went away. I'd just found out he was staying at Miss Red's. I went down to the beach to find him, and Chester . . . Chester. Chester. It wasn't the first time Chester . . . "

"It's okay, Anna Lee," Uncle Johnn said. "We understand, honey." I was crying, and he handed me his handkerchief and stroked my hair.

"Why in the name of God didn't you tell us?" Daddy began.

"I was afraid. Then when I did, you wouldn't believe me. Nobody listened to me."

"I'll kill that slimy son of a bitch," Daddy said and knocked his chair over getting up from the table.

"Robert, haven't we had enough trouble?" There was a pleading in Mama's voice. "Let the law handle it. What good's it going to do any of us if you go to jail?"

"She's right, Robert," Uncle Johnn put in.

"She may be right," Daddy said in a low voice, "but this here" — he stood over us and jabbed my shoulder with his finger — "this here is my youngun, and there ain't nobody gonna mistreat her. Not and live to tell about it."

Like a moving picture, Mama's face changed, fright giving way to hurt. "Yours?" she asked in a trembling voice. "Seems to me she should be ours."

Daddy walked back to his chair and righted it with his foot. He patted his holster and cleared his throat. "That's just what I'm a-sayin', Stelle, except I'm the only one's actin' like she's ours. This ain't just any girl. This is our own youngun, and I intend to even the score with Mr. Tight Ass Chester."

"I would think, Robert," Uncle Johnn said slowly, "that by now you would understand that scores aren't always evened. Even if they could be, they shouldn't. Do you know what I mean?" He lowered his head slightly and leveled a gaze at Daddy.

Daddy's face paled at the threat. We both knew what Uncle Johnn meant.

"You'd best follow a mother's advice. Killing Chester won't undo what's happened. It'll just be one more hurt we'll have to handle, and I for one think Anna Lee has had more than her share of that already."

We all watched Daddy as he pushed his chair up to the table. Without a word he walked over to the china closet and reached his hat down off the top. Holding his left hand at the back of the brim and his right hand just inside the front crease, he adjusted it forward somewhat. He sniffed loudly and walked into the living room, where he picked his leather jacket up from the couch. Slowly, still with his back to us, he put the jacket on and squared his shoulders. When he reached the front door, he turned to face us. He stretched his neck and thrust his chin upward in a half circle as though his tie might have been too tight. I could hear Mama's indrawn breath when he hitched his belt up and patted his holster. Sucking air through his clenched teeth, he said in a steely voice, "Okay, have it your way. Still and all, I'd like to bury the bastard. I just hope they'll let me be the one to drive him to Raiford. I want to watch them lock that bastard away forever."

They talked him out of it just that easy. I thought he couldn't help himself. I really believed he could kill a man. Especially for me.

W. T.'s second funeral was on December 31, 1943. Miss Amy had him buried in the old cemetery next to their baby. "He always did love children," she said. "There he can watch over our little girl." She didn't put a headstone up for him. She had a marble sundial installed instead. The epitaph was simple: W. T. — FOR ALL TIME REMEMBERED

"She does have funny ways," Mama said, "but I have to admit that was a beautiful idea."

"It ought to be," Daddy replied. "She's sure had enough experience."

"Robert! Don't be disrespectful of the dead. We owe him a great debt."

"I'm not talking about the dead. I'm talking about her. The truth never hurt nobody."

Daddy was wrong. It hurt Chester.

Daddy didn't drive Chester anyplace. Word of what he'd done reached the men on the *Blackwater*, and they knew the police were coming for him. Afterward nobody knew why he jumped. Never a favorite with the men, this bit of news hadn't improved his standing any. They heard him hit the water and weren't sure if someone forced him overboard or if he was trying to swim away before the police arrived. He nearly made it. The men saw him reach the shallow water at the edge of the swamp when the half-submerged log rose up to become a giant gator that grabbed his leg. Like a trailing lure, Chester slowly disappeared beneath the water, screaming for help that never came.

19

Every day I stared at the pile of ashes that had been Miss Red's house. It looked like a war zone. The blackened remains of the kerosene stove lay on its side. Some pipe, the bathtub, things like that were still there, but, like grave robbers, people came by and carried things away. I longed to walk through it, too, to pace it off room by room, but Mama wouldn't let me. She claimed it was dangerous and, anyway, it would get my shoes dirty. Verna wrote Mama that she had a job in a defense plant. When the war was over, she'd come back to Bay Harbor and rebuild. In the meantime, she'd hired someone to clean things up, but they were too slow to suit Mama. "It's like somebody's been cremated over there," she said every time a wind came up and blew in and out of the wall-less rooms. She didn't know about the box of hair. And I knew now that I could never be rid of it.

Miss Red's house was gone, but the picture show stood firm. The newness had worn off though. Like the unwilling good-bye to a favorite friend, I saw my passion beginning to dim. My breathless, hurried steps were slow and heavy as lead. No matter how I tried, I couldn't recapture its former magic. And it wasn't Hazel. I knew that now. If I thought of Hazel at all, it was to feel sorry for her shut up there behind the candy counter all the time. Even the red paint on the candy counter looked faded, and it wasn't as big as I'd always imagined. So faded and small, and it could still hold Hazel. Maybe growing up wasn't going to be fun after all. Would anything be fun anymore?

Uncle Johnn and Miss Amy planned their wedding again. They'd decided on the time and place: springtime in Miss Amy's garden. They would be married when the flowers were new and the leaves that tender green of first love. I prayed that it would rain.

It began to look as though we would be spared nothing. It wasn't enough that Miss Amy was taking Uncle Johnn away. She invited us to dinner at her house, where I'd have to see him sitting at the head of her table. Mama told us about it at supper.

"I guess we're going to get broken in, Johnn," Mama announced. He looked up, puzzled, and Mama smiled. "Amy's invited us to dinner this Saturday, and . . . "

Daddy interrupted. "There ain't no way I can go out to eat in the middle of the day," he said in a disgusted tone that told us his opinion of Miss Amy's intellect.

Mama smiled weakly and gave an embarrassed little laugh that made Uncle Johnn more than ever an outsider. "Robert, Amy is referring to the evening meal. I'm sure you can get off for a few hours. It's not often we go out together in the evening as a family."

"She's lived right here in Bay Harbor all her life," Daddy said. "For the life of me, I don't know why she can't talk like the rest of us."

"Robert," Mama pleaded, inclining her head in Uncle Johnn's direction.

"It's all right, Estelle. I don't think any of us care what the meal's called, Robert. The point is, Amy has invited us to eat with her. We're going to be a family soon, so we might as well start acting like one, whether it's dinner at her house or supper at yours."

Daddy swallowed a mouthful of biscuit and shook his head.

Mama closed her eyes. "Robert, please don't make this difficult for us."

He did, though. He couldn't help himself. We went to Miss Amy's for dinner, but it would have been better if we hadn't. Except for Uncle Johnn, who sat at the head of the table as though he belonged there, everybody seemed uncomfortable, especially Mama and Miss Amy. Daddy wasn't so much uncomfortable as he was disgusted. The minute we were home, Mama had to start frying chicken and warming leftovers for him. He was starved half to death.

"Well, Robert, I, for one, thought it was elegant. I haven't seen a table that nice since I was in New York City. From the linen napkins to the silver candle holders, it was like a picture."

"Why the hell did she have to light them damn candles? I like to see what I'm eatin' for Christ's sake. If she'd had the lights on so I could of seen what I was eating I would've known that wasn't strawberry jello."

"That was tomato aspic, Robert."

"Well, you don't know how close I come to spittin' it on the floor."

"Robert, I would have died right on the spot," Mama said, as she placed steaming bowls of food on the kitchen table at ten o'clock at night.

"I don't envy Johnn none married to a woman with them kind of airs. Earl never had to put up with that kind of foolishness."

Mama looked at Daddy funny and he added, "And me neither, thank God."

For weeks everything was directed toward Uncle Johnn's wedding. I had trouble studying, and Mama was a nervous wreck. I wanted to enjoy Uncle Johnn's last days with us, to make the most of every moment, but he kept slipping further and further away, even in my dreams. When I was able to talk, I was able to dream again, dreams that were tormenting at times but lacking their former terror. The lady still waited for me with outstretched arms, but now she had a face, and it looked like my own. One night I dreamed I was a stranger passing through town. It was cold, and the wind blew my skirt. I kept fighting to hold my skirt down as I walked along the uneven sidewalks outside in the dark alone, watching people moving around inside their lighted houses, happy, doing things together, belonging to each other. A little girl ran through the yellow light to a screen door and stared at me. I had only the wind, but she stood in the warm light of her house looking out at me. Seeing her there, I cried. She was in our house. Mama and Daddy and Uncle Johnn were inside. I should have been at that door, not some stranger.

The little girl should have been me. My pillow was wet when I woke up, but I was filled with relief. I was the little girl. Uncle Johnn was still with us. For now.

"Amy sure is a planner," Mama said to me one day. "She's an absolute whiz at funerals and weddings. Johnn better watch his step or she'll have the rest of his life planned before their wedding night."

Despite enjoying talking to people like she was on the inside of things with Miss Amy, Mama was not joyous over the wedding. But our feelings didn't slow Miss Amy's plans one bit.

The ceremony was to be a simple one with Mama and Daddy the only attendants, but simple was never quite the same thing to Miss Amy that it was to other people. The size of their wedding cake was her only acknowledgment that there was a war on, and even at that she caused quite a stir by ordering a pale green cake. Nobody in Bay Harbor had ever heard of a green wedding cake, but that's what she wanted, a cake tinted the color of leaves in spring. That still didn't make it a first love.

No matter how pale the hue, Mama thought a colored wedding cake was about the tackiest thing she'd ever heard of. She felt that way right up until the time Uncle Johnn came home bringing her a new dress to wear to the wedding. It was of pale green lace, and she cried when he gave it to her. But it was the cake that was the talk of the town. Miss Amy and Uncle Johnn asked me to serve it, but I wouldn't. Mama was furious. She thought Uncle Johnn might buy me a dress, too. He did want to, but I cried every time he brought it up, so they finally dropped the subject. I wasn't like Daddy. I couldn't be talked out of something so easily. I did wonder, though, if it would have made a difference had I known Mama would end up crocheting a dress for me. At first I thought it was only another lamp shade. Her own composition, it was a symphony of stitches. Chain and netting stitches supported single crochet, double crochet, treble, and double treble — she knew no bounds. Rose stitches competed with love knots, and shell stitches held their own. In its own way, it was quite remarkable. And it itched.

The wedding day finally arrived. It didn't rain. The sun came up like any other day, except maybe it was brighter, better, for them. Daddy wore his funeral suit, and Mama was so nervous she spilled a whole box of Lady Esther face powder on the floor and left it there.

I guess it couldn't have been any other way. Mama said all brides are beautiful, but Miss Amy was radiant, and Uncle Johnn was as handsome as I'd ever seen him. Maybe I was crazy after all. It was all I could do to keep from yelling, "Hey there, Miss Amy, how'd you like to be in a wedding when Jesus comes?" I didn't because Uncle John was there, too. We would be moving his things into her house while they were on their honeymoon. Mama said she'd fix his room up for me, but that didn't make up for his leaving.

Pearl served the wedding cake the same as she would have done for an ordinary occasion. Since I refused to serve it, Miss Amy wouldn't ask anyone else. I knew she was trying to be nice. She felt special about me now because of Ashley. And I really wanted to do it for her. I wanted to be able to take the plates from Pearl's hands and serve the cake myself, but I couldn't. I just stood there, frozen in my lamp shade dress. My mouth was dry, and even the punch didn't loosen my throat.

Helen came to the wedding. After all, she was Mama's best friend, and we were a family now. Untouched by all that had happened, she looked so nice, almost like a bride herself. Queens are like that.

Miss Amy's dress was pale yellow, and it shimmered like sunlight. The brim of her big straw hat held pale green and yellow roses. It didn't seem right for one person to be so beautiful.

The photographer was still snapping pictures when they got into the car to leave on their honeymoon. Uncle Johnn had hired a Nigra man to do the driving, but I knew when he looked at Miss Amy that he wasn't helpless at all. They were in the car smiling and waving. I tried very hard at that moment to smile, but when I opened my mouth, all I could do was taste the salty tears sliding down my face. Uncle John leaned over and whispered something to her and then got out of the car. The crowd of people went, "Ah," but Miss Amy just smiled at them and looked down at her lap.

Uncle Johnn walked over to me and took my hand. We walked into the house, where we were alone. He stuck his hands in his pockets and gave me a long look. "Don't let it be this way, Anna Lee. You're making it so hard."

Unable to hold back the tears any longer, I leaned against him. "I love you so much, I'd rather be dead than see you go."

"Don't say that!" He spoke angrily and gripped my shoulders. Then more softly, "You don't mean that. You'll be falling in love yourself one day."

I shook my head and tried to pull away, but he held me close, and I loved the feeling of his coat beneath my cheek.

"Yes, yes you will, and then you'll move away, too. Even if I were still there, you'd move away. I don't know . . . " He turned and stared out the window. "Maybe you won't know how much this means to me until then. I would like you to try, though." He turned and faced me again. "Won't you please?"

I looked into his clear blue eyes. "Love shouldn't hurt so much."

"If it didn't hurt, then it couldn't make you happy, either."

"It won't ever be the same with us again."

"No, Anna Lee, not the same."

I looked at his coat and saw that it was all wet. "I'm sorry, Uncle Johnn. I'm sorry for everything."

"Oh, God, Anna Lee, not you. You've nothing to be sorry for." He looked at his pocket watch. "I have to go now. If I had one wish, it would be that you could share my happiness." He started out of the room.

"Uncle Johnn?"

"Yes?"

I swallowed hard. "May I have my choice of the wedding pictures? One to put on my dresser in a silver frame?"

He walked back for a minute. He looked so happy. "Sure you can! You can have all the damned pictures you want!" He winked at me then and without even apologizing walked out of the house. I watched his tall figure until it blurred and disappeared. He didn't come back again.

When it was all over, we returned to an empty house with face powder spilled on the floor. So much had changed, but out back the tender buddings of Miss Red's chinaberry tree were as fresh and full of promise as if there'd been a house to shade. Like misguided talent, it spread protectively over a pile of rubble. Everyone had someone, everyone but me. I hadn't even found my light. All I'd found was the responsibility that is the true heart of love, the starch that keeps it from being a weak and flimsy thing. Maybe I could even kill somebody for love.

Uncle Johnn thought he'd gone, but he hadn't. He could never leave me. When the pictures came, I chose the one taken just before Uncle Johnn got out of the car to talk to me. It was the only one I wanted. In the rest of them he was looking at her. In that one he was looking at me.